GW00392729

TWISTED BLOOD

BY

KEV CARTER

Copyright

2021

Second edition

Please visit my web site

www.fancyacoffee.wix.com/kev-carter-books

CHAPTER ONE

The water was calm. A few pieces of wet, soggy bread were floating on top of it. The Ducks had enough and were losing interest in the situation. They began to float and move away from the side where they had been fed for the last fifteen minutes. Effortlessly moving through the water, they left a slight ripple behind them. This time each day, bread was thrown in for them and they had come to know and be ready for their feed, but soon got bored and disinterested. The day was warm and still. It was time for the local school to let its young pupils out. Many of them walked along this way, through the park, and out the other side; it was a short cut around the busy road. He sat watching as the ducks went away from him and his gaze stayed fixed to the spot, motionless and quiet. He could hear the girls coming up behind him but he did not turn; he knew it was the same ones who always made a point of saying something to him. He knew who one of them was, but they didn't know who he was. One of the two young pretty things walked up to him. They were giggling to each other. The man stayed still saying nothing, not lifting his gaze or changing his expression. One girl walked to his side and held her hand to her mouth as she looked back at her friend laughing at her. Both were dressed in the same uniform. They hated it and did not see why their school had to insist on it, when other schools didn't. She stood by his side, close enough to touch him if she wanted to or him to grab her if he wanted. She looked out across the large stretch of water and ran her fingers through her long, brown hair and stuck out her well developed chest, looking down at him through the corner of her eye. She saw he did not bite to her invite and looked back at her friend who was encouraging the childish performance with a grin and a nod of her head. Turning back, she put her hand down and began to scratch her leg, then moving up she started to lift up her small skirt to reveal her thigh, but it had no effect. She looked back at her friend who was laughing at her. She smiled, turned back and shouted at the young

man with venom in her voice and a frown on her face.

"What the fuck you looking at you sick little pervert? I'm going to report you to the Police; you should not be looking at us innocent little girls like that, with your dirty thoughts and disgusting ways." It had no effect, and she was angry. He did not look at her and did not move his gaze from the still water in front of him. She turned in a huff and walked back to her friend, who shouted back at him as they walked away laughing. "You sick little shit, you want locking up." It was soon quiet again and he took a deep breath, then a deeper sigh. Looking up, he stared in the direction they had gone. He could see them in the distance, watching as they disappeared over the hill. He turned back to the water and the ducks. He had no bread left and just watched them floating around. He had no expression on his face and blankly looked at the water. The girls went out on to the road again to walk home. They were close friends and had been since secondary school. Lisa was the loud one and the one who tried to tease the man in the park, while Sharon was quieter, but still as unfavorable when she wanted to be they were well matched and complimented each other perfectly.

After walking to Sharon's house, they parted and said their goodbyes. Lisa kept going the short distance to her home and was soon there. It was a modest semi-detached house with a very well kept garden mainly because it was a bit of a hobby of her mother's. A double garage suggested they had two cars, but in fact they only had one. She walked up the paved path and to the front door, letting herself in with a key she had in her little bag and closing the door behind her. The house was warm and clean, welcoming and modern. She did not appreciate it. She had all she ever wanted. She did not know what it was to go without, what it was like to want for something, to have to wait or have to be denied something in life. She went to the kitchen and opened the fridge taking out some cheesecake. She put it on the side, took a knife from the rack in front of her and cut her a large piece. She left it and the knife on the side, walked to the main room which was spacious and tidy, switched the television set on, and sat in front of it with a thud.

"Lisa, is that you?" a man's voice came from the adjoining room.

"No," she shouted and paid it no more attention.

The voice was her father's who was sat in a large, leather chair facing his friend who was sat in a similar chair. Each had cans of beer in their hands and were in conversation. Her father was a sturdy looking man who had worked hard all his life to get what he had. Married, and with two children, he was contented but his friend made him feel he had missed out on a lot in life. Peter was a sneaky looking man, going slightly bald but tried to hide it and never talked about it at all.

"I tell ya Graham, your daughter is becoming quite a woman these days. I remember when I use to bounce her up and down on my knee.""Keep your lechering eyes off."

"Hey no way friend." He held up his hands, smiled, and took another sip of his cold beer.

"But I can look, can't I?"

"They grow up much too fast these days."

"My sister is just the same, mate. She is going out with a bloke eleven years her senior. She is only seventeen. He is too old for her and what she wants to start doing now he has already done. He is entering a different stage in his life. She is just beginning and he is just leaving, but you can't tell them anything, bloody sisters, who needs them?"

"Have a word with him then." Graham suggested sternly.

"No, fuck it, it's her life, you learn by mistakes, old man. A man who does not make mistakes makes nothing."

"A woman at our place is having an affair and she came home the other night and told the husband, 'yes I'm getting shagged.' She then threw him some knickers and told him to wash 'em."

"Fuck off," Peter said unbelievingly.

"It's right, all he did was cry, apparently."

"Soft bastard, I'd tell her where to get right off."

"Strange things, women."

"Only if you give them the chance to think, I mean they're stupid at the best of times, so when you ask them to use their brains it sends them all in a flutter."

"That's a very sexist remark." Graham frowned at his friend and took a sip of his beer.

"Fact, they're handicapped before they start because they're stupid. Let people shit all over them then go back. I've shagged loads of women, you just tell them what they want to hear and you're well away." he said shaking his head in a matter of fact way.

"I bet you get up to some stuff in that police force."

"You wouldn't believe it mate, it's the authority that turns them on, and the size of my truncheon of course." He winked and took a long drink of his beer.

6

"No wonder your marriage broke down."

"Look, there is just too much opportunity, you are too close to the opposite sex all the time, and in lonely places like the back of patrol cars and stake outs and all that. Anyway why buy a book when you can join a library? No offence meant."

"My son asked me what a hard on was yesterday."

"What did you say? I don't know, it's been that long since I had one." Peter laughed and rocked his head back.

"No, I told him to ask his mother." They both laughed loudly.

"Do you remember that dyctylographyist, who I told you about?"

"What the hell is a dyctylographyist?"

"Fingerprints." Peter said bluntly

"Oh yeah," Graham nodded as he remembered.

"Well, Sue from accounts always used to walk past him and say, 'have you got anything I can suck on?' and he never clicked. He used to give her a Polo. We always thought he was bent, well it turns out he was shagging his dog."

"Oh piss off; you do come out with some shit at times Peter"

"I'm telling ya, he was caught putting cream on his balls and having the dog licking it off, it's fact. He left yesterday."

"I'm not fucking surprised, are you?"

"Mind you, Sue is nice. Big tits, firm you know." He gestured with both hands and grinned at his friend.

"You're a dirty bastard," and smiled back at his friend, shaking his head.

"Don't tell me you have never thought about it. I mean Gloria is a nice woman and all that, but you must get bored shagging the same hole all the time. Why don't you come to one of our do's and we will get you fixed up, old man?"

"No, it's alright, I'm happy with what I have."

"Don't tell me you have never had another woman. Now that will be fucking sad. I've only known you since you have been married. So tell me, what did you poke before you became tied up with a wedding ring?"

"A couple or three."

"Three?" he asked, disgusted and alarmed.

"Dozen." They again laughed and finished their cans of beer.

Graham reached down to the side of the chair and picked up two more cans from the floor. He handed one to his friend and they opened them simultaneously.

"No mate, I tell you, it's best to shag 'em, all of 'em, because if you miss one, then your regretting and wondering about it all your life. If it's there, screw it."

"Yeah, well I thought like you once."

"I'm telling ya, they all have holes between their legs, find 'em, finger 'em, fuck 'em, forget 'em, simple as that old man. Do ya good to have a bit of fresh now and again, what Gloria does not know will not hurt her. I mean women are content to stay with one man. They get what they want and that is them satisfied because they're stupid, but men are more intelligent and have got to have more. I tell you in Hong Kong if you have money then you have mistresses. It is an accepted fact, women over there know what the score is and all is well." He nodded and agreed with himself

"So what is your limit then?"

"Over sixteen and under fifty, although there are a few exceptions to that rule, clean and under twelve stone. I don't like 'em too fat, but then again not too thin. I like a good pair of tits, a firm arse. I don't like prunes and 'I won't do that' all the bloody time. If I want something then they have got to do it." He looked up and nodded as if to say that was the way it was and the way it should be.

"You'd shag your own mother, you dirty bastard."

"No, not me ma, she was like a mother to me." He laughed into his beer and Graham did the same.

"Shagging, it's all you ever think about." Graham told him.

"Well, it's my favorite pastime; happiness is your cock in a woman's mouth."

"You're a sexist pig."

"Can't help it, it's the way I am. Take me or leave me." He looked up as if he was making some great speech and Graham shook his head at his old and best friend. They were close and had been for some time. He enjoyed their afternoons together and found his company relaxing, and funny at times, but not always agreeing with his ideas.

"Anyway, women love to be treated like shit, it turns them on."

"Bollocks," Graham protested

"I'm telling you Graham, you listen to old Pete, he is in the know."

"Old Pete is in a fantasy world, old friend."

"Hey, I'm a copper. I have seen things you would faint at old man. What I have seen is too disturbing to mention here, that's why I live while I can. I like women so I'll have as many as I can before I go, because there is nothing when you are gone. I tell you, no bloody afterlife, no God, no nothing, you just don't know when your time is up so live for now and let the future happen because you can't stop it when it does happen to you."

He nodded his head at Graham and took a big drink of his beer. Graham sighed and said with a slight smile

"Your philosophy is a strange one for a policeman, Pete."

"Strange or not, there is a lot of truth in what I say. You mark my words, you'll see, you just do not know what is round the corner, and it might just hit you smack in the face. You have got to be prepared for it the best way you can. I've seen the scum of this country, this Earth, and believe me you have got to live while you can, it's no bloody good worrying about what is going to happen. Live your life how you want to."

"Without breaking the law of course." Graham added

"Oh yeah of course." Peter smiled and sat back in his comfy chair. "Well, I'm happy with my life at the moment, a business doing well, I can go in when I want, or stay at home when I want, house, loving wife, two good kids."

"Well, if you are happy then that is alright my friend, but do you know of the other pleasures that await you?" He rolled his eyes at him and smirked a little cheeky smile. Graham narrowed his eyes and asked suspiciously:

"What you on about?"

"A stag do, I want you to come along this time, it will be good."

"No bloody way, not after the last time, thank you." He sat up in his chair and was adamant about his decision.

"Oh come on, that was a mistake, I didn't know it was a man." He started to laugh at the thought of what had happened.

"Bollocks, you knew alright, I felt a right twat."

"It's not all you felt, was it?" He rolled his head back laughing and Graham joined in at the thought of it all.

Peter straightened up in the chair pulling his suit jacket from under him. He sighed and calmed down. He sat forward resting his elbows on his knees with the can of beer in both hands. He looked round at the attractive room, then back at Graham.

"When is your lovely wife coming home?"

"Any time now, why?"

"I want to look at them perfect tits of hers. I must say Graham; your wife has got the best pair of tits I have ever seen, and I have seen a few."

"I know, you tell me every time I see you."

"Well, there you go then, it must be true. I bet you have a time with them don't ya?" He winked at his friend and smiled cheekily.

"We have our moments, tits and all."

"Come on then tell, I want all the sordid details. What does she wear for you? Will she dress up and all that?" He looked on, in anticipation of the answer.

"Well, Peter my perverted friend, she does anything and I mean anything." He teased, with a wide-eyed look and cheeky self indulgent grin.

"Yeah, like what?" His eyes opened wide and he waited eagerly for some details. Graham leant forward and looked round to see if anyone was there. Then he went close to Peter, who was getting excited at the thought of some sexy talk.

"Mind your own bloody business," Graham shouted in his ear.

"Bastard." Peter sat back up saying, "mind you I bet she is a right swinger, the quiet types always are. You have a good woman there,

Graham."

"I know that is why I want to hold on to her."

"Well yeah, each to their own my friend each to their own."
Just then the door opened and in strolled Lisa. She walked up to her
father and stood next to him. He wrapped his arm round her giving
her a little hug. She smiled at Peter who smiled back.
"Dad, can I go to Sharon's house tonight till late?" She gave him a
false smile.
"Why?"
"Watch a film." she answered instantly and a little too quickly.
"Better ask your mother, dumpling." He smiled at the disappointed
girl knowing it was not what she wanted to hear.
"Why not come and sit on my knee and make an old man happy?"
Peter suggested. She smiled and headed back out of the room,
trying to find another way to get to her friend's house. She knew
her mother would not let her and hoped her dad would say alright,
and she would have just gone. She had done this before but it had
stopped working lately. She strolled out of the room and closed the
door behind her. She headed upstairs to the shower. Graham
watched her go and then turned to Peter, who was looking at him
through the corner of his eye.
"Keep your eyes off, or I will cut them off and feed them to you."

"Hey, man, I'm only kidding, bloody hell," he said in protest.

"She is getting to that age now you know."

"Oh yes, mind you, you can tell she takes after her mother."

"What do you mean?"

"She is becoming a big girl, you'll have to watch that you know, all the young lads will swarm to her like a moth round a flame. Tits are always a big draw. When I was at school there was this Italian girl who used to charge for a feel of her tits, fifty pence for a squeeze on the outside, and a pound if you wanted to touch skin. She made a bloody fortune."

"Yeah, off you no bloody doubt."

"First breast I ever felt, I had an hard on for two days."

"How much did you charge for them to touch that?"

"Very funny Graham, very funny," he said, sarcastically. He took another sip of his beer and sat back in the chair.

"What shift are you on this week?"

"Late, so I won't be round next week old man, it will be the week after. Tell you what you and Gloria, making sure she wears a low cut dress of course. We could go for a meal." He nodded enthusiastically.

"Alright, yeah sounds good, I'll arrange a baby sitter for that weekend then."

"Sorted, I will try and bring someone presentable this time."

"Er, yeah; it would make a difference if they did speak English this time like."

"She was a nice girl, a student on an exchange, and did speak English."

"Yeah, only the words you learned her, it was disgusting what she was saying, embarrassing in fact .She had no idea what she was saying, or the meaning of the stuff you were telling her. What they would have made of her when she got back home I dread to think."

"I bet she was very popular in fact." Pete smiled to himself.

"It wasn't fair Pete, was it? the poor girl trying to learn English and you telling her to order a blow job for her starter?"

"Did you see the waiter's face?" He sniggered and started to laugh, until he spilt some of his beer on his jacket, but did not mind because he was laughing that much. Graham joined in and they enjoyed the joke.

"Whatever happened to her anyway?" he asked with a wondering look.

"She went back home." He calmed down and took another sip from his can.

"Where was she from again?"

"I don't know some island, somewhere; it was a young PC who was going to take her out but I put him on something that tied him up for the night and took the nice lady out instead." He smiled and Graham shook his head saying:

"I suppose you shagged it."

"Of course, had to keep England's end up, she was very forthcoming I tell you, and she had the softest hole I have ever had the pleasure of filling, lovely."

"You're a bastard at times."

"Got to be, life is a bastard."

"Don't you ever want to settle down?"

"No, tried it once, did not like it, does not suit me mate. I'm happy with what I'm doing,

and so long as I'm happy I'm staying the same."

"Fair enough." Graham nodded drinking his beer.

 Lisa was in the shower. She let the water cascade down her firm, developing body and relished its freshness. The shower gel she had rubbed in was now washed off and she was ready to get out. She stood there for a moment and let the water cool her down and refresh her skin. Pulling the curtain back, she switched the water off by turning a gold colored handle next to her. She stepped out, water dripping off her body. Taking a clean soft fluffy towel, she started to dry herself off. Standing in front of the mirror, she looked at herself. She let the towel drop to the floor and looked at her body. It had developed rapidly these last few years and she was becoming a woman. Her periods had already started and she wanted to go on the pill but her mother had said no, it was too early for her. Her friend had been on it for over a year, but she was having a lot of pain and trouble, and the pill calmed it down.

She looked at her firm, large breasts and did not know what all the fuss was about with the boys at school. She found them boring; she had played with them one night and got bored with it.

Taking a deep breath, she picked up the towel and finished drying herself, wrapping the towel round herself above her breasts. She went on the landing and into her room, closing the door behind her and leaving the bathroom in a mess, her clothes on the floor and the shower gel bottle left open on the side. She knew her mother would clean it up for her.

Gloria was a fine looking woman, tall and long hair but she wore it up more than down. She would have liked to cut it all off but Graham liked it long. He found it sexy so she left it for him. She came through the front door wearing a short skirt and white blouse, which she had unbuttoned a third of the way down. She closed the door behind her. She smiled as her husband's voice rang out from the back room.

"Is that you love?" he asked

"Yeah, it's me." She took off her shoes and put them neatly by the side of the hat rack. She walked into the main room and put away a paper Lisa had been looking at. She also replaced the television remote control. She walked in the back room and smiled at her husband. They kissed. She smiled at Peter as he said to her in a husky voice:

"Gloria, come and sit on my knee, it will make an old man happy.

"We'll talk about the first thing that pops up, eh?" she said blankly

"You know baby, you know." He winked at her and took a drink.

Gloria sat on her husband's knee and looked at Peter, who was transfixed by her heaving bosom. He could see more than usual now she had unfastened a few buttons. She looked at him and asked in a serious voice:

"What the hell you looking at Peter?"

"I'm afraid it's your lovely tits Gloria," he said without hesitation.

"Oh well, that's all right then." She smirked at them both as she got up and walked to the door, leaving them too their little boys talk.

"Lisa wants to ask you something, if she can stay at her friend's house I think." Graham told her while it was still fresh in his mind.

"Ok, I'm just going to get a shower, darling. If you want to join me and wash my breasts for me, please feel free to come on up." She winked at Graham and sent a nod to Peter when he was not looking. Peter sat up and said with envious enthusiasm: "Fucking hell man, you are a lucky sod with a pair of tits like that at your disposal." He looked towards the door, then back to Graham. "Why don't we go up and wash them for her? I can just watch."

"You have no chance, my perverted buddy, she has only eyes for me and everything else for that matter"

"Well, if I have no chance then I'm going to have to go now I'm afraid. I've seen what I've come to see, that being your wife's mammaries. I can leave a happy man, so until next time I will bid you farewell, old lucky bastard of a friend." He finished his drink in one gulp and stood up, straightening his suit. Graham stood up and they both walked to the door.

"I look forward to us going out then," Graham told him as he opened the door.

"Yeah, it should be good. We will arrange it, I'll ring ya and see what we are doing, and We'll have a laugh."

They walked through the house to the front door. Graham opened it for him and he stepped out into the daylight. He turned back to face his friend who was now stood in the doorway, and asked him: "Now you're not driving are you officer?"

"No sir, I'm going to get the bus, I'll see ya." He walked away and headed off down the road. Graham watched for a short while then closed the door. He went upstairs and could hear the shower at full blast. He decided to wait for his wife in the bedroom. He sat on the bed and rubbed his eyes. The beer had taken effect and he was feeling a little tipsy. He lay back on the bed and looked up at the peach colored ceiling. It was not long before his wife entered the room. She was drying her hair with a towel and he looked at her beauty. She stood there with a perfect figure, long hair and pretty face. He felt a tingling in his loins and an erection beginning. She looked at him and could see and knew that look in his eye. She turned and closed the door, smiling back at him. She let the towel drop from her body to reveal her nakedness.

"What about Lisa?" she whispered

"She will be in her room until tea. Now come here sexy."

"You're a randy bugger when you have had beer." She walked towards him and stood in front of him. He sat up and gently kissed her navel; she brushed her hair back with her hands and looked down at him looking up at her.

"He is right you know," he said

"Who?" she asked, momentarily confused.

"Peter, you do have the most magnificent tits." He reached up and put his hands on the warm, firm, flesh of her bosom, one in each hand, squeezing them gently. She moaned and swayed back with the motion. He stood up in front of her, looked her in the eye and whispered:

"I do love you." But before she could answer he kissed her full on the mouth. She responded by putting her arms round him and pulling him close. They fell on the bed and made love, the way it had always been, good and passionate, loving and caring. They knew each other well and knew just what to do. They had not lost any of the fire they had when they were first married and both were grateful for it.

Sam, the golden Labrador, loved fetching sticks, and Sebastian liked to throw them for him They were close and the love was strong between them., The field was within walking distance from the house and he brought his canine friend here every day after School for their ritual bonding time together. He was the first to get home and always beat Lisa, but she would not walk Sam anyway. This was the rest of the family, Sebastian was only nine-years-old and he had had Sam for five of those years. The bond was strong between them as they had grown up together. Loyalty went a long way and he loved his dog. Sam loved his master and ran to bring back the old stick. He was panting and lay down after dropping it at Sebastian's feet. He waited in anticipation for him to throw it again, which he duly did, far down the Field Sam went running after it eagerly, always willing to bring it back. Sebastian could not figure out if his loyal friend liked the game or thought he was doing him a favour by bringing it back, but it did not matter; they both seemed to enjoy it so all was well and good. Looking at the small watch on his wrist, he saw it was time for home, so he shouted his faithful dog to his side. Without hesitation, the animal did as was commanded and sat next to him. He clipped the lead to his collar and they walked away back up the field. Sam walked protectively by his master's side, not pulling or dragging but keeping the same pace as his friend. His tongue was hanging out and he was panting as he trotted on. Sebastian felt proud to walk with his friend and would do anything for him, no one dared touch the child while Sam was around. He was protective and the bond they had was for ever growing stronger. Graham had bought the dog as a family pet, but both child and dog hit it off right away and ever since they had been inseparable. It was good protection for his son and he knew he would be safe so long as the dog was by his side. He welcomed it and the rest of the family accepted it. Lisa was dressed in dirty jeans and a loose t-shirt. She came out of her room and walked past the closed door of her parents' room, down the stairs and into the kitchen. She opened the back door and looked out, the air was fresh and clean taking a deep a deep breath. She could see her younger brother walking towards the house and watched as he got closer. When he was within earshot, she said to him:

"Oh look, it's sir bastard with the hound."

"Watch what you say woman, or I will instruct my dog to attack," he said with a playful tone in his voice. She looked down at the exhausted dog and gave a slight sarcastic laugh, saying to him: "What that thing, it's like an old man, it won't live much longer you know."

"It will live longer than you if you don't get out of my way, woman." He pushed past her and took the dog's lead off. It duly went to its water bowl and lapped up some much needed water for what seemed like forever, then went back out into the garden and lay in the shade. Sebastian walked into the hall and took off his shoes. He put them away under the stairs and walked into the main room.Lisa followed him in and they sat on the settee next to each other.

"Where's mum and dad?" he asked without looking at her.

"Shagging, I think," she said bluntly.

"You are a dirty person Lisa," he said seriously, but then it got the better of him and he started to laugh, holding his hand up to his mouth. As he did, he had a funny laugh, and it always set Lisa off laughing. She was not amused by what was said but by his daft infectious laugh. They both sat there giggling and sitting back on the settee, knowing when their parents came down they would start again and not be able to help themselves.

After supper, Lisa was still disappointed that she could not go to her friend's, so she went to bed early as a sign of disapproval. Graham was doing the washing up and Sebastian was getting ready to go to bed himself. He gave his beloved dog a hug and a kiss, then without hesitation shouted good night to his parents and went up to bed. Gloria came into the kitchen and stood behind her husband. She put her arms round him and gave him a tight, loving hug, he put his head back towards her and enjoyed her touch.

"I'm sure he thinks more of that dog than he does of us sometimes," she said

"Best friends. I had a dog when I was young, I told him everything."

"Did he ever answer you back?" she asked, teasingly

"Yes, he did actually." He carried on with his washing up. She pulled away and stood by his side folding her arms.

"Lisa is pissed off again." she said with a slight sigh

"She'll get over it, wanted to stay at her friend's didn't she?"

"Yeah, maybe I should have let her. What do you think?" He could tell she felt a little guilty and wanted some reassurance from him.

"You have made your decision, so stick to it. She is going to have to learn she can't have everything her own way. Anyway she has got to get up for school tomorrow, so it is for the best." He finished the washing up and emptied the bowl of water into the sink. He reached over and pulled a small tea towel off its hook on the wall and dried his hands on it, then replaced it neatly.

"We should just get a dishwasher," she suggested.

"We got one." He smiled and pointed to himself. "Fancy meeting me on the settee for a bit of a cuddle?"

"Go on then." They walked into the main room and settled on the settee. Gloria sat across her husband's legs and snuggled up into his chest. She felt safe and wanted, loved and adored as he gently stroked her hair.

"By the way, Peter wants us to have a night out with him and a friend again."

"What friend? Not that poor girl from last time?" she asked, slightly alarmed.

"No, she is gone; he will bring someone else this time."

"Yeah, alright, When?"

"Week after next."

"Should be ok, have to ring the baby sitter."

"He wants you to wear something revealing."

"Oh surprise, surprise, the man is a pervert. Mind you, you're not much better when you get going." She lifted her head and kissed him softly on the lips.

"You love it really."

"That's besides the point." They kissed again and settled back down into each other's

arms. Graham liked these moments together. He felt the valuable time together was important, and would not change it for the world. Gloria started to doze off and Graham was not too far behind. It was half an hour later when Sam suddenly pricked up his ears. He could sense someone. All was quiet but he knew he was not wrong. He was standing and looking intensely at the back door. His eyes were staring and he was listening for any little sound. He walked to the kitchen door and stopped again, listening. Then the silence was shattered with his ferocious barking. He was protecting his territory and someone was on it. He stood at the back door, barking and growling. Graham was awakened with a fright, so was his wife. They looked at each other and stood, staring into the kitchen. Gloria rubbed her sleepy eyes and looked at the clock. Graham walked into the kitchen. Something was bothering Sam. Graham turned the light on. He went to the back door and also turned on the outside light. The garden emerged from the darkness and was lit up.

"What is it boy, eh?" He patted the dog and opened the door. Sam dashed out down the garden before he could stop him or grab hold of him. Graham looked out and saw Sam at the bottom of the garden barking at the fence. He was jumping up but the fence was too high and he could not get over it. Graham ran down and looked around. He could see nothing, but knew Sam knew someone was there. Graham calmed the dog down and took another look round. Gloria shouted from the backdoor to him her arms folded across her chest.

"What is it love?"

"Dad, what's wrong with Sam?"

"Nothing son, go back to bed. There's a good lad."

"Is he ok?"

"Yes, he's fine. Go back to bed." The window closed and he did what he was told.

"Sam, come here boy!" Gloria called the happy dog and patted him at the door. Graham looked round once more and noticed the lawn indented with a footprint. Someone was there. He looked back to the house, where Gloria was making a fuss of their dog. He was pleased they had him and he decided not to alarm his wife by telling her about the imprint. He walked back to the house and went in. Gloria was giving Sam a biscuit. Graham locked the door. He double checked it and the front door. They turned out the lights and went upstairs. Sam stood in the kitchen keeping guard. Someone was there and he was not happy about it. He lay down and eventually fell asleep. In bed, Gloria looked up at the ceiling. Graham was next to her. She had a puzzled look on her face, and asked him:

"Who do you think it was?

"Who?" he said, looking at her.

"In the garden tonight."

"Oh, just some kids probably. Sam will make sure they don't return. Now they know there is a vicious dog on guard, they will keep away. Stop worrying about it. No harm will come to you here."

"When I was talking to Lisa tonight she said she had seen the duck feeder man again." There was a concerned tone in her voice.

"Oh for god's sake, that girl is going to have to stop thinking everyone's at her. She told me about it too. A man who feeds the ducks keeps looking at her and her friend." He sounded disinterested.

"Yeah, but what if there is something in it?"

"I told her to come home a different way and avoid the park. Sharon told me he has never even spoken to them. You know what Lisa's like, she is getting to think all men are after her, and all the lads at school want her. I think she is just exaggerating again. What about last month when she said her room was haunted? It's all attention seeking, love."

"I'm not sure. I'm going to tell her to come home a different way in future."

"Yeah, well I told her that. Anyway she can take care of herself, and she always has a friend with her. I wouldn't worry about it." Graham insisted

"No, well maybe not." She leant over and kissed him on the cheek. He smiled and turned out the light. The room was in darkness and all was quiet, the house, the garden, the street. The shadow of a man was stood watching from a distance. From where he was, the house was in plain sight. He had been in the garden and now was looking from down the street. A dark coat and trousers made him blend into the night and hard to see, but he was there and had been for several nights

CHAPTER TWO

Lisa was unaware her movements were being closely watched and did not know she was the target of much attention. She walked to her friend's house swinging her arms and dragging her feet. She didn't want to go to school today. It was geography and she found it very boring, and Miss Peters made her work which was worse. She called for her friend and walked up the block paving path. She knocked on the brown wooden door and a thin woman answered it, looking very flustered and annoyed.

"Is Sharon ready Miss...?" but before she could finish her sentence she was told very abruptly and with some resentment.

"No, no she is not going today; she is ill, bloody silly girl, partying last night I found them." She shook her head and put her hands up in the air. "No, she will not be coming today." She closed the door and hurried back inside. Lisa smiled. She knew her friend must have had a good time last night. She sighed. She should have been there. Cursing to herself, she turned and walked away, slowly to the around. This was normally where the duck feeder was. She stood by the side of the water and looked out across it. It was calm and still; boring she thought. Shrugging her shoulders, she made one more attempt to get to school, this time it was with a faster pace and she had convinced herself she would get there.

Late but what the hell, So what? She headed off and went through the park and down the road. She could see the large, old building in front of her. It was the school she had been at for the last two years. Her heart sank. She didn't want to go. She'd had enough of school, but at least it would not be too long. She walked into the grounds, through two large iron gates which looked very grand but had not been closed in over twelve years and were rusted at their hinges and would not move now anyway. She was late but did not care, it was going to be a long day without her friend by her side. She prepared herself and was ready to face the music. The day went very slowly for her and she did not enjoy any of it. She even walked around the park on her way home. She could not even be bothered to see the duck feeder today. Slowly, she strolled on home and was looking like an old woman when she got there, bored and fed up. She went past her friend's house. She looked up but could not see any sign of life. She carried on to her own home, and although she saw Sam and Sebastian walking down the road to the fields, she did not call out to them. She just went into the house and straight up for a shower. It refreshed her a little bit. She lay on her bed until she was called by her mother late that afternoon.

"Lisa, Lisa come down here I have something for you," Gloria shouted from the bottom of the stairs, then went into the main room. A few minutes later Lisa came slowly and lethargically down the stairs and went into the room. She sat next to her mother on the settee and her curiosity grew when she saw an empty box, and her mother holding something.

"What is it?" she asked.

"I have bought you this and want you to keep it with you at all times. Do you hear? I have registered it for you and you're ready to go with it." She held up a mobile phone in her hand.

Lisa's face lit up. She opened her eyes wide and sat up straight. "Excellent mum, oh yeah." She took the phone from her mother with a big smile and she was surprised how light and small it was. "Right, I want you to read the instructions and read them well. It does all sorts of stuff and I have already put several numbers in its memory for you. From now on, you will have to pay for it so don't run up an astronomical bill, for Christ sake. It's for emergencies more than anything, alright, so have a play with it and if you're not sure on anything let me know." She told her commandingly "Yeah, thanks mum."

She leant over and kissed her mother on the cheek. She was overjoyed with her gift, and it was so unexpected. She looked at it and started to press some of the buttons on its face. One made it light up and bleep she took the instruction booklet and started to read it. Gloria went into the kitchen, just in time to meet Sam and Sebastian coming in from their walk. Sam was panting and went for his water bowl. He lapped it up and wagged his tail at the same time. Sebastian was also out of breath and sat at the table, breathing heavily.

"You alright love?" Gloria asked sitting next to him at the wooden table.

"Yeah, I've raced Sam home and he won, I think." He smiled and took a big, deep breath of air, trying to get his breathing back to normal.

"Hey mum, this is brilliant," Lisa shouted from the main room.

"What is she on about?" Sebastian asked.

"She has got a mobile phone, I've bought her it."

"Right, and what have I got then?" he asked, looking at her with his head tilted to one side. Sam sidled up to him and sat down, water dripping from his mouth.

"A mature head on your shoulders I hope and you're not going to give me a hard time about it, just because she has got something. It doesn't mean you have got to get something as well."

"Does this mean she is more important than me then?"

"No, not at all I've bought her it because it is a dangerous world out there, and she is out a lot. The dark nights are drawing in and it makes me feel a little better that she can get in touch when and wherever she wants."

"She had a mobile before and abused it. That's why dad took it off her."

"Yes, well she should have learned that lesson."

"I go out a lot too, don't I?"

"Yes, but you have always got Sam there." She looked down to his faithful dog.

"How much did it cost mum?"

"Not that much."

"Who is going to pay the bill mum?"

"She is, I've told her that."

"With the pocket money you give her I suppose." He shook his head.

"Probably look she will be working soon, what exactly, are you trying to get at young man?" she enquired looking him straight in the eye.

"Well, if I can't have a phone ..."

"You can have a phone, but not just yet."

"Well dad never uses his mobile, he is always leaving it behind can I have that?

"You are correct there about that but no you can't" she smiled at his bravado

"Well ok, but if I can't have a phone, yet, and you can buy her that, then could dad buy me something?" He smiled and looked as cute as he could at her.

"What?" she said, slowly and cautiously.

"Well, with my savings and if dad would help me out just a little I could have a laptop computer. There, brilliant mum. You can play wicked games on them, and my home work, and if you get a scanner ..." he said eagerly.

"I know why you want a computer and the internet in your room," she said, pointing her finger at him. "You were caught looking at stuff you're too young to look at round at your friend's house last week. His mum rang me and told me all about it. It's bad for you to be looking at all them dirty women, Sebastian."

"Hey mum, they just keep popping up on the screen, and internet. We could not get shut of them. I was not interested in all that stuff. Anyway, you can get great games on it you know, the graphics are dead good, honest mum. Come on, I'm a good kid, don't give you no trouble." He pleaded and saw she was smiling and knew he was in with a good chance with this one. If she smiled at him then it looked good, he had come to realize.

"You have a games console already and plenty of games."

"Yeah, I know mum and I'm very grateful for you buying me that. I love it, but please a laptop would be so rewarding. I mean its 2009 already we're entering the computer age, we're going to get left behind if I don't get working on one now you know. I mean all the kids at school know how to use them and most have one. Surely, you want me to do well, and if I could get clued up on computers well who knows what I will become." He smiled and Gloria melted .She came over to him and gave him a big, long hug. The love for her family was paramount and she counted herself very lucky with what she had got. She crouched down by his side and looked into his big blue eyes and saw his father in there. She took his hand in hers and lovingly said to him:

"Sebastian, you are so mature sometimes. Now listen, we know you want a computer of your own and I know we have one and you don't use it, much, because you want the privacy of your own room. Now don't you say anything to your dad, but he is upgrading his and getting a new one, so keep hold of your savings and be patient. You might be in for a surprise very soon, but please don't tell your dad I have told you ok?"

His little eyes lit up and he threw his arms round her, giving her a long hug. She did the same and they swayed there for a short while. Eventually, he let go and looked so excited he did not know what to say or do, the thought of it made him stand up and laugh where he stood. Gloria put her fingers to her lips and made the 'be quiet' sign. She winked at him then went to the sink. Sebastian hugged Sam and they both went out into

the garden. He took a brush from the inside the door and eagerly brushed his companion with a smile that stretched from both sides of his face. Gloria prepared tea, and it was waiting for Graham when he came in a while later. They ate as a family and Lisa even helped with the washing up, which surprised everyone. Sebastian did nothing but smile at his dad all through the meal and could not do enough for him. He put all the dishes away and then went up to his room. Lisa did the same and rang her friend to tell her about her new toy. Gloria sat with her husband on the settee; they were close and held hands. Graham spoke but did not look up.

"What is Sebastian being so helpful for?"

"Don't know my love," she said, unconvincingly.

"You've told him, haven't you?"

"Oh well with Lisa getting the phone he felt left out, and his baby blues just got to me. Honest, it was so difficult not to tell him. He wanted to give up his savings to get one, and it just kind of slipped out." She turned and faced him, squeezing his hand.

"Well never mind, if you've told him then the surprise is gone and you have spoiled it all, ruined it, ruined it all," he said teasingly. She snuggled up to him and whispered in his ear in a sexy husky voice.

"I'll make it up to you later, just think about my big, round, firm, perfect tits."

"Stop it!" He sat up and looked to make sure the children were still out of the room. She smiled at him and put her hand on his leg and brought it up to his crotch. She slowly rubbed and he sat straight up on the settee.

"Gloria, what if one of the kids comes back down. Stop it, you mad cow."

"Oh live a little dangerous, my love, I'm getting quite randy. Shall we go upstairs or shall we do it right here and now?"

"I think we will have an early night. Mind you, there is something I want to watch on the television tonight."

"Tape it, or I will go up myself and entertain myself." She put her tongue in his ear and slowly licked it for him. She then took his hand and put it on her firm breast. He leant over and kissed her full on the mouth. They embraced and hugged, kissing on the settee. Graham pulled away and smiled at his excited wife; she stared back into his eyes and blew him a Kiss with a cheeky wink of her eye and lick of her lips.

"You're a very sexy lady, you know that?"

"When I want to be I suppose, and right now I feel like a bit of hot sex." Before he could answer, the phone rang. He walked across the room and picked up the receiver.

"Yes hello." He smiled back at his wife who was looking at him erotically. There was silence then the receiver at the other end was put down and the line went dead. Graham put his finger on the button to disconnect the line then pressed the call back number but a voice told him the caller had withheld their number. He put the phone back down.

"Who was it?" Gloria asked

"Don't know, they didn't say anything and withheld their number. Will it be Lisa messing around do you think?"

"Probably. Do us a favour, love," she asked nicely.

"Anything."

"Make us a cup of tea." She smiled at him from the settee.

"I don't know, one minute you're a mad sex siren, the next you want a cup of tea.

"If I didn't know you better I would take that personally. Tell me, what the hell has tea got to offer that I haven't?"

"Nothing darling, nothing You're better than a cup of tea any day, except when I'm thirsty that is." She winked at him in a playful manner. He turned and went to the kitchen to make them both a cup of tea, saying something incoherent under his breath.

The phone rang again, this time Gloria got up to answer it, but before she got there it stopped. She walked to the stairs and shouted up to Lisa:

"Lisa, are you calling this number with your phone?"

"No, I'm talking to Sharon. Why?"

"Nothing, it's alright." She walked to the phone and dialed for caller number but again it had been withheld.

"Who is it?" Graham shouted from the kitchen. Gloria walked to him with her arms folded .She stood next to him by the kettle, with a quizzical look on her face.

"No number given. I hope we don't have a pest caller; they're a real pain in the arse. Sue had one at the salon the other week. It really got to her ringing the entire bloody time saying nothing, and hanging up. She got withheld numbers barred, but it came from a phone box. She had to change her number in the end. It's so bloody annoying that it's you who has got to spend money for their childish stupidity. Sad tossers with nothing better to do."

The kettle boiled and switched itself off. Graham made two cups of tea, and they went back into the room, each carrying their own cup, and sat down next to each other and slowly relaxed. It was not long before Sam was let out into the garden for ten minutes.

Then they locked up and went to bed. Graham had a shave and wash in the bathroom and when he walked back into the bedroom he saw his wife lying on the bed, naked and looking at him. She put her hand up and gestured him to stand still. Closing the door, he did just that. She slowly slid off the bed and came close to him. She brushed her body past his and stood behind him. She wrapped her arms round him and ran her fingers through his thick, dark, hair and then moved down to his trouser top. She undid them and they dropped to the floor. He stood out of them and she rubbed her body next to his. He turned and faced her. She always got him like this; it never took long and they had exceptional good sex that night.

All ran well in the household for a few days, until the following Tuesday. Sam was getting brushed by Sebastian in the garden. He liked the brush. It made him feel good and he knew he would get a biscuit at the end of it. Sebastian liked to look after him. He was proud of how well and fit he looked. Making sure he stayed that way was his job and he did it well with pleasure.

Graham was in the shower and Gloria was doing the tea She looked at the clock and noticed it was almost half past five. Lisa should have been home by now; her tea was going to be ruined, which would make her in line for a telling off when she arrived back.

She had been told not to be late tonight because her mum wanted to get the tea over with and then spend a few hours in the garden. She did not want to be cooking after the tea had been done just for Lisa. The meal was almost ready and she could not stop looking at the clock. Lisa was late. Gloria was getting angry and the food was ready. Graham came down and sniffed the air. He walked into the kitchen and said:

"Smells good and I'm starving my dear."

"Where the bloody hell is Lisa?" she said, straining the potatoes into the sink.

"Have you tried to ring her?"

"Yeah, but she is not answering or she has it turned off, I keep getting diverted to an answering service. I've left her a message and text, but she's not ringing back."

"Well, don't get into a panic. When she comes in she is going to have to make her own tea. You're not running round after her all the bloody time."

"You know what she is like. She will go without to be stubborn." She brought the potatoes back from the sink to the table then served them equally on four white oval plates.

"Well sod her, she will go without. Put hers in the oven and she can have it warmed up when she comes in, and if she doesn't want it then Sam will have it." Graham insisted He walked to the window and saw Sebastian brushing his dog proudly and with Commitment and it made him smile.

"She is getting worse; I tell you love, worse all the bloody time." Gloria became annoyed and irritated throwing the strainer into the sink.

"Hey, come on love, don't let it start to bother you." He walked over to her and gave her a hug. She welcomed it and responded by snuggling up to him for a moment, taking a deep breath. She pulled away and smiled at him for a moment. He kissed her lightly on the forehead and she closed her eyes for a brief second.

"Sorry, I have had a shit day at the salon," she said to him, quietly.

"Stop worrying, let's have our tea, then you go out into your garden and I will take care of the washing up and our daughter when she comes in. You always get relaxed in the garden, so stop panicking and let's have some food."

"I love you Graham, do you know that?" she told him, softly.

"Cause I do, you're a woman." He smiled teasingly, then walked to the back door and went out into the garden. Gloria finished serving out the food, and it was ready in a matter of minutes. Sam was the first to come running in, tail wagging and eyes full of play. He saw they were about to eat, so knew instinctively to go to his bed. Graham and Sebastian came in after him. Both washed their hands and they all sat down at the table.

"Where is she?" Sebastian asked, reaching over for some butter to put on his potatoes from the centre of the well-prepared table.

"In trouble," Graham said, looking at his wife.

"Good," said a smiling Sebastian.

"Did she say anything to you about being late?" Gloria asked her son.

"No, she is always on her phone these days; you never get a chance to talk to her mum. I think that phone was the best thing you ever bought her, it has shut her up and given us all some peace and quiet."

"Sebastian!" Graham warned him with a low tone in his voice. But he was smiling inwardly at his son's words.

"Sorry," said Sebastian as he began to eat. Nothing more was said except Graham commenting to Gloria how nice the meal was. While she went into the garden and did some overdue weeding and tidying up, Graham got on with the washing up. Sam was taken out for the third time that day by Sebastian, and did not complain one bit. After washing up, Graham looked at the clock. It was now six thirty. Lisa had never been this late before so he decided to ring her friends, but there was no answer. He tried her mobile again but was diverted to the answering service. He looked out of the window and watched his pretty wife working away in the garden. She loved it out there and spent hours on her precious little piece of land, often forgetting the time. It was not strange for her to be out there until late into the night when summer was upon them, He walked to his favorite chair and then started to read the paper. He watched as Sam and Sebastian came back in then Sebastian went back out to his friends. He read the paper as much as he wanted to, and rang Lisa's mobile once more, but still there was no answer. He tried her friends again, but still there was no response. He looked at the clock; it was becoming worryingly late and what had started as annoyance was now slowly turning to concern. He turned from the phone and saw his wife stood in the doorway looking at him.

"Have you found out anything?" she asked.

"No, but she is in for a rollicking when she gets in here, I tell ya," he said, trying to reassure his worried wife she was on her way or would be here soon.

"Something has happened Graham, I know it." Her voice faltered and she was slightly shaking. He walked up to her and put his arms round her and pulled her tight, giving her a reassuring hug for a moment.

"Come on she can look after herself. I have rung her friend's house and she is not there either, so they're probably off somewhere together. She will turn up, don't worry love."

He squeezed her tightly and held her in his comforting embrace "Hope so." She looked at the clock and saw it was past nine. "She has never been this late before, I'm going to ring the hospital." She walked over to the phone. She reached

down for the receiver but the phone rang before she could pick up. She looked at her husband with hope in her eyes. She quickly picked up the receiver and put it to her ear while Graham came over to her.

"Hello, is that you Lisa?" she asked. There was silence for a moment, then a voice she recognised spoke to her. But it was a voice filled with fear and terror. It was her daughter's voice but it was as if she had never heard it before.

"Mum, mum," she faltered in her voice, "just listen to me." She was crying and was obviously petrified. "Don't call the police, don't tell anyone, and don't do anything, please mum do as I say, please." Again, there was silence.

"Oh my god, Lisa," she shouted desperately into the phone. Graham tried to listen to what was being said but he could hear nothing. He didn't have to, his wife's apprehension and panic said it all. She was shaking. He stood next to her and asked concernedly but with a large hint of fear.

"What is it? What's wrong?"

"Lisa, Lisa speak to me," Gloria shouted despairingly into the phone. She gripped it tightly in her hand and held on to it as if it was the only lifeline to her daughter.

"Lisa," she shouted again. Then was silence as her daughter's voice spoke again.

"Mummy, I have been told to tell you to involve no one, not a soul, not the police, not your friends. The house is being watched and he knows everything about me and dad and everything."

"Lisa who is he? Where are you? Are you alright baby? Has he touched you? What does he want? Lisa, tell him not to hurt you and we will give him anything he wants." Gloria was on the verge of total panic; she could not believe this was happening. She wanted the nightmare to end. Graham was getting in a similar state. He grasped what was happening and wanted to grab the phone, but he knew his wife was holding it tightly and would not let it go He stood there helpless and began to shake. Fear and dread took hold of her heart. She began to shake more uncontrollably and could not comprehend it all. She did not want to believe this was happening. Graham put his hand on her shoulder and tried to offer her comfort but he was in much the same state.

"Mum, I'm sorry." Her daughter's voice cut to her heart like a scalpel. She held on to her husband and listened. Tears rolled down her face and there was anger in her soul. 'Who was this man who was holding her little girl? Who had the right to do this?'

"It's alright sweetheart, you will be alright. What is it he wants?" There was an unbearable silence. She could not take it any longer and her legs gave under her. Graham held her up. He took the phone off her and put it to his ear. He could hear a faint hiss. He spoke into it, his voice faltering but still in control.

"This is Lisa's father, who is this? What do you want?" There was a muffled noise, the phone was taken off Lisa and someone else came on. He could not hear him but knew he was there. Then a voice, a man's voice, a voice from the north of the country, a voice of a man who had his daughter. It was a full voice, one with a hint of menace in it, dry and slow.

"I have her, you tell no one, and you do not tell the police. I will know if you do. I will send her back to you in small pieces through the mail, a package at a time, little bit by little bit, piece by piece, body part by body part. You do absolutely nothing, nothing until I say." The phone went dead, but just before it did he heard a muffled cry, a cry of pain, a cry he recognized, the painful cry of his beloved daughter. He was rigid, fixed to the spot momentarily, until he slowly put the receiver down. His tearful wife looked up at his and asked in a quiet shaky voice:

"What did he say? Is she alright? Graham?" She burst into tears and held him so tightly it hurt. He was not about to complain. His heart was struck with fear and his soul cried out of the darkness to be helped.

"We are to do nothing," he said quietly.

"We are phoning the police, right now." She took the phone and started to ring. Graham took the phone from her and put it back. He took her by the shoulders and faced her. He shook her slightly and looked her straight in the eye, speaking to her with a nervous fear in his voice.

"No Gloria, no we're not to phone anyone. She will be alright if we do as they say. He said he would know if we phoned the police."

"You spoke to him?" She became hysterical. "What did he say?

Who is he? What does the bastard want?" The tears rolled down her face and her words would not come out right. She was breathing erratically and had to sit down on the settee, burying her head in her hands. She sobbed uncontrollably, unable to speak, unable to think straight. Graham
was holding back his tears trying to be strong for his wife's sake and his own. He took deep breaths and sat next to her. He noticed his hands were shaking, and not wanting to believe what was happening, he put his arm round her. She moved over and fell into his embrace, crying out loudly and sobbing.

"What, what are we to do? My poor baby, he has my baby, No, no, what can we do?" she asked him, only just being able to speak to him. He looked at her and threw his arms right round her. They sat there crying and hugging. Someone had their child and they felt helpless to do anything about it. The torture was too much and Gloria was unable to cope. They did not know what to do .Trepidation had struck them; they had each other, and that was all they had. Graham had to be strong for his wife. He took a deep breath and looked down at her, seeing her so hurt and upset.

"We can do nothing until we find out what the bastard wants. If it is money then we shall give it to him, we don't know what he wants so we will have to wait. She will be alright if we do as he says. He told me that." Graham didn't sound convincing. He noticed his wife's face was red with tears, look up at him and straight into his eyes.

"What if he just wants her for his pleasure? What if he doesn't want anything? What if he just wants to rape and use her? What if you are wrong? What is he doing to her right now?"

Her voice became louder and more hysterical. "What if she is being hurt right now, at this moment? What can we do?" She shook her head. He tried to comfort her but he was shaking himself. They sat there silently and in emotional pain.

It was over half an hour later before the front door opened and Sebastian came in from his friends. Luckily, he was late and went straight up to his room, knowing he would probably get sent there anyway. Graham let Sam out into the back garden and watched as he ran about sniffing and exploring his territory. He knew something was wrong. It was dark now and the night had brought a chill with it. Sam was called back in and the door was locked. When he went back into the living room Gloria had made herself a drink, a stiff gin and drank it down in one go. She went to make herself another when she froze at the sound of the phone ringing. She looked over at it as quickly Graham picked it up. He ran his fingers through his hair with his free hand and said:

"Hello?" For a moment there was silence. Then the northern voice came back again, the same voice he had heard before, the same one who had his daughter.

"Listen, now that you have sweated for a while let me explain to you. We are going to have to play a game. I will give you clues and you are going to have to find out who I am. It won't be hard. You should know, your precious little girl will be safe as long as you do as you're told." Gloria had come to the phone and was listening. She put her hand to her mouth as the voice of her little girl came back on.

"Daddy, please do as he says. I'm alright but he will hurt me if you go to the police or try and get help. Please, do as he wants daddy."

"I will sweetheart, don't worry, you will be alright, I will do anything he wants. You tell him that, tell him not to hurt you because daddy will do anything he wants. Is he there? Tell him I want to speak to him."

"I have to go daddy, I love you and tell mummy I love her." There was silence until the man's voice came back on the line.

"My second name is Leigh, L.E.I.G.H." He spelt it out to him. From this you might be able to gather where I come from. I'm in control, don't ever forget that. From now on, you will do as I say. Is that understood daddy?" He mocked in a pathetic little voice.

"Right, get shut of your little boy and stay in the house by the phone, I will be watching the house, sometimes, not all the time, but you will not know when I will be there. I know a lot about you, daddy, so don't try and con me. If you inform the police you will get your daughter back in little bits. Alright, you go to bed and shag your bitch of a wife. I will not be calling again tonight."

The phone went dead and Graham slowly hung up. Gloria looked at him with a puzzled frown on her face.

"Who the fuck is he do you know this bastard Leigh?"

"I have no idea, but I think we have to do as he says for now. He does not seem to be hurting her so let's just hope we can get it sorted out, and I'm not taking the chance of calling the police."

"What about Peter? Call him he might be able to help," she insisted.

"No, we don't know if he is watching the house. Christ, he might be right across the road for all we know. If he knows things about me then he might know who Peter is. I will have to get in touch with him on the quiet if I'm going to do it." His voice was stronger now, in a way a little more at ease. He was the centre of this and the voice of this man bothered him. He could not put his finger on it but there was something about that voice.

A northerner, he came from the north. Was it some kind of revenge on him? But he could not think of anyone. They sat on the settee and held each other. They did not sleep that night and had to think of a way to get Sebastian away without causing suspicion. Gloria thought of sending him to her parents and asking them to look after him. But she could not bring herself to do it convincingly. It was another problem they had to deal with this night, the night that was the worst of their time together, the worst of their entire lives, but Graham feared it would get worse. He had hidden fears but dared not tell his wife. This was just the start and he knew it. He also knew he had to be strong for his loved ones. They depended on it. It was all down to him now and he hoped he would be strong enough to cope with it all, whatever it may be.

The next morning Gloria was asleep in bed. She was so tired and exhausted she dropped off in Graham's arms and he put her to bed early that morning. He got about half an hour's sleep himself when Sebastian came downstairs, sheepish and ready for the telling off he would surely get. He walked up to his unshaven, tired and drained looking dad. Instantly, he knew something was very wrong. "I'm sorry dad, I was late last night ..." He bowed his head in confusion as well as shame; there was no shouting, no telling off, and no demanded explanation.

"Forget it son, take Sam out will ya?" Graham walked into the kitchen and made himself a drink. Sam had his lead on and was taken out by his little master minutes later.

They went off down the fields and he was let off to run round and then back up to Sebastian, who searched for a stick, he got one and threw it several times. He looked back up the road. He knew the atmosphere was not right at home so he exercised his dog then headed back. On entering the house he said nothing; it was quiet and strange. What was wrong? He knew something was, but he dared not ask. As he ate his breakfast he looked at his dad who was looking out of the back window. He was not really enjoying his cornflakes. He put his spoon down and asked:

"Is everything alright dad, where's mum and Lisa?"

"Eat your breakfast lad." His father's tone was a bit blunt for his liking.

"I've finished. Have you had a fight?" He watched as his father came over and sat with him at the table. He looked round as his mother slipped quietly into the kitchen from upstairs and stood with her husband. She was smiling but he knew it was false. They looked at their son and Sebastian became nervous.

"Listen, Sebastian I have to tell you something. Lisa and your mother have had a fight and Lisa is going to stay with your gran for a while."

"Oh, I knew it, the silly woman. She's always getting out of it." He threw his hands up in the air. He now knew what was wrong and he didn't want to know any more. He shook his head and sighed.

"She won't be back for a while but we don't want you to tell anyone about it. Is that clear? No one, and listen if you do as you're told you can have that computer you keep going on about in your room. But you must do us this favour.

"Anything, you know that dad." His face lit up with the anticipation of a computer. He eagerly awaited the request.

"We want you to go and stay with your gran just for a little while. Ok? Lisa is at my mum's, so I will take you over to your other gran today and we will let you know what is going on. So go and pack a bag. I will ring her now and off you can go. I will look after Sam for you and when you return your computer will be in your room. Is that alright son?"

"That's spot on dad, thanks. Love you, love you mum." He grinned from ear to ear, got up and went upstairs to pack. Gloria hugged and kissed her husband, then went and phoned her mother. She gave some story they needed some space and asked if she would look after Sebastian for a few days. She knew she would have no trouble and was right; her mother was a very understanding woman. She also phoned in work and played she was ill. Graham's work was next and that was no problem either. She looked at her little boy as he came down the stairs smiling and ready. She hugged him and kissed him. He returned the hug but not the kiss, then went to his dog and put his arms round him kissing him on his wet nose. He was taken out by his dad and driven to his gran's. He didn't mind and it had happened before when they wanted some time together so it didn't look out of the ordinary. On his way back

Graham felt obliged to go and buy the computer he had been after, and then headed back home. He saw his wife with a glass of gin in her hand looking at the phone like a statue.

"Anything?" he asked as he came in. She did not look up and shook her head.

"Gloria, this will work out, love. Everything will be alright, you'll see. She is a strong girl, she will be ok. I will do anything and everything I can."

"What can we do, love? I want my baby back." She drank deep from her glass of gin, and looked haggard and worried.

"We will get her back, don't worry. Don't you ever doubt that." He came and sat next to her putting his arms round her. She moved into him. She needed him more now than ever. He held her close and they found strength from each other.

All they could do now was wait until they found out what was going on, and what they wanted, whoever they were. He found it somewhat amazing that he was able set up a computer, and put the old one in his son's room, while the world he knew was turned upside down. But he had to do something. It was time-consuming and it took his mind away from the terror and helplessness he was feeling.

The minutes seemed like hours to Gloria. She had drank half a bottle of gin and just sat looking at the phone. She jumped out of her skin when it rang. The noise sent a shiver through her veins. She looked up at her husband as he ran from the kitchen to answer it. Standing next to him and her ear next to the receiver so she could listen too, she was shaking at the thought of her little girl in the hands of someone else and she was powerless to help or do anything about it.

"Hello, yes," Graham said with anticipation. There was silence, a slight hiss and then the northern voice came back to him.

"Yes? You answer the phone by saying yes? Very submissive of you .You have got shut of your little brat of a boy I hope."

"Yes, we are alone. What do you want? Let me speak to my daughter please. Is she alright?" he pleaded with the voice.

"Shut up and listen. You should know who I am. If you saw me you probably would know. I have given you a second name, have you done anything with that yet?" His voice became annoyed and agitated. He sounded unstable.

"I know you? Your name is Leigh? I don't know anyone of that name I'm sure, I'm sorry"

He was searching his brain but he could not find any answers. Gloria was holding on to him tightly and shaking nervously.

"I fucking bet you are, now you have shown me you do not listen. I'm wondering if you are taking me serious. I said the name leads you to where I'm from, did I not? You obviously do not listen and your precious little girl will suffer for it daddy."

"NO, please no, listen …" but before he could say anything else he shook with dread and fright, as he heard his little girl scream. She yelled out in pain and it cut through him and his wife like a surgeon's scalpel. "Stop, stop," he shouted, holding the phone until his knuckles were white his hand shaking uncontrollably

"Listen, daddy," the voice mocked again. "My second name is Leigh, it is a clue to where I come from. Now to make it easy I will give you another clue. My first name begins with the letter K and should be familiar to you seeing it is your middle name. How fucking easy do you want this?" The line went dead and Graham slowly put the phone down. He looked at the tears in his wife's eyes. As he thought about it, he sat down and put it together. It was very easy, as he said. His wife sat next to him and asked helplessly: "Your middle name, how does he know that, it's Keith? What is all that about?"

"Where do I come from, love?" he said, deep in thought.

"West Yorkshire," she said, confused.

"The town in West Yorkshire?"

"Keighley" She put it together as he had done

"Keith Leigh, a clue to where he comes from. He comes from my home town Keighley. The bastard comes from my home town." Gloria went to the phone quickly. She desperately rang her daughter's mobile number. It rang and rang, then was answered, but no voice came back. The person on the other end just listened. "Listen, whoever you are, so you come from Keighley. Now please listen, we will do anything, just don't hurt my little girl any more please." Her voice became a hesitant stammer and tears came down her face and she could not speak for a moment. But she swallowed and carried on: "Please, please." She pleaded with him. Graham came over and took the phone from her, "We have played your little game. So you come from my home town, maybe I knew you from back then. But this is obviously between ma and you. It has nothing to do with my family. I will give you anything you want, let my girl go and I will go in her place. If it is me you are after then why not come and get me? I'm offering you myself, exchange me for the girl. What do you say? She has nothing to do with this, it is you and me." He waited for an answer. Eventually, it came, the voice monosyllabic and dull. "You are so fucking pathetic. I don't want you yet, I can have more fun with your daughter. What you trying to do, impress your bitch wife? 'Take me instead,' he mocked Graham's voice. "You have watched too many movies. First of all, you do not tell me what to do. So, you have figured out where we come from. Good. Top of the fucking class, it wasn't very hard, was it? I will be in touch. If you keep ringing this phone the battery will run flat and we won't be able to get in touch, will we?" His voice suddenly became loud and offensive.

So stop fucking bothering me and wait for me to phone you two fuckers. You have scored nothing here, and your little girl will suffer for it, and she screams so sweetly."

The line became silent and dead. Graham stood rigid for a moment before he put the phone down and sat down with a thud on the settee as his legs gave way. Gloria sat next to him. They were holding hands, helpless and afraid. She looked at him, her eyes red and hurting, her cheeks wet with tears.

"Who the fuck is it, Graham?" she demanded.

"I don't know." Slowly, he shook his head, swallowing as a lump came to his throat. He lifted her hand and kissed it, saying "it will be alright, love."

"Some fucked up bastard is torturing my baby. He wants you to suffer, us to suffer, and you are telling me it will be alright?" she said, unbelievingly

"Love, what can I do? I don't know what to do." He held back the tears but found it hard.

He saw distress in his wife's eyes, but also blame. He saw his wife looking at him as if it was his fault.

"Why us, Why you?" she screamed

"You think this is my fault? I have done nothing; don't turn against me for God's sake, united we stand, divided we fall. We will get through this but we are going to need each other so just hold it together, for Lisa's sake. I'm not the enemy here, please for Christ sake love, please." They fell into each other's embrace and sobbed not knowing what fate would become of their daughter.

Sam was watching from the kitchen. Seeing the alpha male and his mate in distress caused him worry, the pack was in disarray and two members were missing. He walked slowly into the room and came next to them. Silently, he sat and looked at them both. He then lay down by their side and stayed there, protecting, comforting and making the gesture of comradeship. The house was silent.

Graham was holding his wife; they were gently rocking together with his arms round her. She was still shaking, she was still angry, and she was still just holding herself together. The last thing she wanted to do was fall apart, not be able to cope, not be there, not be next to her man, and not save her daughter.

The big question she kept asking herself was why? What if she had done something differently? What if they would never see her again? She shook this out of her head, but it kept returning, and each time it was harder to get rid of the thought and stay focused and positive. The household was being held to ransom. She did not know how long this would go on for; she just wanted to get her daughter back safely. It didn't matter what it cost. Tears stained her face, her eyes hurt, she was hungry and she was scared, but she could not eat, and could not control this fear she had inside her.

CHAPTER THREE

The room was dimly lit, bare and cold. The house was away from the road and did not look any different from any of the others in the street. But it held a secret, a secret that no one knew. Inside was a girl held against her will, a girl who was petrified, a girl who wanted her family. She was Lisa, who was tied in a chair in the middle of an upstairs room of the house.

Desolate and lonely, she looked round, scared and shivering. Her fear made her feel ill. She did not know what had happened; she was confused and tired, she had not slept, dared not sleep. Why had she been brought here? The paper was coming off the walls and the place was damp. You could smell the fustiness in the air; the place was in need of decoration, the carpet on the floor was worn but in places it was brighter than anywhere else. She could make out where a bed had been and a wardrobe, the indentations were still in the carpet and all the furniture had been moved before she had been brought in.

She was sat and tied to a chair and was afraid to struggle. She did not know what was behind the door. She stayed still and quiet and her head hurt where she had been hit across it. But she had no recollection of how she had been brought here. She woke up and was told to talk to her mother on the phone. She was dazed, terrified and confused but did what she was told. Her heart missed a beat when the door slowly opened. She sank back into the chair and looked at the opening where the door swung open. She could see a shadow standing outside. She began to tremble as she heard a laugh, a slight mean laugh, then in he walked, looking at her with his head slightly bowed and his eyes fixed on her as if he was looking over glasses. A little devilish grin on his twisted face made her bite her lip with panic. She looked at him with worried, tear-filled bloodshot eyes. He stood in front of her, and looked her up and down with disgust. She looked back at him, shaking and shivering violently. She dared not say a word. He looked about twenty five and she noticed something about him, it seemed familiar but she could not put her finger on it. It was the duck feeder but now she was closer, she could see something familiar about him, it confused and bewildered her.

He was clean shaven and had short dark hair and was dressed in casual but out of date clothes. He stood straight and lifted his head towards her.

"I didn't have any childhood," he said in a northern accent. "I bet you were taken to the fair, on holidays, days out to the fucking seaside, looked after like a little baby." His voice became louder and angrier "bought toys, nice fucking things. You have good fucking memories and what have I got nothing fucking nothing."

"Please," she pleaded, but could say no more. She sobbed and sniffed and cried at his voice and insane-looking wide eyes, as he stared at her.

"Please, Fucking please." His voice came down a level and he spoke to her in a calmer way again. "I didn't have a chance, what chance did I have? I was doomed before I was fucking born; you see we have more in common than you know a lot more. Now if you give me any trouble I will cut you up into small pieces then put bits of you in concrete blocks and drop them in rivers and lakes all over the fucking country. That way you will never be found, I will cut off your fingers and burn them. I will pull out your teeth and grind them down to a powder which I will drink in my tea.

You see I know it's not your fault but I'm using you as my instrument, an instrument to get to him, his little precious daughter. But what am I doing this for I hear you say. Well, if I have to kill you then I might tell you so you can know what sort of man your daddy is. I want daddy to hear the fear in your voice, I want him to suffer psychologically, I want him to suffer, suffer." He shouted and stomped his foot into the wooden floor and came up to her closely. She tried to back away but was restricted by the rope tying her to the chair. His face was close to hers and she turned her head away. His breath smelt horrible and she started to cry uncontrollably. She wanted the toilet but dared not ask. She could not hold it any longer as urine ran down her leg and off the chair onto the carpet. He looked down at it and then back at her. He laughed loudly and tilted his head back. He turned and left the room, closing the door behind him. She sobbed and cried out with shame and humiliation, and could not stop. This was a nightmare she was not going to wake up from and she knew it.

Her knickers were wet and her leg also. She felt even more uncomfortable and ashamed about wetting herself. She looked at the window. It was covered with an old curtain, ripped at one corner. It was plain, thick and not much light came through it. Startled at the door opening again, she swallowed but her mouth was dry. In walked her captor; he was not laughing anymore. He had a serious look on his face and stood in front of her. She looked up at him with a worried face.

"Right, we can work this two ways," he began to say, "one, you are a silly bitch and I have to be heavy handed and beat the shit out of ya, or you can be sensible and do as you're told. Which is it to be?" He waited for an answer. She swallowed again and quietly and hesitantly said:

"I will do what you want if you don't hurt me."

"You will do what I want if I do hurt you, stupid. Now which one is it to be?"

"I will be sensible." She nodded.

"Good, you are learning. Right, I don't want you smelling of piss all the bloody time, so when you want to go to the bog, you tell me, right. Don't ever piss or shit your fucking self again. Is that clear?"

"Yes," she said nodding her head again. He nodded back at her and left saying nothing more to her. She heard him walking into the next room opening a drawer. It was stiff and he cursed as he struggled with it. He returned promptly with some clothes, a short black skirt and a low cut blouse. She looked at them and took an instant dislike to them, but dared not say anything about it they were old fashioned and she could smell the funky smell they had. Surprisingly, they seemed to be her size. They looked cheap and she would not want to be seen dead in any of them, but knew she was in no position to say so. He also had a black cloth bag in his hand. He walked over to her and dropped the skirt and top on the floor. He took the cloth bag and put it over her head. She started to panic and shake. He slapped her across the head saying loudly: "Be still cow, you're going to keep this bag on your stupid head at all times until I tell you to take it off or I take it off for you."

She was in darkness, her sense of sight was taken away from her and it was scary. She did not know what was going to happen, but she felt him behind her undoing her ties.

She was soon free, and pulled up out of the chair. Her feet were a little unsteady and numb, but she soon got feeling back in them.

"Where are we going?" she asked, hesitantly.

"To get you cleaned up you, tart." He took her arm and pulled her from the room, picking up the clothes from the floor as he did. She was taken into a cold room; she could see nothing but could detect a foul smell. It reeked in her nostrils. It was colder here and the floor was not carpeted. She figured out it was the bathroom. "Right cow, you take your clothes off and wash your stinking pussy. Then you put these clothes on for me." He was silent as she started to do as she was told. Scared and cold, she undressed. She could see nothing and the fear grew as she sensed he was coming closer, but he seemed to walk away past her and to the opposite side of the room. She could hear taps being turned on, water flowing, and something put under it to break the noise of the constant gush. When she was naked, she covered herself the best she could with her arms and hand. Feeling embarrassed and vulnerable, she started to breathe heavily. He walked up to her and took her hand. It made her jump at first but he pulled her to him and gave her a damp cloth saying in a disgusted voice:

"Wash your smelly cunt, you dirty cow." She started to wash the urine from between her legs and down her inner thigh. The water was cold but welcoming. When she was clean again, he took the cloth from her then gave her a towel. It was rough and she found it coarse, hard and unclean. It had a bad smell to it. After she had dried herself, he put the skirt in her hand and she put it on the best she could. She was blindfolded and almost lost her balance. The blouse was next and she was dressed again and felt better for it.He grabbed hold of her hand and violently pulled her out of the bathroom and back to the

carpeted room, pushing her towards the chair. She lost her balance and fell to the ground.

She cried out in pain as she twisted her ankle and rolled over as she held it, whimpering.

"I'm sorry," she yelled at him with painful emotion, which was lost on him. He just stood there and told her coldly and very sternly: "Take off your hood, bitch." She reached up and pulled her hood off. She looked up and saw him standing over her holding his penis in his hand. She yelled out in surprised disgusted horror, and backed away from him. Rape was something she had always feared and if it was going to become reality she would die right here and now. She was sure of it. He looked at her and laughed out loudly. He rocked his head back as he put his penis back into his pants. Walking up to her, he grabbed her hair and pulled her up. She was paralyzed with fear, and wanted to run, but her legs were too weak and would not respond to her brain's command. She reached up and pulled on his grip to take some of the weight off her hair. The roots of her hair began to give; she could hear them pulling out. He sat her back in the chair and pulled her arms round to the back and tied her back up and this time it was tighter than before. She cried and sobbed at him, saying through her tears:

"Please, don't hurt me, please."

"Shut up. When I was feeding the ducks you told me I should be put away. You flirted with me then, oh you was the hard bitch back then, well all that is changing now isn't it, not so fucking tough now are we bitch? If you give me any trouble I will fuck you. Do you understand? I will fuck your mouth, I will fuck your cunt and I will fuck your arse. Do you understand?" He sounded demented and she knew he meant it. "Be fucking good and stop giving me trouble bitch." He shouted into her face so closely that their noses were touching. The stink from his breath made her heave. She did not want him to touch her so nodded a frantic 'yes.' He made sure the ties were secure and then left the room once more. It was again quiet. She did not know where she was or what it was all about. She wished she had never teased him now, but it seemed to be her father he was after. She tried to move her hands but the ties were too tight. He had done them tighter than before. She was uncomfortable, cold and hungry, scared to death that she was going to be raped. That was her worst nightmare. She had decided to do anything that he said just so long as he did not abuse and rape her. Escape was in her mind but not knowing where she was or how to get out; it was out of the question right now. She could not even get out of her ties, never mind the room. Sniffling and holding back tears keeping hold of her sanity was hard at this point. She wanted to scream out but dared not. She was going to have to wait her chance, if that chance ever came. Turning in the chair, she tried to make herself as comfortable as possible.

The skirt was a size too small she found when she moved, and the blouse had a stagnant smell. Lifting her head away from it, she sniffed up and screwed her nose up at the stench. Worrying about what her mother must be going through made her sad, but also gave her a lift, a determination to get through this, if not for herself but for her mother and father. She had to be strong and she knew that now. She had not to give up and she knew that as well. Gaining strength from it all, she clenched her fists and breathed out. She was going to give this her best and not let this bastard, whoever he was, win. She was going to get out of here, and alive.

CHAPTER FOUR

"You must tell Peter," Gloria pleaded, with a painful look on her face.

"He said not to involve the police. What if he is watching the house?"

"Oh for god's sake, we have got to do something," she shouted at him and he knew she was right. Picking up the phone, he rang a number. He waited and then said, in as normal voice as he could manage:

"Hello, yeah could I speak to detective sergeant Peter Summers please, Graham, his friend…yes." The line was silent for a few moments then the voice of Peter came back to him.

"How we doing, you old spud? What the hell you ringing me at work for?"

"Peter could you come over right away, but please come in the back way and tell no one." A panic was in his voice he could not disguise

"Are you alright mate?"

"Please, please, please." His voice had a nervous fault in it and his friend knew there was something wrong.

"Alright mate, you sure you want me to come alone? If you're in trouble I could bring reinforcements you know, what's wrong?"

"Pete, please just come round and I will explain. There is no one here but I need to talk to you"

"Be there in twenty." The phone went dead, and he hung up. Gloria came to him and put her arms round him.

"We're doing the right thing, you will see." Her words were comforting to him and he was so glad he had her.

It was only fifteen minutes later when Peter was climbing over the back fence, and was let into the house. Petting the welcoming dog in its corner as it greeted him; he walked in very curiously and could see something was wrong instantly. He was shown into the living room where he saw Gloria sat in a chair. Her eyes were red and bloodshot. He smiled and she returned one to him. Graham came to him and took a deep breath. He looked at his wife then at Peter.

"Pete, we need your help, but first you must promise me something."

"What?" Peter was confused; he had never seen any of them like this before.

"Promise me my friend," Graham said, standing firm.

"Alright I promise, what the bloody hell is wrong?"

"It's Lisa. She is being held by someone and we don't know who or why."

"Abducted?" His voice became official; he looked at Gloria

breaking into tears.

"Yes we think so, now you have got to help me as a friend, not the police. I have been told she will be hurt if I involve the police. I'm not taking that risk."

Looking at his two friends, Peter calmly sat down. Graham sat down beside him. Rubbing his face with his left hand, he thought a while, then looked at Graham and told him with a voice of reason and authority:

"Listen to me very carefully. I know you are hurting and must be bloody petrified, but you must involve the police, you must get some expert help here."

"No, no we can't, he might kill her," Gloria shouted at him, through her tears. He turned to Graham and said to him:

"We have trained and experienced officers who can deal with this, experts, professionals. What has he said and what does he want?"

"We don't know what he wants yet. He is called Keith Leigh, and comes from my home town. He seems to know a lot about me, but we're not sure if he has just got it off Lisa, he is not demanding anything yet."

"How is he getting in touch with you?" Peter asked calmly

"Through Lisa's mobile phone."

"We might be able to trace that. So he is saying he knows you and if you go to the police Lisa will be hurt?" Peter confirmed.

"Yes." Graham was nervous, and he was fidgeting a lot in his seat. "How many times is he calling you in a day? And how long is he on the line, and how long has this gone on for? How long has he had her?"

"A few days, and he has called a few times in that time. He won't tell me what he wants Pete, all we want is our girl back safe. I will give anything for that."

"Yes, of course. How did he grab her? Do you know?" Peter was sounding very professional, and his police persona was coming to the surface."No, she just didn't come home, and then we got this phone call from her."

"So you have spoken to Lisa, have you?" he sounded a little surprised

"Yes, we have She sounds scared and shook up." Graham said with a worried voice

"Well, that is something. At least we know she is alright. You have to be alive to be scared, again Graham, I know you two are at your wits' end, but you must report this.

They always say don't go to the police, they always threaten you with that. It is a classic sign, he probably has made mistakes when he is talking to you, but you being so emotionally involved have not picked up on it. I can have a team here in twenty minutes. We can tap your phone, get in touch with the mobile network provider, find out who he is and …" but he was not allowed to finish.

"No, no I can't risk it. He might be watching the house and I want your help alone or not at all. For god's sake, we're talking about my kid here." His voice was desperate. He buried his head in his hands shaking his head. Peter could see he was at his emotional wits' end so, taking a slow breath, he tried a different approach.

"Alright Graham, I can see and understand you're both upset, but if it was someone else, and you were asked, what they should do what would you say?"

"It isn't someone else's, it is my child." Graham broke down and shouted at his friend, who stayed calm and in control. He knew he would not make them see sense at this stage, so he decided, against his better judgment to go with it and try to help, hopefully getting the police involved later, which he knew to be the right thing to do.

"Ok, stay calm. Now where is your boy?" He looked round for him.

"Staying at his gran's," Gloria said through her tears.

"Does he know about what has happened?" She shook her head, unable to speak.

"What can we do?" Graham said, trying to calming himself.

"Who have you told?"

"You," was his simple and blunt answer.

"You both off work now?"

"Yes, work is sorted out, what can we do?"

"Well, like I said. My advice would be to go to the police, but you're not going to do that. By rights, I should report this but I won't, and the only reason I won't is because I know you and you're both good friends of mine. I can't get your phone tapped without a official permission, and more importantly without causing suspicion, so I want you to tell me everything that has happened down to the smallest detail, no matter how unimportant you might think it is."

"Do you want a drink Peter?" Gloria managed to ask. He nodded. He stood up and took off his jacket, taking a small notebook and pen from his jacket pocket as he did so. He sat with Graham who began to tell him all that had happened, while Gloria went to make them all a drink. She let the dog out into the garden and watched him sniffing around. He missed Sebastian, and so did she. She would phone him tonight to make sure he was alright. She changed the dog's water in his bowl while he was outside and she was waiting for the kettle to boil. She could hear her husband telling Peter all he knew and what had happened. Peter was asking the occasional question and taking notes. She watched out of the window and was lost in her thoughts for a time, wondering if she would ever see her daughter again. She felt sorry for all the times she had punished her, all the times she had shouted at her, and all the times they had fallen out. Bringing the tea in a few minutes later, Gloria sat down, cupping the mug of tea in her hands, feeling the warm glow through her hands.

"This Keith Leigh is a wind up then of course?" Peter told Graham.

"Well, I do come from Keighley"

"Yeah, but Lisa knows that. He might just be using what she knows and what he is asking her. You're going to have to find out what he wants, and ask him to answer a question about the home town that Lisa does not know, something only someone from there will and should know. We have to establish what the hell he wants, and who the hell he is. When we find that out we have a much better chance of getting to a satisfactory end, getting Lisa back and putting this sick fucker away." He took a drink of his tea and sat back on the settee with a deep sigh.

"So what are the chances? Will I ever see her again?" Gloria asked hesitantly.

"If I knew what he wanted and who he was I could answer that question, but we must think positively. Yes, you will see your daughter again. He will come and tell us what he wants soon, will have to. We have got to get him working for us, let him think he is winning when actually he is on a downward fall to capture. We have got to find things out without him knowing, listen for sounds in the background when he calls. I will get you a listening device for your phone that will record your calls."

"I thought you said we can't have it tapped without court permission?"

"I'm not tapping it; I'm recording your calls. You can buy these devices in the high street

now. Leave it to me, but you have got to get him talking a lot. Try to talk to Lisa every time, comfort her and reassure her you are doing all you can. She is a strong girl and she

is smart. That is a plus for us." He took another drink of his tea. Graham turned to face him.

"What is the outcome of most of the abductions you have worked on Pete?"

"The force have been involved from the start, and we have done it within the week. Like I said, we have experts, sophisticated equipment to trace calls and all sorts of professional stuff to help you That is why I pleaded with ya to get it official. It depends on who we are dealing with.

"No, I can't, not yet, it might hurt Lisa I'm not risking that."

"Whoever he is?" Peter said, looking him in the eye.

"Exactly." He shrugged his shoulders in confusion

"You're going to have to rack your brains mate. Who wants you? Wants to hurt you? This could go back years man, you're going to have to try. Did you recognise the voice at all?"

Graham thought for a moment, there was something there but he could not put his finger on it. He shook his head saying:

"No, no not really."

"Well, keep thinking have you upset anyone at work? Do you owe money? Have you stood on anyone's toes? Have you any enemies you know of? Have you come into a lot of money? Anything out of the usual happened?"

"I can't think Peter I don't know. No, none of them, nothing has happened, nothing."

"Well, I will help you as much as I can, but again I ask you to make it official. I can help you a lot more if you do. Please think about it, it is the best chance you have got of getting Lisa back safely."

"We will think about it." He looked at his wife for a moment, then back at his friend.

"But for now no one is to know." His voice was weak and tired. Peter looked at his friend, his friend in need. He turned to Gloria, a woman normally full of life and joy. She was a shadow of her former self. She sat on the chair, shoulders arched round and looking at him with tearful eyes. He took a deep breath and sighed. He should report it, he knew that, but, with a slight shake of his head in disapproval, he took a drink of his tea. He looked at this normally strong family falling apart. It was sad but if he could help them then he would. But he was going to push to get the police involved; he knew that was their best chance. He just hoped it would not turn out to be their only one.

It was the next day when the package arrived at the house. Gloria had just finished talking to her mother and reassuring her everything was alright. They just wanted some space together, but mothers know when something was wrong with their offspring, and Gloria's mum was no different. But she let it go and accepted what her daughter was telling her, for now. The postman knocked and Graham went to the door taking the package off him. It was drizzling and a horrible looking day. The brown paper covering the item was worn and old. It was taped up and felt soft. A confused Graham brought it into the house. The stamp had been stuck on crookedly and the post office date stamp was unreadable; the dampness of the weather had smudged it. He took it into the kitchen and cut it open with some scissors. Gloria came and watched as he unwrapped it. She shook with horror, and a sinking in her stomach made her feel sick, as she saw what was in it - her daughter's clothes, the last ones she had seen her in. Graham took them out and put them on the table. A cold chill went through his body. There was nothing else in the package.

"Oh my god, what does this mean?" Gloria sat down holding on to the shirt that her daughter had been wearing. What was she wearing now? What was he doing to her? She became panic stricken and did not know what to do. She jumped and looked at her husband as the phone rang. They both ran into the living room. Graham picked it up quickly and said:

"Yes, who is it?" He had anxiety in his voice.

"You had the post yet?"

"Yes, where is she? What have you done to her?" he demanded.

"Nothing yet now listen to me, this time it is her clothes the next time it might be a finger, or an ear, or even a nipple. So let me remind you, if I think you are involving the police, private investigator, or anyone, I will send her though the post a piece at a time. Is that understood? I will be watching."

"Let me speak to her, is she alright? I want to know she is alright. I will do nothing until I know you have not hurt her. Do you hear?" His voice had a desperate urgency in it and he was on the verge of panic, but what he heard calmed him slightly. It was the scared voice of his little girl his daughter.

"Daddy, I'm here, please do as he says." Her voice cut deep into him and tears streamed down his cheeks as he heard the pathetic, petrified little voice of his little girl. She was alive and seemed well, under the circumstances.

"I will darling, I will. What is it he wants me to do, sweetheart?" There was silence for a moment and he could hear voices on the

82

other end, then his little girl's voice said to him again:

"He says I'm wearing what she was wearing when you did it, a black skirt and a low cut blue top. Does that mean anything daddy?"

"Darling, you keep calm. It will be alright we are doing..." but before he finished the man's voice came back at him with a vengeance. It was loud and fierce.

"That is your second clue, Bastard. Figured it out yet?" The phone went dead. Graham put it down and turned to his wife, who was looking at him sadly.

"I spoke to her. She is alright and he has not hurt her. She is ok." He gave a faint, quivering smile. They hugged and held each other. Graham was thinking about what had been said, a black skirt, and a blue low cut top. It meant nothing to him. He was confused and getting worried. His next move was to ring Peter. Lisa was sat in the chair, hungry, thirsty, cold and tired. She had not slept all night. Fear would not let go its grip to let her get the much needed sleep her body wanted. She looked up at the duck feeder in front of her. He was holding her mobile phone with a look of hatred on his face. Slowly, he took his gaze from the floor to her. His eyes pierced hers and she looked away to the floor.

"Do you know what your daddy did?" he said in a cruel mocking voice.

"No," she said shaking her head, not looking at him but keeping her eyes fixed on the floor.

"What do you think of your father?"

"I love him very much."

"Love an overrated emotion. Blind and stupid people fall in love. It does not exist; it is the weak looking for an excuse to be wanted."

"Please tell me what you want," she asked biting her bottom lip with anxiety.

"I want the oldest emotion known to man, I want what is mine, I want the years back, I want the fucker to pay, I want to know why I was not told the truth, I want to know why I had to extract it, I want what I want, revenge." He shouted his last word at the top of his voice which made her crouch down and bow her head. He left the room, slamming the door behind him.

She could hear him storming into the other room next to hers, then go downstairs and slam the room door at the bottom of the hall. Looking round her prison, she was helpless and knew it. It was uncomfortable and cold; her stomach rumbled for want of food, and her mouth was dry. She had not dared ask for anything and was becoming weak, knowing she must eat. She decided she must communicate with this man instead of just letting him domineer her all the time. It would be hard but she knew she must do something to try to help herself and keep strong willed, try and keep on top of it, and not get drilled down into submission. Her dad always told her to be strong and look your fears in the eye. Overcome them, and no longer were they fears, and you would go forward. It was the only way. She wanted out of this mess and was going to do it, one way or another. She had cried and was scared but she knew in that state of mind she would not be able to do anything positive for herself. Fighting it head on was going to be dangerous and hard but she was going to try, she had too, she dug deep and gritted her teeth breathing in deeply.

Deciding to talk to try to get his confidence was her first choice. Thinking all the time, she got her mind to work on how to get out of this nightmare, how to make it work in her favor, if that was possible. Suddenly, she looked up and strained her ears as she heard something, a muffled sound. Not sure what it was, she listened again. The noise came from somewhere in the house. It might have been him doing something, but she knew he was downstairs. This noise seems to come from upstairs. She listened again, but could not make out what it was. It seemed to come from the next room or down the corridor a bit. A cold chill went through her as she suddenly realised she might not be alone in the house with him. There might be someone else in here with her. Not knowing if this was a good thing or a bad one, she did not know what to think. Had he got someone else in the house like her? If so, they were allies, but if it was someone like him then she was in even more trouble. Again, she listened. A car went past outside and she leant forward. She was sure she had heard it, a muffled sound of someone moving, maybe. The silence hurt her ears. Sighing and giving up, she slumped back into the chair, repositioning herself and trying to get as comfortable as she could. Looking at the covered window, she wondered where she was, remembering nothing of how she was brought here. All she knew was she was hit from behind and dragged into a car, and then it was all blank. Waking up here in this room, god knows where, wishing she had gone home a different way that day. She bowed her head and looked down at the skirt she was made to wear. She hated it and it bothered her. It shouldn't but it did. The clothes were dated and horrible. Strangely a smile came across her face as to what her friends would say if any of them saw her dressed in this rubbish.

"For fuck's sake, Graham, you have got to get in touch with my boys now," Peter insisted to his friend after being shown the parcel.

"No, I can't risk it."

"Listen to me friend. We have forensic experts who will be able to tell us where this was posted, fingerprints, saliva tests, all sorts of matches. Christ, we might even have this fucker on file, and bang we have got him. Now come on, this is not a fucking game. It is your daughter's life we are dealing with here." His voice was full of hope that his friend would see sense.

"I'm not risking it yet Pete, please understand. I'm not playing any game. He wants me and is using my daughter to get to me. Now when I can figure out what he wants I will be able to deal with it. I have spoken with her and she says she is alright. He has not harmed her. If I thought she was being hurt I would not hesitate to bring you in, in an official sense."

"Fuck man, he is holding her against her will. Kidnappers are not nice people. Just because she says she is well on the phone that doesn't mean shit. He will be telling her what to say. You have no idea what he is doing to her. Listen to yourself, because I tell ya now, if any harm comes to her you will never forgive yourself for not informing the police. That is what we're here for, that's what you pay your frigging taxes for, now come on let's get the ball moving. I'll take this in and we will get it looked at by the experts."

He went to pick up the clothes, but was stopped by Graham, who shook his head, saying angrily and with a loud sharpness to his voice.

"No, not yet, please. Let it be for now. I ask you as the only friend I have Pete." Peter shook his head in disbelief. He knew he was right and his friend was wrong, but, then again it was not his daughter that was being held.

"Alright, I have the surveillance device in the car. I will show you how to use it. All you need to do is fix the microphone to your phone and press record. As you speak it will pick up you and the person ringing you. I'm putting my job on the line here, but I'll take the clothes in and try to have the packaging and clothes looked at on the quiet. I'm owed a few favours but if there are any comebacks I will have to make up some cock and bull story. At least then we can find out where it was posted and if we have any fingerprints on it. Do you agree with that?"

"If you can do it without involvement yes, thank you."

"Right at least that is something." Peter said sighing and shaking his head.

"Thank you, I appreciate what you are doing for us."

"Look, I will help you all I can but again I ask you to get it official. There is a limit to what I can do otherwise." They looked towards the stairs as Gloria came down. Pete could see she was not good. She looked drained and weak. He smiled and she came over to her husband, putting her arms round him, as if she needed the support to stand. Looking at Peter, she asked in a serious, steady voice:

"In your experience, what are her chances?" Peter thought for a moment then answered straight and as directly as he thought safe to do so.

"Well, it all depends on who and why, and seeing we don't know that, it is hard to say.

You would have a much better chance if you made it official. All I can say is I will do my best, but like I have just told Graham, you can't leave it too late to involve the police. He might be making mistakes that we could pick up on, but you just have not noticed. Try to involve him in conversation, find out what he wants, say you will do as he says, tell him what he wants to hear, try to put him in a clam and secure mode so that he thinks he is getting what he wants at all times. That way he might pay less attention to Lisa and if you can, always reassure Lisa when you talk to her, she is scared and needs you so make sure she knows you are there for her. Right, I will go and get the recorder for your phone." He went out to his car that he had parked a few streets away round the back. Graham looked down at his wife and smiled at her reassuringly. "He is taking in the clothes and the parcel, getting them checked out on the quiet for us."

"Good, Graham, I think we should tell the police. I think Peter is right."

"I don't know love, let's wait and see what he wants." He kissed her on the head and then went to the kitchen to make a cup of tea.

It was less than twenty minutes later when Peter had the recorder set up on their phone. It was simple. All you had to do was press record and that was it. He took the clothes and went a short time afterwards. They waited for the phone to ring but it didn't.

Afternoon came and went. They had some food and sat by the fire. Sam walked into the room. He was missing his little master, and instead of the walks out to the fields all he got now was let out into the garden. He sat down in front of his two human keepers. He knew something was wrong. Graham was unshaven and looked rough, Gloria was frail-looking and in need of sleep, something like her daughter. She was not doing very well at all. Sam wagged his tail and dropped his ears, but no one was taking any notice of him. Slowly, he walked away and back into the kitchen. He took a drink from his bowl and lay down in his basket.

"Graham, what did he mean when he said this morning that she is wearing what she was wearing when you did it?" Gloria asked without moving her gaze from the floor. Graham took a deep breath and told her:

"I don't know. I have been trying to think about that myself. I just don't know."

"What was it a blue top and a black skirt? Is there something in your past you are not telling me some secret you are locking away?" He closed his eyes for a second before saying to her in a low voice:

"No."

"You would tell me, I would understand, I would not love you any less no matter what you have done, you know." Gloria insisted

"I don't know what he is talking about love, honestly."

"I wonder why he is doing it then. He seems to know about you a lot, and from Keighley. Do you know of any enemies up there?"

"Well, I suppose there are people who don't like me, but nothing to warrant this. Christ,

I've been left for over sixteen years. I have no friends there now, the only person who lives

there who is related to me is my sister, but I have not seen her for almost twenty years."

He stopped. His mouth dropped open, and a thought flashed through his mind. He looked away in case his wife saw his reaction as he remembered something. He swallowed and nervously rubbed his head with his hand. Sighing, he calmed himself.

"You alright love?" Gloria asked him noticing him move.

"Yes, as well as can be expected. I'm going to take Sam for a walk, I won't be long. If he rings don't forget to press record, will you?"

He stood and she nodded her head. From the settee, she watched him go to the kitchen and put the lead on an excited dog. He smiled and looked at his wife laying on her back. She had a sad look on her face and he came close. He bent down, gave her a kiss on the cheek and whispered to her in a quiet and soft reassuring honest voice:

"I do love you."

"Love you too," she smiled and watched him leave. The door closed and she was alone.

The house seemed bare and empty, no noise, no children, no dog, and no husband. She looked at the phone and curled up on the settee holding a cushion for comfort and security until her husband came back.

Night fell and the darkness brought a chill in the air with it. They locked up and settled in for another long night, all secure, dog fed and asleep in his basket. They had a light supper and watched the television, neither of them taking any notice of what was on it. Every now and again, Gloria would look at the phone, wanting it to ring, but then again hoping it would not.

"I thought Pete would have got back in touch by now," she said.

"Probably take time doing it on the quiet. He is calling in some favors, he said. I will thank him properly after all this is over, he is risking his job for us."

"He is a good friend, Peter. We need them right now."

"Yes, have you rang your mother today? How is Sebastian?"

"He's alright. She thinks we're going through a divorce because I'm not telling her what it is all about."

"What have you told her?"

"That we just want some time alone and together. I think she knows something is wrong but is not saying so. She's not stupid, she knows when her daughter is lying to her, but what can I do?" She shrugged her shoulders.

"I'm sure she will understand when we can tell her it is all over."

"I hope it is all over soon. Christ, I'm going insane just thinking about what he might be doing to her. For fuck's sake, why us? What does he want?" Her voice was full of dread, and she became worked up again. Graham came close to her and put his arm round her. He held her tightly and she snuggled into him. It hurt him seeing his wife so upset. He tried not to show it and stayed strong for her but he was bothered about something, something that had come to him, something in his past, something he had never told his wife, and it might, just might, have something to do with all this but he was not sure, not sure at all. He had closed the door on it a long time ago, a door he would never open again, but he feared he would have to bust this door down and face the demon behind it. He was not sure but it all added to his pain of the situation, a pain he would have to suffer alone for now.

Eventually, they both fell into a haunted but much needed sleep. The house was dark and bare, the love and family life had left it. It was cold like a prison cell, not a home any more but a place of upset and worry, somewhere the love had gone and been replaced by torment and emotional torture. It was much like the room his daughter was in. She looked up at the bare, single light bulb hanging from the dark ceiling. It was a low wattage and did not do the job for the size of the room. It had been left on for some reason tonight. She jumped as the door opened and in came the duck feeder, a drill in his hand and a wall bolt with a round sealed hook on it. She watched as he went to the far wall and knelt down. He pulled on the extension cord and she saw the plug was out in the corridor. She saw for the first time out of the room. It was much better than the room she was in, well decorated and did not look like the same house at all. This room had been made to look like this on purpose, she thought. She looked at him as he pulled the trigger on the red power drill. The masonry bit spun and ate into the wall, going through the plaster and into the brick underneath. Red brick dust came out on to the floor. He went in about six inches then stopped. Pulling the drill out, he blew into the hole and dust came out. He put the drill down and then took a spanner from his side pocket. Putting the wall bolt into the hole, he tightened it up with his hands until it opened in the hole, and bit into the brick. He continued with the spanner when he could not do it any more with hands alone. It was about twenty four inches from the floor, and when he had finished he was left with a round sealed hook, bolted to the wall, sticking out and very secure. He knew it could not be moved and was pleased with it. He took the drill and then went out again closing the door behind him. Lisa was a little confused at why he had done this. She looked at the mess on the floor and at the hook sticking out of the wall. She soon found out why it had been done. He came back in and closed the door behind him. This time he took a strong pair of handcuffs from his back pocket. He fixed one end to the hook in the wall pulling at it to make sure it was fixed firmly. He pulled Lisa's chair by tipping the back down so it was only on its two back legs. He pulled it over to the far wall, set it back down, knelt down and pulled one of her legs over to the other locking loop of the handcuff. He put this round her ankle and locked it in place tightly. He looked down and nodded his head. He had a pleased look on his face at a job well done, then untied her from the chair. She stood and was pleased at the relief of doing so. She was cramped and stiff. He took the chair away and went out once again leaving her standing handcuffed to the bolt in the wall. She stretched and moved her upper body about. It felt good to be able to move again. She rubbed her hands to get the circulation back where the ties were tight around her wrists.

It felt good; it was like she was free again. She saw the handcuff round her ankle, but thinking about it, it was better for her, and at this stage she was welcome for small mercies.

She arched her lower back and it was such a nice feeling to have movement again. Swinging her arms round, she took a deep breath, but stopped when the door opened once again. He walked in with a plastic bucket with a tight fitting lid. He put this down by her side and said:" For your shit and piss." He took off the lid and pulled out a cheap, white toilet roll.

"Thank you," she said. He seemed a little confused that she had thanked him. He looked at her with a curious eye then went back out coming in with a milk bottle full of water. He put this down by the bucket and said:

"Water for you to drink."

"Thank you," she smiled and looked at the water. It was something she wanted so badly. He left for a third time and brought in some sandwiches on a cheap, chipped plate, and he put these down next to the water and said:

"Food for you to eat." He made sure the handcuffs were locked.

"Very kind, thank you." He looked at her and said nothing. Slowly, he walked from the room and said from the doorway:

"The light will be out in one hour." She wasted no time. She made sure it was water, smelling it first, and looking at it with a quizzical eye. Convinced, she took a long drink. It felt so nice and her mouth felt refreshed instantly. She swallowed mouthful after mouthful, stopping when she had drank two thirds of it. She looked at the white bread sandwiches. She opened one and saw it was corned beef. There were six in all and they were the same. It was not her best sandwich filling but she was so hungry. She would have eaten anything at that moment. She put it all in her mouth at the same time; she struggled to chew it at first but managed it in the end. It tasted so good. She was not keen on corned beef but this was the best thing she had ever tasted. It was not long before she had eaten all six. It was not enough; she was still hungry, but it was a banquet as far as she was concerned. She washed them down with another mouthful of water. She stretched and the feeling in her limbs was a lot better than tied up in the chair, although she did not have much movement in her left leg. She could sit and even lie down, but for now she relished the pleasure of being able to stand up and move her arms about. She rotated her hips and did a little workout to get her limbs working again. She was trapped and cold, but at least now she had eaten and drank and that was something.

 The floor was hard and uncomfortable. She was laid out on it when the light was turned out. Again, she was thrown into darkness. She looked at the torn curtain, but there were no street light outside like in her room back home. She wondered where she was, and what was going to happen to her. It was a bad dream and she wanted to wake up. The house was silent, and nothing outside could be heard. She must have been off the beaten track, she thought, as she had not heard a sound from outside since she had been there except for the odd car maybe. She closed her eyes and sighed. The floor was not welcoming and the fact she could not really turn round did not help. But it was much better than tied in the chair. It was quiet and she did not know how much time had elapsed. She might even have fallen asleep; she was tired enough, but she knew what she heard. It was a woman's voice, faint but there. Could it be her mind playing tricks on her? But no, there it was again, a muffled cry. It was loud enough for her to hear. There was another woman in this house somewhere. She lifted her head and listened. A thud, louder this time, broke the silence of the night. She closed her eyes and concentrated on her sense of hearing, then she opened them sharply as she heard a painful scream ring out from somewhere deep in the house. It was a woman's scream. She jumped back and was startled by it more than anything. Not knowing what to do, not that she could do a lot anyway, it was silent again, but she was sure this time. There was no doubt about it; she was not alone in the house. He had someone else in here whom, she did not know. But from this she found strength. She was going to beat this bastard whoever he was. She sat up and leant against the wall, thinking of a way she could get away, a way to survive. It was giving her hope and determination and she liked it, this new-found inner strength, and a possible ally in the house.

CHAPTER FIVE

Her night passed slowly and she watched as the light gradually drifted in through the torn curtain. The sun was coming up but she noticed no shadows. Could it be that a field backed on to the house? Perhaps that was why there was no light at night, no sound. She thought and wondered, only stopping when the door opened and in walked the duck feeder wearing the same clothes as the days before. He had bad body odor and was unclean. Walking over to her holding her mobile phone and punching in a number on the small key pad then signaled her to stand. She did so and was told to come close to the phone, finding it repulsive to stand so close to the man but she did as she was told. The phone rang at the other end. Their faces were close so both could hear what was being said, but the mouthpiece was turned towards her more than him. She felt her heart sink as she heard her father answer the phone, fear and worry in his voice.

"Hello," he said desperately

"Tell him, you are safe for now," she was told to say.

"Hello dad, I'm alright for now. I have been given some water and food in my bare room." She looked at the duck feeder, who saw nothing wrong in what she was said so she gained confidence." Is mum alright?" she asked.

"Yes, love she is here with me. Could you tell me what this is all about?" She looked at the duck feeder and saw him shaking his head at her.

"No, not yet dad, but don't worry I watched the sunrise this morning. It was clear without any shadows like across a field."

"Stop, no, no," the duck feeder shouted pushing her away and down to the floor. She fell hard but was not hurt.

"Lisa, Lisa are you alright?" her father's voice screamed back over the phone.

"She won't be if she tries owt like that again I tell ya."

"Let me talk to her, what have you done you sick little fucker?"

"Don't call me names, or your precious little daughter will suffer for it," he said evenly, looking at the phone as he spoke into it.

"Ok, ok I'm sorry. Can I speak to her again please?" The phone was held out once more to Lisa with one hand, the other clenched into a fist next to her head.

"Hello daddy, don't worry I'm ok. He won't tell me what he wants but he has not hurt me, so you and mum don't worry alright? Please, don't worry. Give my love to Sebastian and I love you and mummy." She began to falter and get upset; the phone was pulled away and the duck feeder was back in charge.

"Right, fuck face, I'm feeding and watering her, and you know she is still living, so if you want her to stay that way you are going to have to do something for me, something you should have done a long time ago."

"Anything you want, you can have anything."

"Can I have your time, your love, your attention? You can't give me back what you owe me, so I'm going to take something else. I'm going to make you suffer a bit. Do you know how much I have suffered? Do you know what sort of life I have had? No, of course you don't, but you should do, you fucking should do."

"You seem to know a lot about me, have I ever met you?"

"No, you have never met me, that is the fucking problem you should have, you fucking should have. I can't believe you have not sorted it out yet. I bet your nice, little wife knows nothing of your disgusting past. In fact I will tell your little bastard here all about you." The phone was then turned off. He put it away in his pocket and looked down at Lisa sat on the floor. She looked up at him and gave him eye contact. She hated him and it Showed, she was not hiding her feelings anymore.

"What the fuck are you looking at?" he asked, annoyed.

"I'm looking at you," she said, scared, but as solid as she could

"Why do you fancy me?" He gave a sarcastic smile and laughed. "Not in a million years."

"When I fed the ducks you were all flirty then you little slag, just like me mother, just like them all. The whole fucking world is full of slags. She was about your age when it happened you know, you could go the same way, you could make one of me. Would you like that?" he glared at her and she tried hard not to look away. "What are you talking about?" She was confused and shook her head at him. He laughed out loudly and walked from the room slamming the door. She watched him go and cursed after him. The hate had taken over from her fear, not only for what he was doing to her, but what he was doing to her mother and father. She hated him the most for that. If she could make him suffer she would, if she could help her father she would, and if she could get out of this place she would. She pulled at the chain of the handcuffs but it was solid and tight. She cursed at it and pulled with all her strength, but it would not budge. She even tried to turn it but he had tightened it up so much with the spanner she could not move it at all. The plaster had cracked and dented where he had screwed it into the wall. She started to pick at it and chip it away, but it went into solid brick underneath. She knew that she did not have a chance with her bare hands. The room was bare; there was nothing she could use as a tool even if she could get to it.

She was stuck, and stuck fast. She let out a long sigh. Fed up and uncomfortable, she wanted to make some sort of effort to get away, but what she could do was limited. She thought hard; it drove her on and made her stronger, it gave her a purpose to go on. Thinking about her family made her more determined. She was going to survive this; she would make sure of that. She wondered what her family was doing and thinking about all the times she had disrespected her mother and father. She regretted it now, regretted all the times she had been cruel to her brother, said some bitchy things, and wished she hadn't. Lots of memories flashed through her mind, things she should have said, things she shouldn't, things she should have done, and not done. She made a conscious decision to change when she got back. Things would be different; things would be much more close and much more faithful. She would tell her family that she loved them and she would go out of her way to show them, show them all that she cared for them and wanted to be cared for.

The next day Gloria was in bed when Peter came round. He was glad because he wanted to speak to Graham alone. He was shown in and they sat down together on the settee.

"Find out anything?"asked Graham.

"No fingerprints we can trace, some on it but they're not on our file. Still, we're having it checked, but it's not easy I can tell you. If the wrong nosey bastard comes along and sees what I'm doing I will have to explain it all so just hope the favors I'm pulling in are good enough. The paper and packaging is standard stuff, buy it anywhere. It was posted in

Keighley, west Yorkshire that we have made sure of. If I was official we could go up there and make some enquiries and might be able to get somewhere, but we're not so I can't. Now does Keighley hold any secrets for you Graham?" He looked at his friend with a questioning eye.

"How do you mean?"

"Well, your daughter is kidnapped, no ransom has been demanded, and she is not being raped used or abused, he knows about you, and he comes from your home town. Now, come on man I'm not stupid. It does not fit no demands, no sexual gratification, no apparent motive except to torture you."

"I don't know, I don't know why he did not take me if that was the case." He shook his head unknowingly.

"Because he wants you to suffer obviously, now, like I said before you hold the key to this, I'm sure of it. You have the puzzle solved in your head you just don't know it. This is not a bloody game, you're dealing with vengeance here and it is a nasty thing that. Revenge for something can go back years, you're going to have to try a lot harder than you are doing I can tell you. It is from your past and you are the only one who can solve it. Think what this is doing to your family, to your life, to everyone around you."

"I know, I know, what am I supposed to do? I don't know who he is for god's sake."

Graham raised his voice then stopped looking in the direction of the stairs so not to awaken his wife.

"Well, if you ask me, in a way you are being lucky. He is not hurting her, as far as we know, yet, and I tell you my friend if you think this is bad wait until you hear her cries and screams. It will rip you apart. I've seen it before and I've witnessed its disaster on relationships and families. It mentally scars you and all around you for life. I would think very seriously about calling in the police, I say again."

"Christ, don't you think I know that. Don't you think my insides turn to shit when the phone rings. It tears me apart when I hear her voice and know that sick fucker is next to her, what he might do to her. Fucking hell man, what do you think I am? Don't you think if I knew anything to help I would do it?" His voice was angry, not at his friend but at himself and the helplessness of it all.

"Graham, listen to me, you are in a nightmare and you're not going to wake up until it is all over, and when you do awaken from it all, it will never go away. Now, have you recorded anything for me? Has he rung again?"

"I spoke to her last night. She tried to tell me where she was I think, said she watched the sunrise without a shadow or something, like across a field. I'm not sure what she meant, you will have to listen to it."

"Did you recognise anything, anything at all?"

"No, I have been thinking what she said but I don't know what she meant. A field Could be anywhere." He shook his head, slowly and dejectedly.

"I will listen to it before I go, but this is good. At least she is trying to tell you. That is a positive thing, a move in the right direction. She is a good kid Lisa, got her head on the right way." He looked at his friend and saw the sadness in his eyes as he thought about his daughter. Peter sighed; he had seen it all before with other cases, but this was his friend and it was not easy for him either.

"I don't know what to do Pete, I have to stay strong for Gloria's sake but I'm hurting. I can't stop blaming myself, if this is because I have done something why won't he just come out and tell me for fuck's sake? I will pay for my mistake, it is me, not Lisa who should be there, and this has nothing to do with her. It's me, not her, not her mother, not anyone but me." He had tears in his eyes and a lump in his throat. He swallowed and took a deep breath.

"I'm afraid it is a hard world my friend. We can't do much until we find out exactly what

he wants from you, until we find out how long he wants to play his sick game, to see you suffer. You could play it by not showing you're breaking and hope he gets frustrated with it, but that could be dangerous for Lisa. You could break down and show that he has won, maybe that way he will slip and we might get something from him. If he wants to destroy you then if we let him think he has succeeded then maybe, I say maybe, he might let off a little. It all depends on what the hell he thinks or what you have done. He is pissed off with you big time and we have got to find out why. It might be a simple, trivial thing to you, but to him it might have great implications. Something small to one is paramount to another. Reality is hitting you hard and you are going to have to hit back just as hard, if not harder." Peter was being candid with his friend and had to be.

"Yes I know, someone in Keighley is holding my kid, someone from my past, someone who knows about me, but who and why?"

"Well, this is what we are going to find out and the best person to answer these questions is you. I suggest you go through as much of your life as you can, from childhood to when you left. Along the way you seriously pissed someone off. They found out where you lived down here, and you are going to have to find out who knew you lived here from up there. That might be a good point to start. How many people from Keighley knows where you live now? Who have you told? Have you had anyone down here, friends or family? Have you told anyone? Have you sent off for anything to be delivered here?" Peter was sounding very professional and official. Graham looked at his friend and tried to think but could not. He shook his head and put it into his hands, shaking it slowly. He looked up and let out a long agonising breath. He turned to face Peter and slowly and quietly said:.

"I can't think, I don't know. None of my family has been here; I don't think anyone has in fact. I don't know for sure."

"None of your family has been here at all?" He sounded a little surprised.

"No, we're not a close knit lot, never have been."

"What about friends then?"

"No, no I'm sure of that. I've lost touch with them all." Graham shook his head

"This could go back years I told you. What about when you go back up for a visit, where do you stay? Who do you see?"

"I don't stay; I'm up and down in the day if I go at all."

"What about ex girlfriends? Have you many of them?"

"It is a man Peter, not a woman."

"A man who might be going out with your ex, or a man who might know about you from someone else and not from personal experience."

"Fucking hell, I don't know." He was at his wits' end and it showed, in his face and in the way he held his head down and drooped. Peter looked at him and felt sorry. He was a hard man but this was his friend and he could see what this was doing to him. He wished he could help more but he knew the only man to help this situation was Graham himself.

"Listen Graham, write it all down. Every time you remember something write it down, places, faces, people, incidents, fights, anything, no matter what, ok?"

Graham nodded and grunted something but Peter could not make it out. He left him sitting there and went to the phone. He listened to the tape, and then listened to it again and again, trying to find any clue at all he could.

"Why? Just tell me why?" Graham said as Peter came back to him. He stood above him and looked down at a broken man.

"How many people have asked that question? Look, you have to be brave, strong and ready, we just don't know what is going to happen. But whatever it is we have to be ready, so do as I said and start thinking of something in your past that could have triggered this off. There must be something. Although it might not seem a lot to you it fucking must be to someone else. What major factor would bring something like this on?

Come on, man." Peter raised his voice trying to snap his friend into some reality. He

didn't want him slipping away into self pity, or depression, and he knew he would not be any good to him then.

"Look, if I knew don't you think I would tell you. It's my fucking daughter that is being kept hostage by this fucker." His eyes were red and bloodshot, his voice a little distant and his face had become drawn.

"Good, Graham, good, start to use this anger, you have to fucking remember what happened to you sometime, something is there, and if you have forgotten, then fucking remember again fast, because I or no one else can do it for you. I have told you, it is you who holds the answer to this, for fuck's sake Graham." He sat next to him on the settee. Peter looked at him; Graham looked back, a little confused and asked:

"What?"

"Is there something you're not telling me?"

"No, of course not. Fucking hell!" He shook his head and leant back.

Peter looked at him and studied him for a moment. His police ptraining and gut feeling took over and he scrutinised his friend. He knew something was wrong but putting his finger on it was the hard part. He would have taken anyone else to the cells and got it out of them, but for now he just had to wait, be patient and hope his friend came up with something, because he knew the longer it went on like this, the worse it would get, not only for his friends, but for Lisa also.

Lisa was sat alone and looking at the wall, trying to keep sane and in control. She had asked herself the question everyone asked when they' in trouble: why? But she had no answers. She looked up as the door opened and in walked the duck feeder. He walked to the bucket and said, with a smile so false it hurt:

"So you have used the bucket little girl? Good, at least you won't stink the fucking place out now." He took it and went away. She could hear him go into the bathroom and empty the bucket into the toilet, then flush it. She could see through the slightly open door into the landing again, moving round to get a better look. The house was well decorated and not what she expected at all. This room was bare but the rest of the house was not, twice now she had witnessed this. She moved back on hearing him returning. He put the clean bucket down by her side and then stood looking at her. She was made to feel uncomfortable and did not like to be stared at she asked him:

"How long are you going to keep me here? Why won't you tell us what you want?" He took a deep breath before answering:

"It is up to me what happens, not you, not your daddy, not any fucker. You're precious daddy is a bastard, a dirty bastard. You will find out and when you do I bet you won't be all nice to him then, not loving daddy then, oh no. If I tell you what he did, if I tell you what all this is about, if I tell you, if, if…" He shouted at her and she crouched away from him. His breath smelt and she found him repulsive. He laughed at her and stood staring down at her bare legs. Her short skirt had lifted because of the way she sat, and her legs were exposed. He looked at her with lustful eyes. She tried to pull the skirt down but it was too short. She became panicky and tried to cover herself. He came closer and knelt down close to her. She began to breathe heavily and get scared. He reached out and she pulled away. This annoyed him and his blank face turned to hate and anger. He grabbed her by the hair and tugged her towards him. She screamed out in pain as she felt the hair pull out from the roots of her head.

"No, please stop," she pleaded

"You are a little tart; I will fuck you if I wish. I'm in control and I can do anything I want, so don't try and stop me from doing anything. Do you hear?" He pulled her close and kissed her hard on the mouth, forcing his tongue into it. She struggled and cried out pulling away. His breath was disgusting and she found him obnoxious. Turning her head away was painful as he still had her hair in his fist. But she had to get away from his face. She struggled and was hit hard across the face by his other hand for her trouble. The pain was excruciating. She had never been hit like that before. She screamed out and sobbed as he hit her again, twice more across the face, shaking her head by her hair violently.

"Stay still whore, fucking like it or I'll kill ya, fucking cut you up, fucking bitch." His voice sounded insane and it scared her more than the hits across her face she was receiving. She tried to cover her face as he hit her again. The pain rang in her head and around her ears. Viciously, he threw her to the ground by her hair.

She fell and banged her head on the floorboards. He sat on top of her and she was pinned to the deck. She tried to lift her legs but could not move one because of the bolt in the wall. She put up her arms to stop him, but he punched her hard in the face once. She could not believe the pain and shock this blow caused. She had felt nothing like it before, her eyes watered, her face felt like it was going to explode, and the pain in the back of her head made her feel sick. She was terrified, the pain was tremendous as her head hit the floor from the impact of the blow.

"No, please, no," she cried out, pleading with him.

"Stop fighting then stupid bitch, the more you fight the more I will hit you." She looked at him through the tears in her eyes and said nothing. Her body was shaking and she was more scared now then she had ever been.

He looked at her eyes, and then put his hand on her breast. She sobbed but dared not do anything.

She could not stand the beating he would most definitely give her if she objected. Sobbing out loudly and uncontrollably and on the verge of panic, she felt him fondle her breasts. He used both hands and pushed them together. He lifted her top and put his rough hands on her flesh, squeezing her breasts together and then leant down to suck them. He bit at her nipples and groped her roughly. She was shaking and could do nothing about the assault she was receiving. Her body was stiff and rigid. This was her worst nightmare, her worst fear, and the most horrible thing that could happen to her, his twisted face had wide open staring eyes as he molested her. She was crying and sobbing as she was subjected to his sexual gratification. He was worked up and excited, slobber was coming from his mouth and he was getting into a sexual frenzy over her. Suddenly, he stopped and sat up again. He looked down at her and her nakedness, put his hand to his belt and undid the buckle. He opened the button on his trousers and pulled down his zip. She looked away and cried a nervous, petrified whimper which turned into a loud cry. She shook her head; she wanted it to all go away. She didn't look at him, she could hear him getting very excited and she could hear his hand hitting his trousers rapidly. She was not sure what he was doing so dragged herself up to take a look her eyes were closed at first then she opened them with a scream. She turned straight away after she saw what he was doing, masturbating himself while looking at her breasts. She was disgusted and frightened at the same time. He began to moan loudly and work his hand faster until it eventually happened. She felt the semen hit her in short bursts, all over her neck and chest.

114

He cried out with joy as he ejaculated all over her. She could do nothing, her body was rigid and she could not move.

The smell of him and the semen made her feel sick. He fell onto her, she could not move.

He breathed heavily into her ear for a moment then sat up quickly. He put his penis away and did up his trousers. He was mumbling to himself and seemed angry at something.

"See, see what you have done? See what you have made me do, you fucking whore? You're all the fucking same. You use your bodies to tempt us and look what happens.

This is what happens, you little slut." He shouted at her with hate in his voice into her face, then got up. She was relieved for a short moment as he got off her, but then, he swiftly kicked her hard in the side which sent her rolling over to the wall in pain and agony. Her ribs felt like they were broken. She screamed, pulling down to her side instinctively to protect her flank. The bolt held her ankle firm and this caused her pain as she twisted her foot awkwardly with the force of the roll. He stormed out of the room slamming the door behind him.

Shaking and not daring to move, she listened to his footsteps disappear away into the house somewhere, she didn't know where and was not at this moment bothered, just so long as he was away from her. She rubbed her ribs; they were sore and painful when she breathed in. Rubbing her leg and ankle, she looked broken and helpless, sad and desperate, in need of help and in need of courage and strength.

Tears were welling inside her, as was fear and panic. She felt like all the fight had been kicked out of her, all the determination she had was going and fading away, her hands were shaking. She could not stop them. She rolled up in sadness and suffering, sobbing uncontrollably. She reached out and took some toilet paper off the roll and wiped away his semen from her body in disgust. She pulled her top back down, threw the used toilet roll in the bucket then sat in the corner, shaking and in a state of shock. She was in danger and it was real, somehow before when he did not hurt her it was almost bearable, but now anything could happen and she was petrified beyond belief. She would rather die than be raped every day. She did not know what was going to happen and did not really want to know. The more she thought of it, the more panic set in. The more the reality of abuse, beating and rape she had, the worse she got. She was not as strong as she thought she was, the situation was life threatening and she knew it. Her captor was unstable, unreasonable and very dangerous. No longer was he the duck feeder she teased and ridiculed, he was now in charge, insane and in her life, and she could do nothing to get him out of it. She was at his mercy, his command, and most of all that scared her, his pleasure. This was the most terrifying time of her life and she wanted her family and she wanted it to go away. She wanted to wake up; she wanted it to be all a bad dream, but the reality hit her hard in the face. Every time he came into the room now she knew he could rape her and beat her. She looked down at the bolt in the wall holding her there like a chained animal. She wiped her eyes and her face with her hands. She sniffed and swallowed and relaxed a little, but the fear was there and would never go away.

Curling up in the corner, she tried not to breathe too deeply because it hurt her ribs. She was hurting and upset, but still didn't know what he wanted. She thought and tried to decipher what he had said but could not concentrate. All that went through her mind was what he would do with her the next time he wanted to pleasure himself. She was his slave, sex or otherwise. The thought made her cry. She bit on her fist and cried, sobbed and shook with fear. She realised she might never see her family again.

CHAPTER SIX

It was late that afternoon when they got the phone call. Gloria answered it. Graham was writing down all he knew and could remember from Keighley, all the people he had known, anything and everything he could think of, in the hope it would jog his memory. He walked over to his wife and listened with her at the voice.

"She pissed me off this morning, and I'm getting tired with it all, so it is time to get it moving and let fuck face know what it is all about."

"What have you done? Is she alright?" a frightened Gloria asked.

"Listen, tell your fuck face of a husband I am going to meet him, but it is going to have to be me and him, no one else, no police, no you, no fucker. Is that understood?" At this, Graham took the phone from his wife and answered in a serious and determined voice:

"Right agreed, when and where?" There was silence for a moment.

"I was talking to your bitch of a wife."

"Well, you're talking to me now, where do you want to meet?"

"You don't tell me anything or what to do. Is that understood? And I think there was a little hostility in your voice then, daddy," he mocked

"I will meet you anywhere anytime, you just name it and I want to see my daughter."

"I bet you will, and I bet you do, but before that you are going to have to do as I say. If I think you have told anyone, anyone at all I will kill her and post her to you in little parcels. Is that clear?" His voice rose a few levels.

"Yes, I have told no one." He gripped the phone Gloria held on to his arm , listening intently.

"Right, you come alone. You tell no one, your wife stays there and tells no one. If anyone comes to the house I will know. It is between me and you. We will sort this out once and for all. I will tell you what you have done, not that I'm convinced you don't already know, because you only have one tie up here now don't ya, no friends, no family except ..."

He became silent, and Graham felt a shiver run down his spine. He asked in an urgent voice, after a few moments:

"Are you still there? Hello, hello," he urged.

"Stop panicking, listen carefully, the writing is on the wall Graham, the writing is on the wall, come up to where the pigeons are, to the sculpture, in your own town. It will take you about an hour to get here. I have your little girl and if you do not do as I say she will suffer, and suffer bad, so it is up to you."

"Where the pigeons are? Sculpture? I'm not sure where you mean."

"Benches, pigeons, sculpture," he shouted at him over the phone.

"The market place," Graham suddenly remembered, and shouted down the phone, as if the urgency of it depended on him getting it right.

"You have one and a half hours to get here and come alone and tell no one, or you will never see your daughter again." The phone went silent and Graham hung up He looked at his wife and then at the recording device. He picked up the phone and started to ring a number.

"What are you doing?" Gloria asked him.

"Ringing Peter." She put her finger on the phone cutting him off.

"No, you can't, not now, he said he would know." She was shaking her head at him

"If he is in Keighley to meet me he can't be watching here can he? I don't want you left alone here Gloria. No, I'm ringing Peter."

"No," she shouted, "you have to go; he might have someone else watching the house. I have Sam, and I will lock all the doors, so please, you have got to go, and go now, go and get all this sorted out, go and get Lisa back, please, please." Her voice was weak with worry but Graham could feel the urgency in it. This was the little bit of hope they needed and it was to be taken eagerly and with optimism and hope.

 "Alright, but you must promise me you will phone Peter if anything out of the ordinary happens, anything. I will phone you as soon as I get there." They hugged and held on to each other tightly for a few moments. Pulling back, he kissed his wife and they looked at each other deep in the eyes.

"I do love you," she told him.

"I love you too." He dashed to get his coat. He made sure he had got his wallet, grabbed his car keys from the side and headed for the door. Gloria walked to the door with him. She watched him go and get into the car. He drove away and she watched until he turned out of the street and was gone. She burst into uncontrollable tears at the sight of him leaving, but quickly went back in and locked the door securely behind her. She walked through to the back door and made sure that was locked as well, signaling to Sam to follow her into the main room and she sat on the settee. She patted the seat next to her for the dog to join her. He did as commanded and she put her arms round him for comfort. She sniffled and looked at the phone waiting, waiting for it to ring, waiting for her husband to ring and say everything was alright and he had their daughter back safe and sound. This was what she wanted but knew it was not what she was going to get, not yet anyway all she could do was wait and hope for the best.

Graham was coming out of the petrol station at this time after filling up with petrol, he then realized he had left his mobile phone but didn't worry about it now, he could use a public telephone easy enough, he had more things on his mind right now.

He was on the way up to his home town, a journey he had made many times but none like this, none so important. He did not know what to expect, he did not know if he was doing the right thing, he was just going and wondered if he would know the man, if he would recognise him, if he would know what it was all about, if he would see Lisa. He drove fast but not reckless. Soon, he was on the motorway and heading north. He usually liked music playing when he drove but for some reason he wanted silence. He was in like overdrive just going and not thinking about driving the car which seemed to be taking itself. All he could hear was the roar of the engine taking him to Keighley to meet the man who was doing this to him and hopefully to reunite him with his daughter. Gloria sat in the same position for twenty minutes. She eventually stood and walked to the table where Graham had been writing things down, trying to jog his memory. She took the piece of paper he had been writing on. She read it and found it all nondescript to her, except one bit that stood out because he had underlined it. It said, 'sister big mistake, can't be, no no no.' She looked at it and wondered. She read the rest of it and nothing hit her like this did. She didn't know why but it bothered her. Why should he underline it? What had his sister got to do with this? Although she had never met her, she knew she lived in Keighley, she knew Graham and they had not seen each other for years. He never spoke about her, so why should he write about her like that, and underline it?. She put the paper down and went to the kitchen. She looked out across the garden and down to the fence, not really looking at anything or seeing anything. Sam came in and stood by the back door. This was his signal he wanted to go out. Gloria smiled at him and opened the door for him. He went out and sniffed round the garden for a minute, then went trotting down to the far end and sniffed round the tree. This is where he cocked his back leg and gave the tree its daily watering. He continued to sniff and explore the bottom fence, and his territory making sure no one had trespassed. Gloria heard a slight tap on the front door. She looked down at Sam who was preoccupied with his sniffing. She left the back door open, went to the front door and asked:.

"Yes, who is it?"

"Special delivery for ya love, need a signature," a voice said from outside.

"Oh right." She opened the door slowly, looking back at the kitchen to see that Sam had a clear run if needed. She was surprised as the door was forcefully pushed in and she saw a hand come down and hit her hard in the face. Someone dashed past her and closed the kitchen door. Sam came charging in but just was not quick enough to get into the house, the door stopped him and he was helpless in the kitchen unable to get in to help Gloria, who was being dragged across the floor by her hair.

The front door had been locked and she was dragged to the centre of the room. A foot came down and stamped on her chest holding her to the floor. She was weak and petrified, not knowing what was happening. She cried out in terror, but it was short lived as a piece of sticky tape was ripped from a reel he had pulled from his pocket and put across her mouth. She was violently turned over and her arms pulled round to her back and again she heard the tape being used. Her wrists were taped tightly together and then her legs were next. They were brought up and taped to her hands. She was now flat on her chest. It had all happened in a matter of minutes and she was confused and scared. She had no idea what was happening or who this was. She could hear Sam barking and scratching at the door trying his best and hardest to get to.

The traffic was light but could have been better. Graham was heading up the motorway to his turn off. He could get off and go through Bradford, a town he hated, but he decided to go over the top and on to the M606. Soon, he was going through the traffic in the fast lane and heading off to his turning for the M62. He turned off and kept going through the system and down on to the M62. He stayed on there until he came off at the M606. He was getting close now and became anxious, looking at the small clock in his car. He had made good time, forty five minutes. He kept going, soon missing the traffic of the city and heading over the top part of it, past the supermarket, over the roundabout and down to the traffic lights. He had to stop for the red light. He looked round and saw a man walking his dog. He thought of Sam for a moment, then of Sebastian. His son had been blind to all this, and would have to be told one day. He was taken away from this thought when the lights turned green. He was away again, turning left and up the hill, through Wilsden and Harden. He soon would be dropping into Keighley. He looked at his watch. It had just been under an hour since he left. He went left at the small roundabout then right onto Keighley road and up the big steep hill, he always thought about a car he had when he was young, a Lada. Everyone took the mickey out of him about it and whenever he went up this hill he had to do it in first gear. It was just too steep and bendy for him to use any other gear in that car, but this car had no trouble. He was in second, then third speeding up the hill effortlessly. He came to the top and headed down the big straight, into Long lee, turning left at the bottom and then there he was as he reached the bottom of the hill. Keighley he was there. It had taken him an hour. He headed for the supermarket behind the market place. He knew he could park up there. It did not take him long to find a space. He locked up his car, checked his pockets and realized again he had forgotten his mobile in the rush to get out. He headed for the phone box next to the car park. All the memories of his childhood came flooding back as they always did when he was here; certain things that meant nothing to others meant a lot to him; certain roads where he had his first clumsy fondle of a woman; first pub he went drinking in; first place he had a fight. It all was there, his roots, his history. He reached the phone box but he did not even go in. He could see it had been vandalised, broken into, and the hand piece missing. Shaking his head, he walked to the market place. He went through the snicket and past the benches. He went past some people who were carrying shopping.He looked round for anyone he might recognise, anyone at all. But there was no one, just empty faces and people he had never seen before. He was stood in front of the market. He looked round, the sculpture was still there, a stupid steel thing he had never understood or liked, a grey contraption of cogs and wheels. He was never impressed with it, so was the market place sign in white on the wall, the Keighley coat-of-arms under it on a shield. He looked up at the pigeons perched on the roof, waiting for the old lady who fed them every day, with a loaf of bread, to come.

He was here, and now what? He thought, looking at his watch, that it had been one hour and ten minutes since he had left his home. He was told an hour and half. Sitting down on one of the benches, he watched a road cleaner sweeping up some rubbish nearby. The town was not busy and less hectic than he remembered it. He sat on the bench and looked round. He knew anyone here could be the man who he was supposed to meet. He wondered if he would see his daughter today. Knowing he had to phone his wife, he again looked at his watch. Should he go and phone her? Should he stay here in case he missed him? He looked again at the road sweeper and getting closer for a moment he thought this was him. The sweeper looked directly at him, then through him and at the wall shaking his head. Graham did not look at what he was looking at, but could hear him talking to himself as he swept the ground with a stiff brush.

"Little fuckers, why do they do it? That wasn't there yesterday." He shook his head and walked past Graham, who for some reason got a chill down his back. He turned and looked at what the sweeper had been looking at on the wall. This had been blind to Graham unless he leant forward and looked back. Slowly, he turned and saw what the sweeper had seen. What he had took as graffiti of children meant something very different to Graham. There on the wall were the words, in spray paint:

"Graham I did not think you was so fucking stupid, I've fucked your daughter and now I'm going to fuck your wife; the writing is on the wall old man."

His heart turned to stone; he shook and did not know what to do for a moment. He looked round, taking deep breaths. He dashed from the market place and up into the shopping centre to where he knew there were some phones. He fumbled in his pocket for some change. He reached the phone, lifted the receiver, put a fifty pence piece in and dialed the number. He wanted his wife to answer and say she was well, but it rang and rang. He became anxious until the phone was answered.

"Hello, hello Gloria?" he said frantically.

"No, not Gloria you fucking stupid fool falling for an old trick like that?" The voice cut into him like a sharp knife. He became weak and could not hold himself up straight, gripping the phone until his knuckles turned white.

"Don't hurt her, I've done all you asked," was the only feeble reply he could give at this time. The fight was gone, the fear was eating at him, his knees were weak and he didn't want to believe it.

"Yes you have. Now I've come here to get the charger for the phone as the batteries are running low, so what I will do now is fuck your wife, nice tits by the way. I can see where your daughter gets hers from. Then I'm going home so I'll ring you later old man."

"No, no listen please, what do you want? What is it I've done? Please tell me." He was breaking down and people looked at him.

This was not the place to collapse on a phone.

He knew that but could not help himself. Gritting his teeth, he tried to fight it all the way and regain his strength.

"You must know by now, you can't be that fucking stupid." The northern voice hit him like a hammer. He felt the anger dwell inside him, he hated this man and wanted to do him serious harm. He stood up and held the phone into his mouth as he spoke into it.

"You listen to me, I'm going to meet you one day and when that day comes I'm gonna fucking rip you apart. That is not a threat, it's a fucking promise. You have beef with me, then come and deal with me. All you can manage is girls and helpless women. Well, why don't you come here to me and see how big you are with the men? You're a fucking coward too weak to stand and fight."

"That's big talk for a man who is over an hour away. I'm here in your house with your wife and fucking dog, which is getting on my nerves barking all the fucking time. I have your daughter to fuck whenever I want to, so don't try and talk big to me. You have done me wrong, you both did me wrong. Do you know how hard it is in that place? Do you know what they do to you? Do you know who you have got to share your fucking day with? Well, I got out and they said I was alright now. I told them what they wanted to hear, they're very stupid really. I did what they wanted me to do. I asked to see my mother and they said no, but mother wanted to see me.

She asked them, so we were allowed to exchange letters. Oh yeah, she wanted to see what her son had become. Fuck him off at first, make his life fucking hell, in fucking homes and institutions, but I'm alright now they said so, and they can't be wrong .Can they? I was a nice man, a good man, did what they wanted. Well, I found out where she lived you see, and when I did they didn't know, and I have not told them. I have seen her and I have made her suffer and I want you to fucking suffer. She told me all about you, oh yeah, you might not have seen her for so long but she knew all about you. I got it out of her, oh yes I did that."

As he was talking on the phone, Gloria was struggling with her tape ties. She had loosened one at the back. She looked up from the floor and saw he had his back to her. She rolled off towards the kitchen door. Sam was quiet for a while but now was barking again. The duck feeder did not hear her because of the dog barking. She struggled and rolled to the door. It was awkward for her but she got there. She worked her hand free from her back and quickly pulled the tape from her mouth. She free kicked the kitchen door and it flew wide open. Just at that moment he turned round, just in time to see Sam charging in at him. Sam leapt from the floor and through the air, hitting the intruder square on in the chest and knocking him down. Sam ripped at the man's face and as he did they both struggled in a fight on the carpet. Gloria was eventually free of her ties. She picked up the first thing she could find which happened to be a lamp. She went over to where Sam was biting and tearing savagely at the man, lashed out and hit him hard on the head. Blood emptied from the wound instantly and he was stunned. Sam was ripping at the man's flesh causing him to scream out in pain. His teeth bedded into his skin, tearing and ripping hard. Sam shook his head and pulled, clawing and snarling and biting. Gloria picked up the phone and frantically said down it:

"Graham I have him. Sam is savaging him, Christ, I have him. What shall I do?"

"Gloria, are you alright? Are you alright?"

"Yes, he did not touch me Graham, what shall I do?"

"Hit him again, tie the fucker up, hit him, and call Peter." His money ran out; he didn't even notice the pips going he was that worked up. The phone was dead. She said his name several times, but realised what had happened. She dropped the receiver, letting it dangle by the side of the phone, and went over to the man again. He was trying to stand and hit Sam. She brought the heavy lamp down hard on to his head again, this time he went still when he dropped onto the floor. Sam, foaming at the mouth, was hold of the man's arm and shaking his head from side to side. He had him and was not letting go, he was tired but would not stop until this intruder was under control, and all were safe, he had trespassed on his land and that was a fatal thing to do.

Gloria stepped back and saw the man was still. She was shaking and felt weak. Her legs were like jelly. Sam held on and growled. She called him back. It took two attempts but he came and sat next to her, panting and breathing heavily. She stood there looking at the man on her carpet bleeding from bite wounds and a nasty gash from his head. She did not know what to do.

Graham was trying to ring her back but couldn't as she had left the receiver off the hook and it was hanging down the side of the phone. He hung up and tried again, but still the engaged tone. He slammed the phone down and rang her mobile, but still there was no answer. He rang Peter's mobile but it went onto an answering machine. He was getting frustrated and was cursing loudly. He rang Peter's office. It rang and rang, for what seemed like an eternity to him. He was impatient and shouted loudly to the phone, much to the amusement of passers-by.

"Come on, come on, fucking answer."

"Hello…" A woman's voice came back but before she could say who she was and where she was Graham told her desperately:

"Peter Summers, I need to speak to him urgently."

"I'm afraid Mr Summers is not in at the moment. Can I ask who is calling please?" Her voice was polite and professional.

"Fucking hell, have you a number where I can get in touch with him? It is a matter of great importance. He will explain, please just get in touch with him for me."

"Is it official business?"

"Yes, for fuck's sake love, please," he pleaded with her.

"There is no need to swear sir, just calm down."

"Look ,tell him it's Graham, and tell him to get round to my house straight away, it is a matter of life and death. Find him and tell him for God's sake, please. It is not a wind up." He hung up and hoped it was enough. He tried his wife again, but still got the engaged tone. He slammed the phone down and ran as fast as he could to his car, dashing through the streets and down to the car park. He got his keys from his pocket as he ran, reaching the car, he was away in record time.

 The traffic seemed busier and more in his way. It was always the same when you were in a rush, everything seemed to be against you, he thought. He knew he had to get home as quickly as possible but did not want to crash or have an accident. He drove fast, but in control, quick, but sensible, taking the fastest route he knew. He raced out of his home town, fear and adrenalin were driving him hard just like he was driving his car. Thoughts were running round his head. Who was to blame?

Swerving, he almost hit a parked car. He swung round it and dropped a gear, speeding away down the road, not even looking in his mirror. Nothing mattered but him getting back home to make sure his family was safe. He headed back up the steep hill. He hit the steering wheel as he got stuck behind a large heavy lorry. He could not get by, because there was too much traffic coming the other way. He cursed and shouted at the vehicle in front of him. He could feel the anger welling up inside his stomach.

 Gloria did not know what to do. She held Sam back; he was growling and was not going to let this man move. Eventually, she got her wits back and went to close the back door. Then she went over to the man and kicked him in the side. She stepped back and waited for a reaction, but there was none. She picked up the lamp and held it in a ready position while she hesitantly searched in his pockets. Finding what she was looking for, she pulled out the tape he had used on her. Sam came close and looked down growling and sniffing at the man.

"Good boy Sam. Rip the fucker apart if he moves," she said as she lifted his hands up together. She wrapped the tape round them several times and instantly felt better knowing he was at least bound at the wrists. She carried on and went halfway up his arms, then did his feet and legs. There was no way he could move out of this. She stood and threw the tape down. The wound on his head was nasty and blood was staining her carpet. She wondered if she should tend to it, but decided not to go near him again.

Sam was now sniffing round him and looking at him with curious eyes. He trotted off to the kitchen and took a long drink from his bowl before coming back and sitting next to Gloria keeping guard and not taking his eyes off the duck feeder. Graham had got past the slow lorry and raced at top speed down the road. He had to get home to his wife and the bastard, who had his little girl. What he had said on the phone had torn him apart. He didn't really know what he was on about but reckoned he must have meant his sister. The secret he had kept with her was one he had locked away but it looked like it was going to hit him right between the eyes now. He would deal with that however when he had to. Right now the main priority was to get home.

Gloria was peering down at the seemingly lifeless body of the man she had knocked unconscious on her carpet, wondering if she had killed him she jumped and made Sam jump when there was a knock on her front door.

She looked up, startled, nervous, but in control and went to the door. Sam came as well barking at the person on the other side. She shouted; she was not going to make that mistake again.

"Who is it?" She listened for an answer.

"Gloria, can I have a word? It's Sharon." She knew the voice of her next door neighbour, and it was a relief to know it was safe. She held Sam back and told him to be still. She put the chain on and wished she had been this careful the last time. Opening the door a little, she gazed out. Seeing her neighbour was not in the best of moods, she asked:

"Sharon, hello, what is it?"

"Well, Gloria I don't want to be a pain but your bloody dog has been barking for the past half hour and what the hell is all the banging about? My Burt is working nights this week and needs his sleep in the day, you know."

While Gloria was explaining away the noise to her neighbour, the duck feeder opened his eyes. He struggled and found himself bound. Without a second thought, he brought his hands up and reached inside his jacket pulling out a small pocket knife. He lifted it to his mouth and with his teeth he opened the blade. He held the handle in both hands and leant over to cut the tape from his legs and feet. He was soon free and turned the knife so he could cut the tape from his wrists, a little at a time. But he soon worked the cut enough to be able to get the blade under the tape and rip it right off. He worked quietly and slowly got himself out of the ties. He listened to the two women arguing at the front door.

Dizzy and groggy, he shook his head and rubbed his eyes; he took a deep breath and felt the pain in his head from the gash.

He moved silently to the back and slipped out of the back door. He was limping where the dog had sunk its teeth into his leg but he moved quickly.

Soon out into the garden and at the bottom of the fence, he struggled to get over it with the pain tearing at his wounds. But he managed it and was away. Luckily for him, there was not many people about and he was soon in a car and driving away in pain and cursing.

Gloria was oblivious to all this and had just managed to get rid of her irate neighbour.

Sam watched her lock the door and walked back into the room. His ears pricked up and he smelt the floor, following the trail out to the back and down the garden. Gloria panicked. She was shaking and could not, did not, want to believe what she saw. He was gone. She cried to herself as she followed a few drops of blood on her carpet. She went to the kitchen and saw the trail lead to her back door and out into the garden. She saw Sam sniffing the fence at the bottom of the garden and she knew he had gone. She fell where she was stood and sat on the kitchen floor, weeping into her hands. She could not believe it. Shaking uncontrollably, she could not take any more and wanted it all to be over .She heard the telephone make an alarm noise. It was a feed the telephone company sent down the line after ten minutes if you had not hung up properly. She didn't move for a moment but the sound got on her nerves. She shouted the dog back in and she locked the door behind him. Dazed, she went and hung up the phone. She looked down at the bloodstain on the carpet. What if he had not gone out? What if he was still in the house? She spun round and looked about her. She went to the kitchen and took the largest knife she could find. This was her weapon and she would use it. Keeping the dog by her side, she started to search the house. She deliberately walked about checking all the rooms but found nothing. She stood at the bottom of the stairs and looked up. Sending Sam up in front of her, she began to climb the stairs to the upper floor. Sweating and shaking with the knife held out in two hands, she steadily climbed the stairs a step at a time and when she reached the top she took a deep, broken breath. She searched the rooms one by one carefully and was relieved to find nothing. He had gone; she stopped at the door of Lisa's room. Slowly, she pushed open the door. It swung and stayed open. She dropped the knife on the floor of the untidy room and went in. She filled up with emotion. She curled up on the bed and held onto the pillow, her daughter's pillow. She could smell the distinctive perfume she used and the memories came flooding back to her of when she was a small child and the things they had done and the places they had been.

Sam sat next to the bed and watched in confusion. He knew there was something wrong but did not understand what. He lay down and stayed with her; she fell into a haunted sleep and did not move until she was awoken by a hammering on the door. Sam was already downstairs. She went out of the room and picked up the knife off the floor as she did. She dashed down the stairs and saw Sam wagging his tail at the door.

"Gloria! Gloria!" It was Graham's voice. She thought the sound of his voice was music to her ears. She opened the door and he rushed in. She grabbed him and pulled him close to her. He looked over her shoulder and kicked the door shut with his foot. Sam waited patiently for his greeting, the one he always got when he met someone from the family at the door, but on this occasion it did not come. Graham pulled Gloria away from him and took the knife from her.

"He is gone?" she said, sadly.

"What?" He sounded disappointed and angry. "What happened?"

"I was at the door and he went out while I was arguing with Sharon. She complained about the noise." She was crying as she was telling him and he held her close again. "I tried Graham, I tried. I'm so scared. What can we do? What can we do?" She sobbed into his shoulder and he squeezed her tightly. He walked with her into the room and noticed the blood on the carpet. He looked at her in the eye and felt the tears welling in his own.

"I'm so sorry, so sorry; I should not have left you alone." He kissed her and they went to sit down on the settee.

"What now? What will he do now? He will kill her, I know it," she said looking at the floor and the blood drying in on her carpet.

"Did you phone Peter?"

"No." She shook her head, dejectedly.

"I did but they could not get in touch with him. We are going to have to go to the police Gloria. We should have done it in the first place."

"We can't, not now; it has gone too far, we have to get Lisa back."

"Tell me everything that happened, everything." He turned and looked at him for a moment. Graham saw his wife go from a hysterical state to calmness and back. It was not like her and was doing her harm, physically and mentally. He was in pain and knew that he was near breaking point himself, so he could feel for his wife, the heartache and torture she was going through, the mental anguish and now this attack and the thought that it might be all over for them and what he might do to Lisa because of it. He tried to push it out of his mind and listened to his wife as she told him painfully what had happened and how she had been left alone with a madman, the same one that held their daughter, and the same one that knew so much about him. He cried with her and held her as she explained the terror she had felt and the disillusionment of him escaping, the fear, the horror, the helplessness, the deep down disappointment and destitution she felt.

140

CHAPTER SEVEN

It was some time before Lisa heard the front door slam shut. She listened as the duck feeder came running up the stairs, cursing to himself, but she could not make out what he was saying. He went into the bathroom and was in there for quite a while. When he finally came out he went into another room somewhere. It was silent for a while then she jumped at the sound she heard. It was a woman's voice, screaming out in absolute agony. She was in tremendous pain, and then it was quiet. The silence was broken by a door slamming and someone going back downstairs, slowly and again mumbling to himself.

Lisa listened for another sound but none came. Wondering who this mystery woman was, she sat on the floor with her back against the wall, her knees lifted up to her chest. She wrapped her arms round her legs and rested her head on her knee, pointlessly looking round the room, wondering what was going to happen and if she would ever see her family again. Sadness took over her and a tear rolled down her cheek. She tried to be strong but emotion took over her sometimes and it was heart wrenching to think she would never get out of this alive, or see her family again.

"Listen Gloria," Graham said determinedly. "I have an idea he is trying to terrorise me. If I don't answer the phone then he can't do that, it might defuse the situation." He regretted saying this as soon as it had left his lips.

"I don't fucking believe you have just said that. What do you think he will do to Lisa if he can't get in touch anymore? Christ, pull it together man." She shook her head at him in disbelief; the phone rang at that precise moment.

Gloria answered it and froze to the spot when it was the duck feeder's voice. All he said in a cold voice was:

"The game is over, she is dead." The phone then was silent. Gloria dropped the receiver back onto the phone and fell onto the settee. Graham walked up to her and said in a concerned voice:

"What? Who was it?"

"He said he is going to kill her," she told him in a daze. She was shaking and did not know what to do. Graham felt his legs go weak and he almost dropped to the ground where he stood. The phone rang again and Gloria dashed to it and answered it asking in a terrified voice:

"What have you done to her, you fucking bastard." She screamed into the receiver.

"Did I scare you?" He laughed loudly and heckled down the phone.

His warped sense of humour did not seem funny to Gloria at all, and she blasted down the phone and shouted at him, in sheer hysteria.

"Give me back my daughter, you sick fucker. Why are you doing this to us?"

"Well, it is about time you found out what sort of man your loving husband is. Why don't you ask him what he did when he was sixteen? Ask him about his sister."

Again, the phone was dead as he switched the mobile off. Gloria found energy in rage and slammed the phone down; she turned to her husband and asked in a demanding voice:

"What the fucking hell is all this about Graham? What have you done? He told me to ask you about your fucking sister and what you did when you were sixteen.

"What is this? What have you fucking done?" She looked at him for an answer.

He went weak at the legs and dropped onto the settee. She could see something was terribly wrong, she had never seen him like this before, and she came over and sat next to him, waiting for an answer.

"Gloria, I'm so sorry," was all he could manage to get out. His voice was weak and breaking. He was shaking, and shaking his head, and she put her arm round him and told him in a calmer voice:

"Listen love, I know your family is not a close one. I mean my god the children still think your mother's alive. We lied to Sebastian and told him Lisa was there for God's sake, if you don't want them to know then fine but for fuck's sake what is all this?"

He looked at her with tears in his eyes, all the years she had known him she had never seen him cry. It struck a chord within her and she felt for him. He looked worried and sad; he did not think he could tell her. Feeling cold and drained, he leant forward on his hands and sunk his head in them.

Taking a deep broken breath, he tried to compose himself. She was patient and waited, seeing it hurt him to do this. She became more and more curious by the second. Finally, he looked at her and swallowed nervously. This was hard for him but he started.

"We had a lot to drink; I was young, drunk, adventurous and very naive. My sister was drunk and wearing a short black skirt and a low cut blouse. She had been out that night and her boy friend had left her. She was upset and we talked, laughed, got drunk, held each other close. I was comforting her for Christ's sake, and, and …" He shook his head and stopped struggling to catch his breath.

"Come on love, no matter what it is let's get it into the open. We might be able to find Lisa if you come out with it. Come on." She held his hand and through her fear gave it a reassuring squeeze. His mouth was dry so he swallowed and carried on.

"Holding on to each other on the settee we, well we were young and like experimented a little. It all got out of hand, God I'm, so ashamed of it Gloria, I'm too ashamed, no, I can't." He again shook his head, he could not bring himself to say it, and a nervous shiver went through him.

"What happened Graham?" she demanded. She was becoming scared at what she thought she was going to hear. He looked up with shame in his eyes and fear in his heart. He had told no one about this and it was something he had locked in his mind, now he was forced to let it out. He took a quick breath and told her: "We fucked." He looked straight ahead and said no more. Gloria did not want to believe it. She let go of his hand and backed away, frowning and taking in what he said. She shook her head not wanting to listen. Breathing heavily, she looked away and then back again, disgust in her eyes.

"You fucked your own fucking sister?" she said, loudly and unbelievingly.

"Yes, and I think this is my son who is doing this, to get back at me." His voice was cold and his gaze was equally as cold. He was not proud and he knew his wife would probably not forgive him. She stood up and looked down at him, something inside her told her to hug and pity him, give him support, but she could not. She was full of abhorrence for him.

"You're' fucking disgusting, my god, my baby is being held by some mad fucker you seeded with your own sister? Why should Lisa suffer? It is not her fault. He should have taken you. Why my baby? I hate you for this. Do you hear me? I hate you." She screamed at him and shouted in his face He did not move and said nothing. She ran off and went upstairs. He could not move, feeling disgust in himself. He sat there tears rolling down his cheeks. He could not move, the memory of that night came back to him He made love to his own sister, no one knew except for them. She became pregnant and told her mother she did not know who the father was; the child was put up for adoption.

He lived with fear of it all his life, and now it was back here in his face. He had to reach his sister. It all dropped back in place now, what he had told him about finding her, wanting to make her and him suffer. He must have had a hard time in the homes; he obviously was not of sound mind, which made it worse, if it could be any worse. He shook his head and dropped it into his hands. Perched on the end of the settee, he cried, cried with shame, with fear and with regret. His little girl, his wife had all gone through this pain because of him, because of what he had done, and he was helpless to do anything about it.

He wanted the ground to open and swallow him up; he wanted his baby back; he wanted it all to be right again; he wanted it to never have happened, but it would not go away and he knew it. He looked up to where his wife had gone. He wanted to go up and hold her, but he could not. He did not even know if he could face her again, if he would ever see

Lisa again. His strength was draining away, his confidence was shattered, his life in tatters. Feeling empty and lonely, he stood and had to fight to stay up. His legs were like jelly, his stomach felt hollow and he breathed in short bursts. Wiping his eyes dry, he stood by the phone and sadly looked at it alone and mentally exhausted.

Oblivious to all this was Lisa. She was trying to make herself comfortable; the handcuff was digging into her ankle and she was trying to find the best position to sit. She was hungry and thirsty; she had no water left, and no food. Suddenly, the door was kicked open, and there stood the duck feeder naked.

He was looking at her with the devil in his eyes. She was instantly petrified. He was holding the phone and was looking at her as he walked in. She looked away from his nakedness. Standing above her, he started to talk in a low calm voice, but with a hint of menace.

"Do you know what the most painful form of death is? It is being boiled alive. Did you know that? It is like being on fire all over your body. At the same time, the pain is excruciating. Do you know what I'm going to do to you? I'm going to tie you down Spread eagled on the floor, and above you I will hang a bucket. The bucket will have a hole in it, so whatever I put in it will drip out one drop at a time, the Chinese water torture. I will fix your stupid fucking head directly under it, so the contents drip on your forehead a drop at a time. You will be able to see them drop out and down onto your head, and I will watch. It will drive you slowly insane, but I won't use water, no, I will use acid, one drop at a time on your head. Your flesh will burn, then your skull. It might take hours to get through but it will, then it will hit your brain a drop at a time, burning into your skull, fucking painful. You will be screaming out for me to kill you but I won't. You're isolated, no one to help you, no one, here in this house, in here where it all began. She lives here now, bought it you know, but I found her. She could not hide; she ran but could not hide. I made her tell me where he was, and she knew, oh yes, she knew, and when I saw you I knew, I knew what to do. You're a little fucking slut like them all."

He walked directly over to her. She was looking down at the floor. She would not look up knowing he was naked and only a matter of inches away from her. He reached down with his free hand and grabbed her hair. She whimpered when he pulled her head up violently, forcing her face into his inside leg, smiling at her as he moved her head with her hair up and down his leg.

She looked and saw he was getting an erection. He phoned a number with his other hand and put the phone to his ear, and it rang and was picked up instantly on the first ring.

"Listen Graham, or should I say daddy? Or should I say uncle? Or just fucker I want you to listen to something." He put the phone on the floor and moved over to Lisa. He knelt down by her and without warning backhanded her across the face. She cried out and fell painfully to the floor. Graham felt the blow and sat down listening to his daughter being beaten on the other end of the phone. Her screams cut into him like a scalpel. He dared not put the phone down but could not bear to listen. Luckily, he had picked up the phone before Gloria had heard it ring. Again and again, he heard the slaps and hits inflicted on his daughter. He had never been so frightened in his life, the torture was too much.

He tried to shout down the phone but could not get any volume in his voice; it came out as a pitiful whimper.

"Stop it, please stop it." He broke down and tears flooded down his pain-stricken face.

"Can you hear her scream, daddy?" The voice was hurtful and terrifying to him. He listened as Lisa screamed out and the sound of him slapping her harder.

"Daddy, make him stop dad, please come and get me, dad." She hit the floor with a bang. He crawled on top of her and held her down forcing his lips up to hers. He tried to kiss her but she turned away she looked at the phone, she looked at the curtains, the tear was there and she did not know why but she just shouted out as if her father was there ready to come to her rescue.

"Daddy, he said it is where it all started. He said she had bought the house, field, torn curtain. Dad, help me, help." He put his hand over her mouth but she bit it, and she shouted out at him, as he pulled his hand away.

"You fucking bitch," he blasted and lifted up to strike her again She fought back and lifted her knee. It was a direct hit and crushed one of his testicles. He fell and rolled over in agonising pain holding his groin, heaving as if he was going to be sick.

She kicked out and caught him square in the face with her foot. He rolled off and out of her reach. She laughed at him seeing him hurt, turning and trying to reach the phone, but she was inches short so shouted into it as loudly as she could.

"Dad, dad, I have hurt him. Come quick. He said it is where it began. She, I don't know who, bought the house and he has found her, dad, please come, I'm in a room with a torn curtain,

I don't know anything else." But she could not say any more. He had rolled over and onto the phone. He turned it off with his hand while his other held his groin. He was pale, almost white. He lay there glaring at her with an evil look in his eye. She was petrified but at least she had tried to do something, at least she had done that. She looked back at him with hate and did not care what he did to her. Somewhere deep inside she knew her father was on his way. It was quiet and he was unable to stand.

He looked at her, hurt and in pain. She was ready if he came again; she would lash out and fight likes a devil if she had to; if she was to die then at least she would die fighting, she thought.

"I'm going to kill you," he said.

"I would like to kill you, you fucking sad bastard, you don't scare me anymore." She shouted

"I'm going to make you suffer like I made her suffer. You are going to die slowly and painfully, very painfully." He moved and a flash of pain went through his face. She noticed this and smiled.

"It hurts, does it?" she mocked.

"I will be alright in a moment, then you won't be laughing, you little bitch. You are going to be sorry for hitting me like that, very sorry."

"I'm glad I did, and I will do it again, when I can."

"You think your daddy will come, don't you? Well, let me tell you, he is my daddy too, we're sister and brother, you and me."

"You're lying, you're fucking lying." She shook her head violently. He smiled and nodded at her, mischievously.

"It's true, I have the proof right here in this house. It all happened here. He won't come, he won't dare leave mummy alone again, not after what I did to her. I stuffed her like a pig."

"Shut up, you're fucking lying." She shouted at him in horror at the thought of him hurting her mother.

"It's true, I got him away, then I went down killed that stupid dog, fucking thing, and I rammed your whore of a mother. She squealed like a stuffed pig, fucking big tits like you my dear". He laughed out loudly as he saw the fear in her face once again. She got to her feet and stood up straight, feeling she would have a better chance of defending herself this way. She looked at him and said nothing for a moment but backed off as he struggled to his knees. He was in pain and she obviously had done a lot of damage hitting there as she had. She felt it crunch as she hit him. He rolled back down again and across the floor towards the door. He took the phone with him, reached up and closed the door behind him. She listened and heard him moving away somewhere in the house. She was alone again, scared and shaking, but she hoped her father knew where she was. It was the only chance she had, and she was clinging to it with all she had. Hurting the duck feeder made her scared but it also made her feel less helpless and it gave her a feeling of achievement, she had won a battle now she hoped her father would come and win the war for her.

As soon as the phone had gone dead, Graham gained strength, hope, a chance. He knew where she meant. He put the phone down and ran upstairs. He went to the bedroom where he knew his wife would be. The door was locked so he banged on it demanding:

"Gloria, Gloria, open up now, quickly!"

"Go away Graham, go away." His wife's voice was scared and sorrowful, but he did not waste any time. He backed up and with all his weight and power he rammed the door with his shoulder. It bounced him back but gave in under the force of the hit. He stormed in and surprised his wife as well as scared her. He walked to the bed and looked at her.

"Listen, I know where the fucker is. I'm going now; you are going to your mother's. It does not matter what you think of me, this is for Lisa. Now get ready, you're leaving straight away, there is no time to lose."

"Where is she?" Gloria sat up on the bed. She wiped away a tear from her face and could see the hope and determination on his face.

"Never mind, come on." He reached down and pulled her off the bed with her arm and out of the room. She did not resist and allowed herself to be escorted out and down the stairs. The hope in his face gave her a glimmer of hope too. She had to hurry her step to keep up with him and could see he meant business

"Graham, what is happening? How do you know where she is?"

"I'll explain in the car, come on." He called the dog and took them both to the car, locking the door behind them. He got into the car and drove fast. He had found hope and courage.

"Graham, tell me." She was worried and confused."I'll drop you off at your mother's, phone the police, get Peter, don't take any shit, get him, tell him I've gone to my mother's old house at Keighley. That is where she is. Get the police involved, tell them everything. We should have done that in the fucking first place, I don't believe I have been so fucking stupid."

"How do you know, how do you know? What has happened?" she demanded.

"I will explain everything when I get back." He drove round a corner a bit too fast and had to fight to get control of the car again. Gloria could see the determination on her husband's face. He was ready to do whatever it took and she felt the love she always had for him coming back. Fear and excitement rolled into one hit her again and again like a consecutive barrage in her head.

"Let the police handle it Graham, get Peter to go with you. I will go with you. Get the Keighley police to go round now, ring them."

"No," he shouted, "no, I started all this with a big, terrible mistake. I will end it. It is me he wants, it is me he is going to get and now I know where he is. I will ring you as soon as I know anything. You stay at your mother's no matter what until I ring. Is that clear?" He didn't look at her; he kept his eyes on the road ahead.

"Yes," she said without argument. She could see it would do no good.

He stopped outside her mother's house. She turned to him

with a tear in her eye, leant over and kissed him on the cheek whispering:

"I love you, I'm so sorry." She got out of the car and let Sam out of the back. He pulled away without saying a word to her. Looking in his mirror, he saw his son run out excited to see his mother but more so his dog, it seemed.

"I love you all too," Graham said as he put his foot down on the accelerator. He was going to Keighley once again, this time he knew where and he knew what for. He raced off as fast as he dared; he could not afford to be pulled over by the police now. He was soon on the motorway and turned on his music centre, an instrumental piece of music filled the car. He was not listening to it but he wanted the noise, it took his mind off things slightly. He shook his head and tried to dismiss them. When he saw the man he was going for he did not know what he was going to do, or in fact if they would even be there. But the police were soon to be involved.

He regretted not involving them sooner but could do nothing about it now. Lisa could hear a lot of cursing and moving around the house, falling then dragging on the floor. He must be hurt more than she thought. She saw droplets of blood where he had bled from his wounds, a nasty one on his head and some vicious bite marks on his body. She had hit him hard in the groin and knew she must have done some damage. She just hoped it would be enough to save her own life. She looked at the door, jumping at every noise and movement, expecting the door to open at any time and him to come dashing in, in a rage of hate and kill her where she stood. But she was determined to go out fighting. She remembered something she had read somewhere. 'It is better to die on your feet than live on your knees,' and she had made this her quest. She was going out fighting if nothing else. She knew he was hurt and she had done it and clung to the hope her father, or someone else, was on their way. Graham was speeding along the motorway and did not care if the police followed him. He was not going to stop for anything, not until he had got his child back safely. He was gaining his self esteem again, his strength was coming back and he was coming to terms with it all even if it was only for now. He knew he would need to be strong if he was to get her away. This might be his one and only chance.

The car was doing well and he knew the way like the back of his hand. He kept in the fast lane and got annoyed with a motorist who pulled out to overtake. This made him drop his speed, but tailgating this man was dangerous and something that normally annoyed him. But under the circumstances, he felt justified. The man eventually pulled back into the middle lane and Graham put his foot down again; this was going to be the fastest he had ever done the journey and it had to be. His fear was becoming anger, and he gritted his teeth at the thought of his daughter being hurt. He kept the belief that she was still alive firmly in his head. Holding the steering wheel tightly, he manoeuvred round a car by undertaking it in the middle lane. Lights flashed at him in his mirror but he was not bothered. He pulled back into the fast lane; his vision was set on Keighley and his mother's old house.

  Lisa was becoming more and more worried; the time seemed to be dragging painfully along. What was minutes seemed like hours. She kept hope and was stood ready but she had heard the woman's faint cry again. She could not hear much but the odd noise, the odd word, and the faint cries of agony and sorrow. She thought she had heard him fall over at one point. He was obviously in pain and she was at least glad of that, the more pain he suffered the better in her mind.

  Graham pulled off the motorway but did not decrease his speed any. It was risky. He knew he could not afford a crash at this time but time was his enemy now and he had to get there, and get there as fast as he could. Heading over the same way he had done before, he overtook the traffic in his way and sped on.

The roads were slower and it seemed much too slow for him. He took the corners too fast and had to fight to regain control of his vehicle on several occasions. He kept going and knew he was close. He came down the big road into Keighley, his heart beating faster.

He was almost there; he was almost with his daughter. He just hoped she was still alive. Coming to traffic lights, he was contemplating going through on red, but the traffic the other way was too busy and the car in front wasn't going to get through so he was forced to stop. It was the first time since he had set off which was quite surprising, but he was glad of it. He knew he could not have got here any faster. The lights shone red, they seemed to stay like that for an age. He became impatient and hit the steering wheel cursing out loudly. Eventually, the traffic on the other side stopped and he knew the lights were about to change so he started to lift his clutch in anticipation. But the car in front was not moving. The lights went to green and they should have been away but the car in front was slow at getting away. He shouted out but it did no good. He pulled at the wheel and put his foot down, his impatience causing him to take drastic action. He overtook the car and sped away. He headed through the town and up West Lane. He knew he could get some speed up here, you always could. He passed the pub he used to drink in, the reservoir, and up past the shop. He was heading for a small place called Laycock, the village where he used to live. It was quiet and out of the way. Fields surrounded it as there were two farms on either side of the place. He was soon coming across the road into Laycock. His mind was alert and his heart was pumping. He was almost there. Round the bend, past the large stone village sign. He slowed down knowing the small roads were windy and narrow. He drove past the small grave yard that was one of the oldest in the area. He had spent the night there when he was a kid for a dare with his friend. He went slowly round the corner and hit his horn. It was the thing to do, it was a very sharp bend and you could not see what was coming the other way. If you heard a horn sound back you knew there was a vehicle coming the other way. He had known of many an accident here with people not knowing and just racing round the blind bend. There was no horn back so he carried on, driving through the village where he had spent his youth, heading for the house he was brought up in, going to get his daughter. As he turned the corner, he saw it; the large house his mother had owned, the same one he hoped his daughter was in, and still safe.

He looked at it looming in the distance, not a big place compared with the other houses nearby, but still sizeable. It had three large bedrooms and a large living room, next to a dining room. The kitchen was spacious and the fields to the back gave it a stately feel. He came to the bottom of the road, stopped and looked round. It was quiet, always was in these parts. He took a deep breath and blew it back out. He depressed his accelerator and went up to the front, slowing to a stop. He got out and looked round. He was breathing heavily and a shudder went through his body.

The red, wooden, front door was in need of a coat of paint. He knocked and knocked again. There was silence. He could not see through the windows as the curtains were drawn. He moved the short distance to the rear of the house, the back door was on the side of the house, but was always known as the back door when he was a child. He knocked loudly, but once again no sound was heard. He tried the door, but it was locked.

He went to the back and down the three stone steps to the back garden overlooking the farmer's large field. He looked up and saw the back curtains were also drawn, and in the back bedrooms, one large and one smaller, he noticed the smaller room had a tear in its curtain at the corner. He went to the door again, banged it and shouted loudly:

"Lisa, Lisa, can you hear me? It's your dad."

He was becoming more and more anxious. He tried the door once more but it was locked. He went to the front, thinking that he might be horribly wrong about all this. The front door was also locked. He didn't know what to do, his fear was returning and his hope was dying. The empty, hollow feeling in his stomach ate away at him. Maybe it was another lie to get him away. Part of the cruel game he was playing with him. Running round to the back again, he went out into the garden and looked up to the house, It was haunting and quiet, stood like a large dormant animal holding secrets.

"Lisa," he shouted again, more in anguish than expecting a response.

"Dad, dad, is that you?" The voice of his little girl came faintly back at him from inside the house. She was there in the house and she was alive. Dashing to the back door, he pounded on it like a man possessed. Turning and putting his shoulder to it, he rammed into the door. It was solid and he bounced back.

In a fit of panic and with pain rippling through his shoulder, he began to kick the door fiercely and with all the force he had in him. His little girl's voice shouted out again as he bombarded the door with all his anger, fear and determination.

"Dad, I'm here daddy, daddy." Her voice turned to little cries of relief and excitement.

"I'm coming darling, I'm here," he shouted as he felt the door start to give under the force of his kicks. Again and again he kicked at the solid door. His shoulder hurt as he once again banged into the door. He could feel the lock give in and the latch or bolt on the door burst away from the wooden frame. The frenzy of kicks and shoulder rams had done the trick. He gave one more final kick and that was it. The door swung inwards on its hinges; he was in. He knew the place well, and went through the kitchen and into the large living room. Everything looked normal and clean, well kept and you would not know anything was wrong; he looked up and shouted out:

"Lisa, where are you, love?"

"Up here daddy." She began to cry at the sound of her father's voice. He looked to the door leading up the stairs and went without hesitation through it. He was running up the wooden stairs several at a time, shouting out as he did so.

"Lisa, talk to me Lisa, where are you?" His heart was pumping and he could feel the adrenalin running through his body.

"Oh daddy, daddy," his daughter cried out from the room. He heard it and knew exactly where she was. It was his old room when he was a child. Reaching the red door, he stopped and looked round. Seeing nothing, he was breathing heavily and said at the door so his daughter could hear:

"I'm here darling, I'm here." He opened the door and went in. He feared she would be hurt or in a mess of blood or worse. But the relief was too much for him, as he saw his little girl stood there crying and shaking, shackled to the wall like an animal, wearing the horrible clothes, and looking scared and drained. He went up to her and threw his arms round her. She held on tightly so it hurt but he did not mind. He had his daughter back and she was safe. He pulled her up but saw the handcuff holding her foot to the wall. She was crying and could not believe she was seeing her father again. It was too much for her and she started to sob. The nightmare was over, she was safe. He saw the room was bare.

"Where is he, love? Where is the bastard?"

"Gone, gone I think." She shook her head unable to say anything else Looking down at her ankle he took the handcuff in his powerful hands and tried to turn it, to screw it from its holding, but it was too tight. He moved her away and made room between her foot and the wall. He put his foot on it and the combined weight and power of his leg forcing it round loosened it and it moved. He did not want to leave her here while he went to find something to free her so was determined to get her out now.

With it turning a little, it had loosened the tight grip the thread had on the wall plug. He went back down and tried to turn it with his hands again, this time he was able to do it. He soon was unscrewing it from the wall, and it tightened up on Lisa's ankle. She did not have to be told what to do. She lay on the floor and turned with it as her father undid her shackle from the wall. It was soon out and she was free. He took her by the hand and looked at her, asking:

"Are you ready? We're getting out of here. Now listen, if he is here or if anything happens, you get to the car round the front and lock yourself in. Do you understand? If you must, you get away, anyway you can. You know the basics to drive. I have taught you before so if it comes to it, you get away and phone the police. Is that clear?" He took his keys from his pocket and gave them to her, closing her hand round them as he did. She nodded and held onto the keys tightly. He took the lead and they went from the room. He marched her down the stairs and into the main room, out through the kitchen and out into the open air. Her heart soared as they went into the daylight. She ran to the car and passed her father before getting in. She looked at him as he got in beside her.

"Dad, there is someone else in the house. I heard her screaming." She wanted to get away but the muffled cries he had heard bothered her. Someone was going through worse than she had, and if she could help her she wanted to. Her father started the car, then turned to her and said:

"I'll go and have a look. You lock yourself in, get into the driver's seat and stay ready. Remember what I have taught you about driving and if you see anything happen, you get out of here. Is that clear?"

"Yes dad, be careful. I thought I heard him leave a short while ago but I'm not sure he might still be in there." Her bravery was commendable and it made him proud. He should have just driven her away but he had an idea who the woman was and he had to find out. He gave her a reassuring smile and got out of the car. She did as she was told and locked the doors and got into the driver's seat ready. She had not passed her test but her father had taught her the basics of driving and she was ready to put them into practice if need be. She watched him go back up to the house and to the side to re-enter the house where had been prisoner. She had a good view all round her and felt relatively safe in the car. It was locked, the engine was running and she was ready. All the time, she kept the area under a watchful eye.Graham entered the house slowly and cautiously. Going into the main room again, he felt the pain in his arm where he had rammed the door more than ever. He rubbed it as he went. He looked at the cupboard on the side and saw a framed photograph. It was of a little old lady and it brought a lump to his throat. It was his mother, a grey old lady smiling with her mouth shut so as not to show she had no teeth. He averted his eyes and looked back at the stairs. Slowly, he walked the short distance to them, and went back up the staircase not wanting to find what he might, what he hoped he would not and what he dreaded. He went past the small room where he had found Lisa, and came to the largest room next to it. He looked back and made sure he was alone. He opened the door as he went in. It was a tidy room but empty. He turned and went to the opposite room. He put his hand on the round knob, slowly turned it and gently opened the door halfway. The room was in darkness and the curtain was closed. It was his mother's old room. The smell hit him at this point; it was dreadful and made him heave. It all looked fine until the door swung fully open, then he saw what made his stomach turn. At the end of the room was a bed, no mattress just the bottom half of a divan. On it was the body of a naked and blindfolded woman. Her fingers had been screwed down to the wooden framework on the base of the bed. Dried blood soaked the material and new blood was coming from her wounds. He did not know what to do at first; the sight riveted him to the spot. The horribly inflicted wounds all over her body were sick to look at. He noticed her nipples had been cut off and her vagina had been painfully sewn up with thick cotton. She had marks of a terrible beating, cuts, and bruises all over her. There was excrement where she had gone to the toilet, urine stains all down the base of the bed. The smell was terrible. He held his hand to his mouth, the sight made him weak at the knees. What kind of animal could do this to another human being, he thought. It was unbearable; he never seen anything like it. He took his hand away from his mouth and tried to dismiss the smell. Slowly, he walked over to the lifeless body. The woman was a bit older than himself, he thought, but it was hard to tell with the state she was in. He shook his head at the barbaric way she had obviously been tortured and beaten, abused and mutilated. He shook and jumped as a slightly agonised moan came from the body.

He leant forward and undid the blindfold, pulling it away from the head and over the eyes.

They hit him instantly as soon as they were revealed. All her hair had been cut off, she was swollen and bruised but as soon as he saw the eyes, full of fear as they were, he knew who he was looking at. She stared wildly and madly at him. She recognised him, the wide eyed look narrowed and a ever so faint smile came across the face. He swallowed and tears welled in his eyes. A lump the size of a football came to his throat. Both knew they were looking at sister and brother. He could not hold her. He just looked at her crying and his tears fell and hit her face like a shower of rain. Slowly and painfully, she opened her mouth to say a word. He leant forward and listened. He heard the last word she said, the last bit of breath in her damaged and beaten body. It was a simple 'Sorry'. Her eyes stayed open, he dropped his head and cried. The sister he had not spoken to or seen for so long was dead in front of him. He shook his head and cried out loudly. He looked up and around the room; the pain and agony she must have gone through was tremendous. The only good thing was that he had got to his daughter in time, before the same had happened to her. He looked down at the lifeless body, no more pain, no more worry, no more hurting, no more torture.

He knew she was dead. It was as if she knew he was coming and just held on for that last word. This would never leave him, he knew that. He stood and wiped his eyes. He went down the stairs and into the living room, opened the curtains and saw Lisa ready, poised, at the wheel of the car. She looked at him as he opened them. He waved an "I'm alright" gesture and went to the phone on the wall by a chair. Slowly, he picked it up and rang the number of his wife's mother; it rang only once, and then was picked up by his wife. It sounded good to hear her voice, anxious as it was.

"Yes, Graham?" she said, eagerly

"Yes, I have her and she is safe. I'm coming home now. Get Peter to meet me, and tell him to phone the police up here. I can't do it. Get them round to 184 North Dean Road Laycock, Keighley. There is a dead woman in one of the upstairs rooms. I don't know where he is and I don't fucking care at this time. I've got to get out of here. Please tell him to do it and phone his colleagues up here. I'm coming home with Lisa." He hung up the phone before hiswife could answer. He walked slowly from the house, saddened and sick to his stomach. The house where he had had so many happy times in as a child was now a torture chamber of death and insane happenings. He had to get away and get his daughter back to her worried mother. He walked from the house; he did not look back. He was trying to keep strong for Lisa's sake, his head was bowed and his eyes sad. She opened the door for him and got into the passenger's seat. He got in and calmly put his seat belt on. She asked him:

"Did you find anything?"

"No, there is nothing there now." He pulled away and headed back the way he had come, to face the police, his friend and his family and trying to get it all back to some kind of normality. He did not know where the madman who had done this was but at this point he did not care.

He would leave that to the police. They drove off out of Laycock and through Keighley, onto the motorway and back home. Lisa was incredibly calm. She sat there saying nothing, holding back her tears, looking at her father from time to time, seeing a tear roll down his face now and again. She did not ask. He was hurting, she knew that. She had grown up a lot in the last week and her mood and attitude would change, had changed.

Although she was now free, something was hold of her father and she could see it was gripping him tightly. This was far from over; she at least knew that much. As he drove calmly down the motorway he kept as quiet and as collected as he could. He wiped his eyes every so often. The thought of his past hit him like a thunderbolt. He had no family left now, except his wife and children. His past had been wiped away it seemed, no brothers, no parents, and no sister. They had never been a close-knit family and now he was regretting it. They were all gone. He had to hold on to what he had now, not knowing if his wife would ever forgive him and not knowing what his children would think when they found out what it was all about, what he had done that night in a juvenile, drunken state. It was wrong and disgusting to all, but what he had done was done. It was not something he was proud of but something he could not change.

 He felt he had paid the price; all he cared about now was that his daughter was safe and well. He looked over at her as they stopped in traffic. She smiled at him and he smiled back.

"Alright, love?" he asked, quietly.

"Yeah," she said smiling at him but holding back the awful memories of the last week. They set off again and were soon heading at speed down the motorway. He was tired with all the driving he had done during the day. His shoulder hurt and he was in emotional agony. He kept his eyes on the road and took it easy. He had got his daughter back; it was up to the police now. He was going to work on the hard task of rebuilding his life and regaining the confidence of his wife and children.

"Who was he daddy?" The question came from nowhere and made Graham close his eyes for a second in dread. It was a question he did not want to answer right now. He looked briefly at his daughter who was waiting patiently and curiously for the answer.

"We will have to find out later, my love. Peter is working on all that side now. He will want to ask you some questions. Is that alright?"

"Yeah, I will help all I can, just as long as they catch the bastard."

"I'm sure they will, I'm sure of that. He won't get near you again I can tell you that, so don't worry about a thing alright? You will be seeing your mother soon then we will be a family again and all will be well." He was reassuring himself as much as his daughter.

He wanted it more than anything but he was not sure what he was going to get. The drive was coming to an end and soon they would be there. Lisa became excited at the thought of being back with her mother again. As they pulled into the road they could see two police cars outside the house, and Graham noticed Peter's car there also. This was the time for explanation and confessions. He was not looking forward to it. The front door opened as he pulled up and a hysterical Gloria came out followed by a policewoman. When Lisa noticed her she dashed from the car and they embraced and burst into tears. Graham stood by the car and watched. It was a happy time coming from a horrible one. He saw Peter coming towards him. He was serious looking and he stood in front of him stopping him from going to his wife and child. He looked into his eyes and said, sternly:

"They found the body. Who is she?"

"My sister" was the answer; he leant back onto the car.

"You have a lot of questions to answer my friend."

"Yeah, well I have plenty of time. I got her back and that is the main thing."

"True, but where is he? Have you any idea?"

"No, and at this point I don't fucking care." He watched his wife and children being escorted back into the house by a policewoman. He looked down the road and at some people gazing out of their windows at the commotion.

"Be talk of the fucking town now, I suppose."

"Listen Graham," Peter leant on the car next to him, "Gloria told me who you think he is.

Now it's not up to me to judge my friend. But you are going to have to explain everything you know, even painful details. However you want to handle this, it will not be easy. I will help you all I can, so don't turn off from me, alright? I'm here when you need it." Graham turned and gave a little appreciative smile. He patted his friend on the back saying thankfully

"Thanks, I'm going to need a friend."

"Yes, you are. So you did not see him at all then?"

"No, he was gone when I got up there"

"You should have told the police. Let them go round. They might have got the bastard. Why didn't you phone me?" He sounded confused.

"I did. They said they could not get hold of you."

"That's bollocks; I'll be looking into that, fucking bollocks." He shook his head and put his hands in his pockets. He looked down the street then back up it again before he looked at his friend, who asked him:

"Will it take long to get him, do you think?"

"Well, that depends on a lot of things. We will get a good description from Lisa I hope and Gloria has given a good one to us already. How is Lisa? Is she ok?"

"Seems so, she is a strong lass, I just hope she will get over it. Christ, Pete you should have seen what he had done to ..." He stopped and could not bring himself to say it. His friend put his arm round him and comforted the man he had known some years and someone he regarded as one of his best friends.

"Hey, come on, let's get sorted out then we will get down to the statements." Peter said

"If he had done that to Lisa, then I don't know what I would have done. It was fucking inhuman I tell ya." He shook his head in disbelief.

"Save it for the statement. Let's go in and see your family."

"Does she want to see me Pete?" he asked, weakly.

"Of course she does. Look, you can't keep feeling sorry for yourself man you will bounce back from this, you have to. You have too much to lose if you don't. He has won if you let it grind you down. This is not going to destroy you, I tell you that. I won't let it and neither should you. Do you hear me?" He shouted at him, but in a supportive way, nodding slowly. Graham pulled himself off the car and took a deep breath. He looked over at Peter. He wanted to smile but couldn't so he just closed his eyes for a second and bowed his head and they walked to the house. He knew he now had a long haul ahead of him as they all did, but it was far from over and deep down he knew that. Deep down he knew it had only begun. This was the start and the end would be a long way away yet.

As they walked it all seemed in slow motion to him. He followed Peter and his strides were full of weakness. His legs did not want to carry him, his mind was running overtime and his heart was sad. He did not know what his wife would do, what his life held with her, what she now thought of him. He slowed a little as they reached the pavement and he looked up at the house. He could not see anyone. It looked empty but he knew it wasn't. His whole life was in there, his reason for living, his whole being. He just hoped they all felt the same way about him, knowing things would never be the same. The scares were there for life. It was how they all handled it that counted; if they all could pull together and be a family again. His heart started to race faster as they reached the front of the house Peter looked back as he went up the few steps to the front door. He noticed his friend lagging a little behind. He didn't say anything, just stopped and waited. Graham reached him and opened the door himself. They entered the house and the door was closed behind them. The street was quiet, but a lot of eyes were peering from behind curtains and windows, at the police cars and the house in the street that had become a point of interest all of a sudden.

CHAPTER EIGHT

It was a very painful five weeks for them all, including Peter. He had to get his story right with Graham about his involvement, questions after questions, living through a nightmare time and again, going to see therapists, the counselors, and people wanting to help, Graham was not sure if any of them did. He was sat in a quiet pub in the corner, with his quarter drunk pint, waiting for his friend Peter, who had been a tower of strength for him, for them all, helping in lots of ways and protecting them from a lot more.

The pub was quiet and he had been there many times before. There were only a few people in but with it being mid-afternoon it was not unusual. He looked over to the door as it swung open on its old hinges. The large, wooden, traditional oak was pushed open and in walked Peter. He nodded at Graham, who thought he looked like a cowboy entering a saloon. He watched him go and get a drink at the bar and then come over and join him. He sat down, stretched and made a loud, grunting noise.

"Tiring day, old man?" Graham asked.

"Fucking back breaking mate, back breaking." He took a long drink of his traditional ale then sniffed up taking a quick loo around the pub.

"You in for a cold or something?" Graham enquired

"Hope not, it won't be able to take the pace"

"So have we had any news?" he asked hopefully.

"Not yet." Peter shook his head and saw the disappointment in his friend's face.

"Well, where is he? What the hell is going on? It has been over three weeks now. What is being done Pete?"

"Listen, Graham. Let the police do their job. It is not easy, but we will find him. We have a good description and we know all about him now from the homes and all that. Mind you, with the dog bites and the bash Gloria gave him on the head, then the kick in the bollocks Lisa delivered, I wouldn't be surprised if he was ..."

"Good,." Graham said before his friend had finished his sentence.

"Yeah, well it will only be a matter of time. I told you before you should have told the police up there, then they could have gone round and sorted it all out. They would have the fucker by now, but we have been through all this before."

"I know, I know, but I was so fucked up, I still am I suppose." He shook his head and bowed it slightly, then took a drink of his pint.

"You know, I can't help thinking how slack he was, how unprofessional. He let you find her very easily didn't he? Almost as if he wanted you too. I mean after what he did to your poor unfortunate sister, the sick bastard. He did nothing really to Lisa."

"No, because I got there too fast that's why," he protested.

"No, he seemed to hand it to you on a plate. Why did he just leave?

He knew it would take about an hour for you to reach there. That would have been plenty of time. Why give you all the clues? Why just leave it at that? I mean he had your sister for weeks there apparently, made her eat powdered glass for fuck's sake. We have a real sick bastard on our hands here I tell ya, which is why I don't understand why he left Lisa relatively unharmed. Not that I wanted any harm to come to the girl, God forbid." He stopped when he saw Graham hurting at the thought of it all. He looked at Peter with sad eyes.

"I wanted to kill the fucker; I tell yeah, if I had seen him I would have killed him."

"Well I would say in a way you were lucky because of his lackluster amateurism."

"Lucky? Oh yeah, lucky as fuck me, yeah lucky alright." He raised his voice and had a frown across his forehead. In fact, he couldn't believe his friend had just said that. He looked across at him, but before he said anything Peter defused the situation with a question. "How is Lisa, is she ok?"

"Well yeah, she is coping very well, still the nightmares. Sebastian is chuffed with the computer, which I'm fucking taking back because the frigging monitor is shagged.

Anyway, it's Gloria who is taking it the worst. I mean she won't let Lisa out of her sight, very protective, very protective indeed."

"Well, you can't blame her, can you? She has gone through a lot. It will take time, my friend. Time is a great healer. She will come round. Absence makes the heart grow fonder and all that. How are they all anyway?"

"Fine, I got a postcard yesterday. The villa is nice and they're all enjoying it, sounds good. It was great idea for them to go away."

"Well, I say you should have gone with 'em mate, I'm telling yeah."

"No, I had my work to sort out. Mind you, I have not been able to do that, I've left it to the foreman. No, it's Gloria; she is not the same, Pete. It's not as it was, I mean the garden is a mess; weeds are coming through and everything. You know how nice she used to keep that garden. She just can't forget; there is sadness in her eyes all the time, and we have not had sex since. It's as if she just wants to keep me out." He rocked back in his seat and finished his drink. He walked over to the bar, ordered two more drinks and waited. Peter noticed nothing out of the ordinary. Then again, he wouldn't, but if he looked a little closer to the left, about ten yards, he would see him, a quiet man, minding his own business having a quiet drink alone, glasses and a growing beard, black curly hair. Nothing curious, except if you looked very carefully at the hair you would see it was a wig. If you took time to look at the glasses you would see they were plain glass It was the eyes that gave him away the most. Graham would not recognise it nor Peter. They had never seen him before, but if he spoke Graham would then know who the voice belonged to. He should, he had heard it on the phone enough times. If Gloria and Lisa were here they would know those eyes, without a doubt and Peter would have his man. It was the duck feeder. When Graham returned, he put the drinks down and sat down again.

"Thanks old man." Peter took a long drink of his first pint and put it down again almost empty. He was getting ready for his second that Graham had bought.

"I don't know what to do Pete, I really don't." He sounded dejected.

"Well, it won't be easy. It's like a journey, there is no map for; you are going to have to find your own way, my friend."

"That's very philosophical of you where did you hear that one?"

"Well, I do have my moments. What you need is a night out. I'm looking at this new temp we have in, I tell you she is a spanner."

"What the bloody hell is a spanner?" Graham asked confused

"When she walks past she tightens your nuts up. You need cheering up and we will have a good time. What do you say?"

"No thanks, I'll give that a miss." Peter could see his friend was hurting and mixed up. He pulled back and looked at him for a moment. He was not the same person; the eyes had no sparkle in them, his face looked tired and he had a drained look about him. "Alright mate, alright I'm sorry very insensitive of me. So, when are they coming back from Spain? It's your mother-in-law's villa, isn't it?"

"Yeah, at least I know they are safe there. The bastard has no chance of finding them there, no fucking way, I tell ya. He wanted to make me suffer, he said. Well, he is still doing it now. How the fuck it all happened, I don't fucking know." He took a large drink of his pint and his hand was shaking uncontrollably as he did. "He was adopted, went from home to home, no one wanted him, got moved around a lot, and did not have a good time in the places he was put. He tortured some kid when he was twelve because he said he was weird. When he was old enough he wanted to know who his real mother was. He wanted to write to her, but they don't give out the addresses of course. Apparently, your sister had shown an interest as well, wanting to know all about him and all that. Then some smart arse social worker decided to break all the rules and arranged for them to write to each other. They exchanged letters and it all seemed to go very well. With her writing to him it seemed to calm him down, then they were suddenly stopped for some reason or other, and he went berserk, and threw an orderly through a plain glass window. She lost her face, two fingers and an eye. He was out of control again, so the letters were allowed to continue. It went on for years. I find it bloody amazing really. Anyway time came for him to be released, they could not hold him anymore because he had done nothing else wrong and they passed him of sound mind. Silly bastards! He was released and somehow, I don't know how, he got your sister's address.

The officer in charge of the mail censorship seems to think she told him secretly in the letters, like a code or something. Anyway, he found out, and from what we can gather he went there, tortured her for weeks. For fuck's sake, she must have told him about you, his real dad, and then one thing led to another and we know what happened." Peter told him in a very informative way then finished his first pint and put the empty glass down.

"It's a fucking mad world; I can tell you that, it's all my fault." He was becoming depressed and Peter noticed it instantly, and started to regret telling him everything. He spoke straight at him in a firm voice.

"No, no it's not, now you are going to have to stop blaming yourself Graham. For fuck's sake man, you're falling apart. Don't let it get to you like this, be strong, be brave, be a bastard, be anything but don't cave in. Gloria needs ya strong and so do the kids. We will find him and he won't be let out again, I can assure you of that little fact. Put it behind you and get on with your life,

182

because if you let it get to you, then he has won, hasn't he? You're fucked, lost everything, your wife, your kids, and your whole life. You don't want the fucker to hurt any of you again so get out of it Graham, and stop feeling sorry for yourself. All that time has passed and it's time to move on. You have made mistakes and we all do, so for fuck's sake fight through it, or it will fucking destroy you man." Peter leant forward and looked at Graham determinedly in the eye. Graham looked back and a little appreciative smile cracked his lips. Slowly he nodded.

"Yeah I know, you're right, but it's not bloody easy."

"Course it's not, nothing in life worth having is, if your kids are getting over it, then so can you. It will not help anyone if you're down all the bloody time, will it? It will just make everyone depressed, and make the situation worse."

"Yeah, but I don't know if Gloria will ever be right with me again." He looked dejected and Peter sighed at him.

"Come on man, of course she will, it will just take time. I think if she was going to leave you she would have done it by now. She will stick with ya, she is a bloody good woman that. You're a lucky man. It will just take some time for her to adjust and get over it all. She will feel better when we have caught him. There was so many things in the house we can get him on. We know what he looks like, who he is. His face is in the paper, his description is with every copper around, and it is only a matter of time, believe me. Have you decided what you're going to do with the house yet? Your sister left it to you in her will, did she not?."

"Oh, I haven't thought about it yet, not had time. It was the house I grew up in, but after what happened there I can never go back I don't think."

"Did you search the house before you left?" Peter asked again. He had been through all this with him before but thought after all this time he might have remembered something new something he had had forgot to mention last time.

"No, I told you. I went in, upstairs, got Lisa out, saw my sister then left. It was bloody horrible." He shook his head and took a drink of his pint. "I tell ya Peter, I will never forget what I saw that day. The way she was nailed on the bed and the things he must have done to her. It makes me sick to my stomach."

"Yeah well, it will have to be something you will have to come to terms with I'm afraid. Are you still seeing the counselor? Is she helping?"

"No, not really, I have stopped. It was doing my head in. I don't know if I will ever come to terms with it you know. You must have seen some sights in your job. How do you cope with it? How do you forget?"

"I have to switch off. It is a job I don't take it home with me, I can't afford to. I have seen a lot of suffering, a lot of mindless violence and I have seen murder. It is a very disturbing world we live in my friend. I get called a bastard. I am, but it is bastards like me who make it safe for other bastards to live safe in this world. I've seen stabbings, kickings, beatings, muggings, hit and run. It is a very stressful job, and underpaid may I add. But what keeps me sane is the fact I know I'm on the winning side. It does not seem it all the time, but I still believe I am doing right. We have stupid rules that are outdated and work for the fucking criminals half the time. We are told what to do by tossers, male and female, who know fuck all about coppering and have never done a real job in their life. But when I get a result, when I get my man, when I send some vicious fucker down, it makes it all worth the pain it took to get them there, and I will keep doing it until I get disillusioned with it all, until I can't see me doing any good any more. That is when I will call it a day; get some stress less job, security or something, telling others to do the work while I sit about and get paid for what I know not what I do. When that day comes and I suppose it will, it will be a sad day for me, because then I will know I can no longer function as a police officer and that will be a very sad day for me, I tell ya"

"You could always come and work for me."

"What, and have you as a boss? Bloody hell, that would be worse than giving up my pension." He smiled as he took a drink of his second pint. Graham smiled back and stretched out looking round the pub. He turned back to Peter and said:

"I have to take the frigging computer monitor back today; it has packed up, bloody thing."

"Too much internet porn, it blows their fuses you know."

No, not porn, Peter."

"There is nothing but porn on the bloody thing. Every time you click, some porn comes up on screen."

"Well, I'm taking it back today. I have to have it fixed for when Sebastian comes home. I'm borrowing his at the moment. He loves the thing, never off it."

"No, I bet he isn't." Peter raised his eyebrow. "Porn you see, he is a growing lad, inquisitive you see."

"Christ, you have sex on the brain."

"I know, I want it lower but the doctor said there is nothing he can do."

"You want to ask him for some fresh material as well."

"Oh very funny, not like you." Peter laughed

"No. maybe not." He lowered his eyes to the floor.

"That computer shop in the high street, is that where you're taking it?"

"Yeah, the one that says their customer care is next to none. We'll see about that. Just see what they say when I walk in." Graham acknowledged

"He is bloody Scottish, can't trust him." Peter stated firmly

"I thought it was the Irish you didn't like?"

"Australians, Germans, French, and Indians."

"There is not many people you do like really is there? You know for a copper you are very xenophobic."

"What the bloody hell does that mean? Is it legal?"

"A strong dislike of foreigners."

"Oh that's what it means, does it? Well, they don't like us, so sod 'em."

"Probably because we have been at war with every fucker at some time in history, there are not many countries we have not had a war with, is there?"

"There are always going to be wars my friend, unavoidable."

"It should be avoidable. Greed and religion, that is what wars are all about, bloody religion, what a hypocritical way to live."

"Now who is getting philosophical?"

"Well, there is too much violence and deceit in the world and the world is a big place ,room for everyone"

"Don't give a shit. We're an island and we should stay one. I will never be European, British or anything else. I'm English and proud of it." He nodded proudly with a noble, eminent look on his face.

The afternoon was bright when he left the pub. After having another drink with Peter, they said their goodbyes and he left to drive to the electrical shop. He listened to some music in his car and was relatively calm. He thought there should be no trouble with the monitor being exchanged. After all, it was still under warranty. He parked up in the little car park outside the shop. He locked the car door and went inside through a glass door atthe front. There was piped music coming from the hidden speakers and he looked around. He stood there with the monitor in his hand. Normally he thought when you walked into this shop they couldn't do enough for you. They were straight up to you asking if they could assist. He noticed none of the assistants wanted to approach him, which made him slightly angry. He went to the customer care desk. There was a woman behind the desk, very smartly dressed and well made up. She looked as if she was going out on a Saturday night. When he approached she smiled at him but walked away. She had some papers in her hand and disappeared through a door, taking no notice of him. Putting the monitor on the desk, he waited and saw a couple being approached by a smiling assistant, as they walked into the shop. He wants bloody commission, Graham thought. He became impatient, sighed and got the attention of an assistant who made the mistake of walking past him. He was a young lad with a shirt that was too big for him and hung baggily off his skinny body, and a tie that was not tied up tight to the collar.

"Excuse me son," Graham said, loudly and firmly.

"Yes sir," the lad said, unenthusiastically.

"I want another monitor. This one is knackered. I bought it only a matter of weeks ago and it does not work."

"Have you a receipt sir? Did you buy it from here?"

"Of course I bought it from here." Graham put his hand in his pocket and pulled out the receipt and gave it to the lad, who came round the desk. He typed something into the computer and looked at the screen. He looked confused and tried again. Shaking his head, he went into the back without any explanation to Graham, who was becoming very annoyed. It was at least ten minutes before the little, light brown, wooden door opened again. It was the woman who had gone through it the first time. She again smiled and went to the till, with no intention at all of dealing with Graham's problem, Graham held his anger and asked, calmly:

"Excuse me love, I have brought this monitor back. One of your young pups messed about on the computer there, and has disappeared. Can you help me?"

Suddenly, she stopped looking pleased and stopped smiling. She came over and said, in a voice he instantly disliked:

"Have you a receipt sir?"

"Yes, and your little helper in the big shirt took it in there. Now, I want a new monitor and I would like it sorting out, now, please." Graham was becoming angrier and it was made worse by this woman shaking her head slightly, in a cocky manner as she went into the back once again. He felt the exasperation building up inside him. Another five minutes went by, which seemed like an hour to him. Finally, the woman and the young lad came out. She gave him the receipt back and said:

"Someone will be out to see you in a moment, sir." She turned and went back to the till.

The young lad strolled off and went to stand by the door, waiting for a potential customer to come in. Before Graham was about to yell at her, the door opened once again and an older, more mature, man came out. He looked at Graham, then the monitor, and came up to stand directly in front of him

"Right sir, you have a problem?" he asked, in a slight Scottish accent. It seemed he was trying to hide it.

"Yes ,finally, this monitor is fucked and I want another one. There is my receipt, which you told me is my guarantee and it has only been just over a month, so can you please sort it out now, because I've been waiting here for half an hour?"

Graham pointed to the receipt on the counter and then the monitor. The man did not even look at either. He looked at Graham and said, in a tone Graham did not like at all:

"I can do nothing with it sir. It will have to be sent off. You have had it more than twenty eight days, and if there is a fault then it will have to be determined if it is a product fault or a customer fault. If it is a customer fault then you will have to pay for it to be repaired, I'm afraid. However, I can do you a good deal on a better monitor than that. You can upgrade to a seventeen inch screen for a very reasonable price." He smiled so smugly that Graham wanted to knock off his face. He felt himself boiling up inside. He was in no mood at all for this, so tried the calm approach first. He spoke in a composed way.

"I have a twelve month guarantee with this. You said so when I bought it. Don't come the fucking crap with me, I'm not in the mood. Just replace it and I will leave, otherwise we are going to have a scene, are we not?"

"Sorry, no can do. You have not taken our advance cover out on the equipment."

"The equipment is only a month old, your guarantee covers it."

"Well, like I said, I can send it off for you but it will take up to four week. I would say your best bet would to upgrade. I mean for what it will cost you to do so, it will probably work out cheaper than paying for it to be fixed anyway.

"Now you fucking listen to me, you smug smart shit," Graham

intentionally shouted to get the attention of the whole store in a matter of seconds. "I'm not fucking upgrading. I want it replaced. If you don't replace it then I will take you to trading standards. You are selling things with promises you don't keep. But first …"

The man behind the counter stopped him by putting his hands up in front of him and saying:

"Calm down sir, there is no need to shout, letting everyone hear." He looked around anxiously at his customers who were all listening, and turned towards the desk.

"I will tell whoever I want." Graham turned round and addressed the whole shop. "Let me tell you good people don't buy fuck all from here they're thieving bastards and don't want to know when it goes wrong. I'd go elsewhere if I was you, because this place is crap. Your guarantee is not worth shit." He shouted loudly

"Please sir, calm down, there is no need for this type of outburst. If it continues, I will have to phone the police," the man behind the counter said with a worried look on his face. Graham turned back and calmly but firmly, said to him:

"Have you another one of these monitors in the back?"

"Well, yes we have but …"

"Good, because this one is coming down on your fucking stupid head in a minute if it is not out here for me to take home, and it better be a good one, because if it is a duff one like this fucker I will be back and give you and your poxy little shop the biggest headache you have ever had. Is that fucking clear?" His eyes looked mean and his voice threatening. The shopkeeper did not think twice. He went into the back and soon returned with a large box, on the side of which was the picture of the monitor Graham had just brought in. Taking his receipt, Graham looked round, and then picked up the box. He did not say thank you. He just walked to the middle of the shop and then turned round. He looked at the man behind the desk, who was looking at him with worried eyes wanting him to leave. He then looked down again at his computer and was typing something in. Graham was going to say something but could not be bothered. He had his replacement and so left it alone. He went out to his car, placed the box in the back and got in. He started up and put his seat belt on. His hands were shaking and he clapped them together. He calmed down. It was time to go.

The drive home was something he needed. He drove past the pub where he'd been spent time with Peter and headed off down the street. The duck feeder was walking slowly from the pub His hands were dug deep into his pockets and his shoulders were arched forward. He walked for some time, just round the small town, then headed out up the hill. Soon, he was passing the school and down into the park. At the edge of the water he looked out across at the ducks. He had no bread for them today. They sat and took no notice of him and he took no notice of them. He looked up towards Graham's house, his father's house, the man he hated with a passion, the man he thought had to pay for all the torment he had suffered in his childhood, and young adult life, a man he would never forgive.

He had satisfied himself his mother had learned her lesson and now it was time for his father to learn his, and he was ready to teach him. He stayed here for some time, motionless and looking in the direction of his father's house. Eventually, he left and walked to a newsagent's. He bought several newspapers and then went to the little room he had rented with cash, cash he had found in his mother's house. It was enough to get him by for some time and he knew he would not need much anyway. The little, bare room was a basement flat type, situated on the outskirts of the town, a bit of a dump with damp patches, but he was not bothered. When he paid in cash for a month the landlord did not seem bothered once he had the money in his hand. He handed him the key and asked no questions. It was a dirty place, with a musty smell and damp feel about it. It had only a single old bed, with a dirty mattress and miss matching bed clothes, a sink, and a small cooker in the one room, very basic with one chair and a soiled settee. A round table and a picture of two white galloping horses, that would have looked better on the wall of a 1960shouse wall. The toilet was behind a partition, which had been purposely built by an amateur.

The windows, which were in need of a clean, looked out onto the pavement. It was not a desirable place and not in demand, so he would be left alone here. He knew that, and that was just what he wanted. Not many people would live here which is why he got it as cheaply as he had and why no questions had been asked and no references needed.

He locked the door behind him and went to a small suitcase which he pulled out from under his bed. He opened it then took off his coat. He pulled at the wig and then took the glasses off at almost the same time. He rubbed his hands through his hair and scratched his head. He put the case on the bed and dropped the wig and glasses on the floor. Lifting the battered top, he searched through its contents and took out a pen and some paper. He went to the table, sat on the chair then started to write his letter. It was in big, bold writing and it took him some time He seemed to struggle with a lot of the words and wrote slowly, hunched over the paper and reading the letters out loud as he wrote, but he eventually finished. He went back to the case, took out an envelope and put his letter inside. He sealed it and wrote Graham's address on it, then went to sit on the settee to read his papers. He would post the letter tomorrow when he went for a walk, he decided.

He stayed there for the rest of the day, looking at and slowly reading every page of every newspaper he had bought.

Night fell and he fell asleep on the settee. The light was left on and from outside you would not know it was a room let out. It looked like someone's cellar, the large building above it was used as flats but the people who lived there did not come into contact with him at all. He avoided all contact as much as possible, speaking to no one and not making himself known. No one saw the light go out at about two in the morning as he woke from the settee and went to bed. He fell into a haunted and restless sleep. He often had nightmares, and had learned to come to terms with them. Horrible things happened to him in his dreams, nasty and terrible things. He had them all his life and knew when he woke he was safe, but he did not know how safe he was at this moment. He had put the first part of his plan into operation, now he had to continue with it until the end. It had taken him a long time and a lot of effort to put his idea into action and get out of that place and do what he had to do. He had a lot of people to convince he was stable enough to be released and let out. It was not easy but he did it, telling them things that made them nod and smile, letting them think he was on the way to recovery, on the way to be cured, on the way to a normal life and not a threat to anyone anymore. And all the time he had his father on his mind, his mother, and his idea, and planned to make them pay and suffer the way he had, They just did not know what had hit them, and it pleased him what he had done so far, but he knew there was more to come.

He knew it would be the end of his father or the end of him, but he did not want to go on living the life he had, an outcast, a reject. People had always seen him as odd, different, someone to keep clear of. He wanted revenge and he was going to get it, get it from the man who was responsible for him being here, his father, Graham. As soon as Peter got the telephone call he was round at Graham's house, knocking on the door It was early in the morning. He was let in and then shown the letter. Graham had an angry look on his face as Peter took it and asked:

"Was it delivered by the postman or hand delivered?"

"Postman, I had it with some other stuff. It is postmarked from here, the bastard is here," he said sitting down on the chair next to his kitchen table. Peter looked at it and read it out loud:

"Hello daddy, how are you? It is your number one son here. How is Lisa? Give her my love. I will be seeing her again very soon, and will be repaying her and her mother for the pain they inflicted on me. I have not met your other son yet, but I'm sure I will. I know all about you all now, and know he takes the fucking dog for a walk on the fields down from your house. There is no need to let your policeman friend send this to his people; it is me, it is your son. The fingerprints and saliva tests and all that bollocks, oh and the handwriting experts, they will all be a waste of time and taxpayers' money. I'm here close, very close. You will not find me, you will not recognise me, but I am here, I have watched you, I have followed you, I will continue to do so and when the time is right I will hit, and I will hit hard. I know how to make people suffer, I know what suffering is. A father should play with his son. Are you ready to start the game again? We have so much to catch up on; what I did to mummy, how I watched her suffer, how I watched her plea for mercy. This will be nothing to what I'm going to do to you. I gave you your smelly little daughter back because she made me ill, and I wanted to show you I can do anything I want. I had the power over life and death with her. I chose life, the next time I will chose death. What you did was wrong, and I have been punished for being wrong, so you must now be punished for being a bastard to your son. Daddy, daddy, daddy, I will be in touch. Have a wonderful day because I don't know how many you have left."

Peter turned over the page over and saw there was nothing on the back so turned it back again. He looked at Graham and ran his tongue over his top teeth.

"Sick little fucker, he is around here Pete," Graham said, unbelievingly.

"Possibly, don't take all he says for granted he might be here, and then again he might just wants us to think he is. He could have travelled to post this down here, could he not?

He might know about Sebastian from when he was watching the house before. You stay calm and don't let him get you riled. That is what he wants; he wants to play mind games with you. We're not taking any chances this time. You are going to be watched, and tell Gloria and the kids to stay away, well away, while they're abroad he can't get to them. You are the bait and we have set a trap to get the fucker."

"How did he know about you Pete?" Graham said, shaking his head while clicking his tongue in worry.

"Don't worry about that now. He could have been watching you for months before he snatched Lisa He probably saw me coming out or something. What we have to work on is how to get the bastard. He will be different, so we can't rely on people seeing him. The description we have out could be bloody useless if he is changing his appearance. You are going to have to keep a look out for anything unusual, any strange people hanging about. Watch your car mirror, watch your back wherever you go. Do not go anywhere without telling me first. I will get someone over here and we will have a watch on you round the clock. You will not fart without us knowing about it. We will get the fucker. I'll take this down to the station and get it looked at anyway, and get the ball rolling. What we will do as well is look at all the CCTV footage. You will have to compile a list and give me places and times you were there. If we can get you on camera, we might be able to see someone following you, you never know. He is as good as banged up now Graham. I tell ya, it is a matter of time."

It didn't take Peter long to get the operation under way. Before Graham knew it, he was under close watch, his phone was monitored and he was again testing his nerves. But this time he didn't have the fear of his daughter's kidnap on his conscience. He just had to sit and wait. It was all taken care of without him seeing it. It was moving into operation behind the scenes, he was just a part of it. The police wanted him now, and it was their job to get there man. He left it to them and tried to get on with his life the best he could. He knew the police were following and Peter told him how to react if anything unusual happened so the police would know if something was wrong, and if anyone approached him he did not know. He had a gesture to make so they knew he had been approached. Running his fingers through his hair was the sign they would be looking for. He knew if a strange man came up to him, all he had to do was run his hand across his head, through his hair as if he was thinking of something, or to scratch an imaginary itch, and the police would be there. He felt comfortable with it and after a while stopped looking for them and trying to spot the following police officer. He knew they were there and it gave him confidence and security.

Walking Sam was a chore he had to do, but he had come to enjoy it lately. He watched the dog sniffing round a tree in the bottom fields. He took a deep breath and filled his lungs with fresh air; it was clean and refreshing. He looked as Sam pounced around and then fall on his back rolling in the grass, with all his four legs in the air. He scratched his back on the grass by swiveling his body from side to side. The happy look on his face indicated he enjoyed it immensely. He stood up and shook himself, then continued sniffing around in the grass as Graham looked on and watched. He knew he was being watched too, but had come to terms with it and hardly noticed them anymore. It had been almost a week since the letter arrived and he had heard nothing since. Peter had told him it could take quite some time; they just had to be patient. Sam picked up his ears up at a dog barking down the way. He wanted to go and investigate but was called back by Graham. He looked at him and then ignored the other dog. He had been told and obeyed the command, and was again now rummaging through some dropped leaves. He cocked his leg to relieve himself on them.

Graham looked out across the field to the trees beyond. It was a nice day and he remembered all the times he came down here with his family when Sam was a puppy and they played with him in the grass. He smiled to himself at the thought of Gloria rolling around with the puppy dog making little barking noises at it, and they all looked on laughing at her childish antics. Sam was now grown and part of the family, the family he wanted back so much, the family that he hoped would forgive him, and the family he had hurt terribly.

Calling Sam, he started to walk back to the house. He turned and noticed his dog was not by his side. He looked up for him, noticing the animal in a rigid position staring down to the trees. His ears pricked up, his tail was still and he was snarling.

"Sam, here boy, come on." Graham thought he was after the other dog again but no, this was different, he had noticed something, someone in the trees. Graham walked up to the dog and looked down in his direction. Sam was poised and ready to go; it seemed to be waiting for something or someone to move from the trees. Graham could see nothing. He looked across at the trees but still saw nothing. He looked back up the hill and noticed the policeman who was watching get out his car and look down at him. The dog growled and it edged forward. Graham again looked at the cluster of trees a few hundred yards in front of him, his heart began to beat faster in his chest. Suddenly, he noticed movement, a shadow like figure moved from behind one of the trees. It was gone again as quickly as it appeared, but it was there, now hidden again behind another tree. He felt the hairs go up on the back of his neck. Was this the man? Was this him? Was this his son? Was he being watched by the man the police were looking for? Sam was waiting and sniffing the air. He had his scent and knew where he was; he was waiting for a command. He knew this man. He had met him before. Graham looked up at the police officer who curiously had moved forward. He was looking down at Graham, who was breathing even more heavily. He was nervous. Suddenly, he put his hand to his head and rubbed his hair. As soon as this happened the policeman was at his car moments later and on the radio. He was soon running down to Graham. Sam felt the tension and was off. He went running towards the trees, barking and growling as he ran.

Graham froze; the police officer ran past him and followed the dog. For a moment he did not know what to do, but instinct forced him to follow. By now, the shadow was gone from the trees. Sam reached there and quickly smelt the area and was off again. He could smell the scent no man could; he could follow just as well, if not better by smell alone, down a hill and along the stream side. He went quickly, followed by the plain clothes policeman. Graham was running after them. He was both excited and anxious at the same time, his heart pounding in his chest his nerves igniting with fear and anticipation.

Sam was difficult to keep up with. He went round a bend and on to a public footpath. He knew he was close and knew soon he would have his man, the same man he had attacked before in the house. He recognised the scent, he ran and growled. The policeman was losing his breath; he was not used to all this running and was out of shape. He was no match for a young, fit, healthy dog. Graham had almost caught up to him and also found it hard going. Both men were getting tired and were gasping for air. Sam was fit and he could still run a long way yet. He pounded on; he could not see his target but he could almost feel him and he knew he was close. Sam ran round the bend of a wall running alongside him. Trees were in front and a stone bridge that used to carry a railway line. He saw a figure disappearing into the trees He had sight of his prey and knew it would not be long before he was there.

 Graham was gasping for air as he caught up with the police officer who was also fighting for breath. Both men ran side by side unable to speak to each other. They reached the bridge and stopped. They had lost sight of the dog. Graham pointed to the trees as he heard a bark and knew it was his dog. He headed off labouringly and was followed by the policeman.

They could hear Sam barking and it was close. It gave both of them strength to go a little faster, opening out into waste ground, they ran on up a hill which at the top was a road. As they scrambled up to the top they saw Sam barking at a brick wall. It was too high for him to get over but not the man he was chasing. Graham hit the wall in exhausted pain, and slid to the floor gasping for air. The policeman took a run at it and managed to get himself to the top. He looked out across the housing estate in front of him and his heart sank as he realised they had lost their man. No way could he be followed and no way could he lift Sam over to do the job. He jumped back down and sat next to Graham, coughing and breathing hard. Sam could not understand why they had stopped. He put his front paws on the wall and stood on his hind legs barking. This was where the man went and he wanted to follow. Graham pulled at the dog and gestured him to sit, which he did reluctantly and with confusion.

"Bollocks," Graham said, shaking his head.

"They're going to nail mine to the fucking wall," said the officer, shaking and bowing his own head. He dropped it into his hands. Sam was walking round smelling the floor; he was so close and was stopped by a brick wall. He lay down by Graham and sighed, resting his head on his front paw, breathing a little heavily but still with plenty of run left in him he could of gone on for much longer and knew he would of caught the man easy.

 It was a few minutes before any of them stood. They had lost him and it would not go down well with the officer's superiors. Graham saw it as a regretful mistake but the policeman saw it as his job on the line. Slowly and wearily, he walked back to the field and to the police car. There was another one there now and Peter was just arriving in his own car. He opened the door and dashed out wanting an explanation from his officer, who sheepishly told him, with his head bowed:

"Lost him, sir."

"Fucking hell." Peter punched into fresh air with his fist. Shaking his head, he turned to his officer and shouted:

"Why the fucking hell didn't you wait? We could have got men here in minutes and surrounded the fucker. Christ, how fucking stupid can you get? You should have kept calm, radioed in and we could have got here without him knowing. You don't go charging in like something from the frigging Sweeney." Peter screamed.

"Peter, it was Sam, he went after him," Graham said in some sort of defense for the man.

"I don't give a shit; you should have called him back. Do you realise how much money it is costing to look after you? We can't afford fucking stupid mistakes like this. We might have had the bastard there. Right you," he pointed to the officer, "take them to where you lost him and see if you can find anything." He signaled to two more officers in the second car and all three of them went down the field again. Peter turned back to Graham and looked down at Sam, who was sat with his ears pricked up at all the activity round him. Peter looked up and around him. He saw a few people coming to their doors and windows. He shook his head in disbelief and went back to his car.

Graham could tell his friend was not in a good mood at all so decided to leave and he walked home. Sam was walking by his side not knowing what all the fuss was about.

They were soon home. Graham went in and let Sam off the lead. He made himself a drink and waited. He knew Peter would be round sooner or later, and he was right. Half an hour to be exact, the front door was opened and Sam went to investigate. He walked back into the room with Peter. Both came to the kitchen where Graham was sat with a mug of coffee. Peter sat next to him at the table.

"Total fuck up," he said, staring at his friend

"What could we do Pete? The dog went off like a shot. I thought your man was right to follow, I mean what if he had caught him?"

"What if … what if … he didn't and it was stupid."

"Do you want a drink?"

"No, listen, if you ever see him again, call me, do not run after him, do not do anything heroic again you're not up to it, alright?" His voice was unfriendly cold and direct.

"Did you find anything?"

"No, clean away. Are you sure it was him?"

"I don't know. Sam seemed to know him. I mean he does not just run after strangers for the fun of it." Sam seemed to know they were talking about him. His ears went back and his tail wagged while he watched them talk.

"Yeah, well maybe I could do with him on my team. Right, I'm off,. I have a shit load to do, and no fucking time to do it in." He stood and went to the door, followed by Graham who watched him go and then locked the door. He went to sit down and relax. Sam came in and laid down by his side, all was quiet and calm again. Graham closed his eyes and dropped his head, it was becoming a strain on him and he wanted it all to be over. He wanted his life back, and he wanted calm and peace again. He wanted this every day and prayed for it. His body ached and he wheezed a little. All that running was not good for him. He was unhealthy and not built or ready for running so much so soon. He would not be doing that again. He knew Peter was right but he didn't know what to do for the best. The stress showed on his face and he felt low and dejected, lonely and in despair. Sadness hung to his heart and he missed his family, missed his life as it was. Most of all he missed his wife to hold and feel her warmth.

The package arrived the next day. It was only small and was pushed through the letter box. Graham was not thinking when he came down the stairs. He was half asleep.

Picking up the brown paper package, he went to the living room. Dressed in an old pair of jeans and a t-shirt, he looked rough, unshaven and tired. He rubbed his eyes and stroked the dog, who came up to him to say good morning. He yawned, sat down, and then pulled open the paper package. It did not dawn on him until he was at the last part of the opening process, that he might be doing wrong. But it was too late now. He pulled the clear tape that was holding it together. His name and address had been written on the front and he should have noticed it, but didn't.

He pulled and it gave way with a sudden tug What he saw and what dropped on his lap made him look in horror. It was red, bloodstained and looked like some sort of human organ. It was in a plastic bag, and he lifted it off his lap with two fingers. It had a note attached, which said in hand writing text:

"I have done this for you and your fucking dog, next time it will be for your daughter, then your son, then your wife, and then you daddy."

He put the thing down on the table. He picked up the phone and called Peter. He let the dog out. He opened the door and watched as Sam ran into the garden and went to his favourite little tree at the bottom, cocked his leg and had a long welcome pee. Graham took deep breaths of air and woke up rapidly. He shook his head, he did not know what was in the bag and deep down he did not want to know. It was all becoming too much for him. He had expected the man to have been caught by now. Sam shook himself and sniffed the garden with his morning inspection All was well and nothing smelt wrong. He came back in and went to his bowl, took some water and was now set for the morning. Graham took the plastic bag and went into the room. He put the bag on the settee, blood was in it and the organ was sat in the blood. He did not recognise it and wondered what the note attached to it meant.

He decided to wait until Peter arrived and hopefully he would be able to sort it out for him. Graham was becoming distant; he could feel it in himself. His life had fallen apart and he wanted desperately to get it back, but he was weakening all the time and it showed in his durable resistance to things.

Peter was not in a good mood when he came round, something that was becoming more and more common these days. He looked at the bag, picked it up by the corner with two fingers and looked closely at it.

"Do you know what it is?" he asked.

"No idea, read the note. What does it mean?" He pointed to the paper; Peter read it in silence, then shook his head.

"Your post should have been intercepted. Why the fuck it wasn't I don't know. With any luck he would have gone to a post office to post this, and it's dated yesterday, so he would be on a security camera doing so. I will take it down to the lab and find out what it is, be interesting to find out I hope its animal and not human"

"I don't like the sound of this at all. Have you any idea what it means?" Graham was worried, and it sounded clearly in his voice. Peter was not his normal self; he seemed not to be a friend anymore and seemed to be doing a job and that's all.

"No, do you?"

"I hope not, I will be in touch. Stay in today and like I said your post will be intercepted, so you won't get any for a day or two. Then one of my boys will bring it round to you."

He turned and left, with the note, bag, and packaging.

Graham was again left alone. He went to the phone and rang a long distance number. He waited. It was ringing and ringing. When finally it was answered, it was the voice of his wife. It made him feel warm and secure and want her more than ever.

"Hello love, how are you?" he said into the phone, holding it as if it was his wife next to him knowing she was on the other end and he missed her immensely.

"Hello love, have they got the bastard yet?" Her tone was a little sharp, the smile he had on his face went, and he sighed. He had a heavy heart when he answered her.

"No, not yet, but Peter thinks it will only take a short time now. He has some new lines of investigation to follow up, and the house is being watched. The phone is monitored; our mail is intercepted, so there is no chance of him hurting any of us again darling." He tried to sound as confident as he could.

"I'm not bringing my kids back there until the fucker is behind bars or dead. I can tell you that. Listen, Graham we have to talk. Mum says she will stay here with the kids. I'm coming back to see you, we have some sorting out to do. I do not know how to handle what you did with your sister. It makes me sick to my stomach and we have got to talk it through." She sounded serious and stern. Graham did not like the sound of her tone, but he did not let his voice show his concern as he answered the best he could.

"Yes, love I understand, I will look forward to seeing you again. I miss you all so much.

Where are the kids now?"

"Out with mum shopping I will be back tomorrow afternoon. I'll make my own way there and tell no one I'm coming. I'm not risking any confrontation with anyone. Shit, the fucking phone is monitored, then they will have this call." She became abusive at her stupidity. She cursed and sounded dejected and mad.

"Love, it's ok, don't worry I will meet you. Let me know what flight you're on and I'll be there. No problem is there?" He was pleading more than asking.

"No, listen I will see you tomorrow afternoon. We will talk it all over then."

"If you are sure, I will look forward to seeing you. Say hello to Sebastian and Lisa for me, and I will see you tomorrow." His voice was happy and exuberant.

"I'm not sure of the time. Expect me when you see me." She told him bluntly with no emotion.

"Are you sure you don't want me to bring you from the airport?"

"No, it is ok"

"Alright love, until then. I love you."

"Yeah, see you tomorrow." The phone line went dead. Slowly, he hung up as if in slow motion. She did not return his message of love, the first time since they had been married. It was a done thing. I love you should have followed and it didn't. He sat and stayed quiet for a long time, lost in his thoughts and miles away, back to the house, the house where he had spent his childhood, the house where this entire nightmare started all those years ago. He was a drunken adolescent child, she an immature girl. They were brother and sister. They had broken the ultimate taboo - incest - and now it had come back to haunt him.

It was easily going to destroy him if he wasn't careful. He shook his head as he remembered the night: the drink, the drunkenness the playful fondling, his sister taunting him that he was a virgin. She had sat on the settee, lifting her skirt up to show him her white knickers. She had been laughing and embarrassing him.

He had taken more drink from the bottle of vodka, she had taken it off him and he had taken a large swallow as well. They had both been drunk and not in control and she had slowly and provocatively taken her knickers off to show him. He had shaken his head and turned away. She had reached out and pulled him close; he could remember her voice as if it was only yesterday.

"You're a virgin and a weak reprobate. Why don't you show me what you can do then, eh?" She had put her hand down between his legs and squeezed. She had laughed and rubbed him. He had pulled away and did not want to know or be there.

"Get off, you mad bitch," he shouted at her.

"Fuck it, you have a hard on. I felt it, so don't come that with me. Do you want me to suck it for you, Graham? Would you like that? Would you like me to put it in my mouth?

Bet you would really." She had smiled at him from the seated position she was in, rubbing her vagina and putting her tongue to the side of her mouth at the pleasure she was giving herself.

He had taken another drink and watched, wide eyed, a young immature lad. It had been the first time he had seen a woman's vagina, all be it his sister's. He had known it was wrong. He had known he was drunk, but as he tried he could not take his eyes off her. She had looked at him and he saw the pleasure in her eyes. She had been masturbating wildly. It was something he had read about and looked at in magazines, but had never seen. She had moaned with pleasure and squirmed about on the settee. He had watched, taking nervous drinks of vodka, but not really tasting it. His attention had been elsewhere, his pants had been tight and he had known why. The room had been swaying, spinning and he had felt sick, but still he could not pull himself away from the teenager sat in front of him playing with herself. His hands had become sweaty, and he was shaking. She had looked at him and smiled, and had held out her hand for him.

"Come on, Graham. No one will ever know," she said, quietly.

"No." He had shaken his head, knowing it should never happen.

"It will be good, oh so good. Come on, please." She had smiled at him and held out her hand once again. He had taken a step forward and stopped, shaking his head. He had wanted to turn and leave but something, he did not know what, had kept him there.

She had pulled herself up and sat in front of him. Slowly, she undid his trousers, letting them fall to the ground. He had been swaying and the room spun faster. He had tried to stop her but it had been a weak effort. He did not want to do this but he had felt the vodka hit him like a bolt of lightning. He had found it hard to keep his eyes open. He had rubbed his face with his free hand, then taken another drink, but it had fallen down his chin and onto his sister. It had been done on purpose; he had no idea of the sexual games adults played. He had been drunk and not in control.

She had moaned as it hit her face. She had licked it off her hand and stood up. Her eyes had fixed on his, and she had started to lick the vodka off his chin erotically. The bottle had been dropped as she kissed him passionately on the mouth, taking him by surprise, her arms round him and holding him up. He had eventually flopped down, his weight had been too much for her to support He had landed on the settee; she had pushed him so he had landed on his back facing up. She had sat on top of him and that was when it happened.

Graham sat up suddenly. He did not want to remember anymore. He looked round and saw Sam, who was sat looking at him and wondering what had startled his master. He went to the kitchen and made himself a drink. He wanted to forget that night but he knew he could never do that. It would haunt him and his family for the rest of his life. It had caused him more pain than anything he had witnessed before and he did not like it, and his family did not like it. His wife was coming home and it should have been a joyous occasion, but he knew she wanted to sort their lives out..

Obviously, she was struggling to come to terms with it all and he did not blame her. He did not know what was going to happen, he would not be able to cope with losing her and he knew it. She had always been there for him and he wanted her there now.

The rest of the day went slowly. He did not know what to do. He rang into work but it was running fine without him. At least he had no worries there. The men who worked for him respected and liked him as a boss and they worked on and kept the place going. He was grateful to them for that.

He had hoped Peter would have rung back, but he did not. It was the waiting around that got to him the most today. He knew his wife was returning and he should have been over the moon about it. The fear of losing her had gripped him and he was preparing himself for the confrontation, which is how he saw it, and all he had in his defence was the love for her and the children. He just hoped she would understand and somehow forgive him.

He tried to think what he would do, but it was no good; it made him feel tormented and crestfallen to think about it and worse, to think of the consequences of it all. He had to be strong and he was determined to win his wife back anyway he could.

The night was fresh and cool. Sam had been fed, and was sniffing round the garden. Graham was stood by the door looking up at the clear sky. The stars were out and blinking down at him. He wondered if his wife was looking up at the same sky and hoping for it all to be alright again. He took deep breaths of night air. It was crisp and pleasing to his lungs. The darkness seemed to cover the surroundings and turn them into something completely different. No longer was the garden a place of beauty, but dark space with shadows and corners of blackness, similar to his situation. He thought where there was once light and love and happiness, there was now darkness, sadness and doubt. He shouted the dog and in he came. He closed the door and locking it, he turned to hear the phone ring He ran into the living room to answer it.

"Hello," he said, hoping it was his wife

"It's me." He recognised Peter's voice instantly. "I'm sending a car to watch Gloria in case she comes home tomorrow and make sure she knows what is going on and tell her to go nowhere without telling us first."

"Why do you have to monitor my outgoing calls as well as my incoming ones Pete?"

Graham asked, a little annoyed at his privacy being totally invaded.

"We are monitoring everything Graham, everything, we have to."

"Have you heard anything? What was in that bag?"

"Well, it is a dog's heart apparently. We don't know what dog yet, but I'm laying bets it will be a Labrador." His voice was distant and unfriendly.

"Why a Labrador, do you think?"

"Think about it, Graham. He said in the note he had done it for your dog. If we are to believe what he said, then...well, I'm not speculating."

"He is killing a dog, then what a girl? a boy for my kids? then a woman, then me. Is that it?" He became infuriating and mad in his tone.

"Look, Graham, let us deal with it. There is nothing you can do at the moment, so stop beating yourself up with this and start building your life back up."

"Yeah, well, it's not you who is a prisoner in your own home, is it? It's not you who could be losing their wife and family. Is it? Why the hell hasn't this fucker been caught yet? Where is he? He must be nearby." His voice began to falter and a hint of panic could be detected. Peter was tired. He had endured a long day and was not in the mood to play counsellor right now.

"Calm down! Fix yourself a drink and go to bed. Gloria is coming tomorrow so look forward to that. We will deal with everything else that is what you're paying your taxes for.

Why don't you try and go back to work? Try and resume your life a bit. We will always be watching, so don't worry about your safety."

"I don't want to go back to work, I can't concentrate. Will you let me know as soon as you know anything, anything at all?"

"You will be the first to be told." His voice was a little cold and sharp.

"Alright then, I'll see ya."

"Good night" The phone was dead and he hung up. The friend he had there seemed a bit distant to him now. He was not sure if it was just his imagination or if there was some truth in it. He would soon find out when all this was over. Then he would know, then he would notice differences. He went to bed and was soon asleep. He fell into that state that we have no power over, the state of sleep, of which we know so little about. Why we wake as we do, why we dream, and why we have nightmares. He had been having restless nights, a touch of insomnia, but this night he was deep in a trance-like sleep. He was deep in himself and what he found there he did not like. Again, he was in the house of his youth, the house where he had found his daughter, the house in Keighley. He was floating from room to room. There was a dull hum in his ears drifting from the silence. He was unable to stop or respond; he was not in control and was at the mercy of his sub-consciousness.

Everything seemed so real and graphic. The door slowly opened by itself and he could hear a noise from within. It was his old room and it was his sister he could hear. She was on the bed in the room smiling at him. She was young, naked and held her arms out to him. He stopped and looked round. He saw his wife come in and sit on the bed. She too was naked. It was then dark and blank. Suddenly, he was in the other room; the bed was in the centre. It was carpeted. He did not recognise the wallpaper or the furniture. He could see a figure leaning over the bed, he could not make out any features of the man, but he was thrusting his fist high then down hard into something on the bed.

Suddenly, he flinched as he heard a deafening shriek, a woman's pain and agony. She was being beaten senseless on the bed. He wanted to go and stop it but he could not move. He was transfixed to the spot and watched the figure strike violently down at the poor woman on the bed. The beating was intense and disturbing. Blood was splattered high up in the air as the blood-stained fist rose and repeatedly came down with force. Whoever it was then stopped and took something from his pocket. It was a needle, a long thick needle with black thread on it. The man forced the legs open with his hands and then went down to dig the needle into the woman's crotch; her most private part, her most sensitive part. He stitched the hole from side to side the hole that gave life that gave birth. The scream was piercing and frightening. Graham moved, finally breaking free from whatever was holding him. He went over to the bed and saw the woman. Her face was twisted with torture, with so much unspeakable pain. It was the poor woman who looked up at him, the poor helpless woman who was being beaten, being mutilated. It was his wife, it was Gloria. He shouted, but no sound came out of his mouth.

Grabbing hold of the man, he pulled him round by the shoulder. He saw the blood soaked needle in his hand. He looked into the face of this monster, this animal, this sick excuse of a human being; he looked at his eyes, the same eyes as his own. He was looking, to his horror, at himself. He was the beast, hitting and torturing his wife. The scream awoke him. He sat up bolt like in his bed, sweating and shaking, breathing heavily. He looked round and saw Sam come rushing into the room. He knew something had startled his master and wanted to see what it was. Graham got out of bed and turned the light on. He blinked as the light hurt his eyes for a moment and he shielded them with his hand as he sat on the edge of the bed. Eventually, he could see and his eyes became accustomed to the light once again. He ran his hands through his hair, then reached down to pet Sam. He reassured himself as he stroked the short hair on the dog's back and head. Then, he went downstairs and into the kitchen. He looked at the time and saw it was just past five in the morning. He made himself a cup of tea and sat alone with his thoughts and fears, alone with the nightmare that had become his life, one he did not know how to get out of. He longed for his wife and she should be here today, and it lifted him a little.

He smiled down at Sam who, protectively and loyally was laid down by his side. Sighing, he went back to bed. He did not sleep much more that night, but lay there drifting from consciousness to sleep and back again. He didn't have that dream again and did not want to. He had once read a book about dreams and what they were supposed to mean He had not paid any attention to it and thought it was a con and rubbish, but he wondered now what this dream would mean, what it was telling him. Was it just a reaction to the terror he was feeling, the fear he had, or was it more, a hidden darkness, deep within himself, something he had no control over, something that was locked away and wanted to get out? Was he some sort of loathsome, sadistic savage? He shook his head and disregarded it, hoping not, hoping he had not passed the gene onto his son, and that was why he was like he was. He knew these thoughts did him no good but he could not help himself having them.

CHAPTER NINE

Gloria had not enjoyed the flight, the magazine she had read was rubbish and she had been sat next to an obnoxious woman who insisted on telling her about her operation to remove a tumour from her stomach in gory detail. She was glad when the flight was over. She got through Customs without a hitch, and was surprised, but a little annoyed to see Peter waiting. She wanted to make her own way home, but when she thought about it she saw the sense in protecting herself with an escort. She was carrying a small hold all bag, which Peter took with a smile to his car.

Graham had been anxiously waiting all day; the morning had dragged on and on and he was excited and nervous..

When he heard the car pull up in the drive, he went straight to the door with Sam. Peter waved and reversed out onto the main road. Graham waved back wondering why he had not come in, even for a short while just to say hello. But ignoring this, he smiled from ear to ear at his beautiful wife. He watched her pet Sam, and cuddled him. Sam loved it and barked with joy at her return. She stroked him and then stood up from her kneeling position. She could see her husband looking pale and weak. She smiled at him. He took her bag. She was gorgeous and he wanted to hug her there and then. He wanted to squeeze her and tell the world he loved her more than anything.

But he played it cool and waited to see what sort of response he would get. It was an awkward moment and a painful one. She opened her arms and put them round him, giving him a big hug, and held him tightly. He closed his eyes and returned the gesture. Tears were in his eyes, but she felt warm and nice. His fears lifted and he held on to her, long and hard, enjoying her firm body close to his. Snuggling into her shoulder for a moment, he smelt her and savoured the moment enjoying the beautifulness of his beautiful wife. He lifted his head and whispered in her ear:

"God, I have missed you."

"Let's go inside," she said, pulling away from him They walked in and Sam followed, wagging his tail. He looked back for Sebastian but he was not there, so went back to Gloria for another rub of his belly, she did it so well for him. Graham made a cup of tea and Gloria went to the bathroom to freshen up and get a shower.

She came down in jeans and a t-shirt. She looked relaxed, sat on the settee and stretched out her arms. It was good to be in her home again. She looked up as Graham brought in the tea. Gloria held her cup in her hand and sat there content. Graham put his down and sat back next to her.

"Why didn't Peter come in?" he asked

"I don't know, he said he had somewhere to go. In fact, he didn't speak much at all. I tell you, I'm getting worried about him."

"Why? What do you mean?"

"Well, they know who this freak is. They have his description, they know all about him, they have clues all over the sodding place, but still they can't catch him. Bloody useless is the word I would use." She shook her head in dismay

"Bloody useless is two words," he smiled, weakly.

"Two words then, what the hell. I still think they should have caught him by now."

"They will get him, I'm sure." He tried to comfort her with his words, but was not really sure himself. She was annoyed and said: "Yeah, but will they? How much fucking longer have we to live like this? When can I have my life back? When will it all be normal again?" Graham, in a way, felt comfort in what she was saying. At least she was in some way admitting she wanted him back, and all would be well again. But while the maniac was out there she was on edge. That he could understand. He put his hand on her shoulder. He reassured her as he spoke softly and quietly.

"I'm sorry sweetheart, I'm so sorry for causing you all this pain. If there was anything I could do I would, you know that don't you?"

"Oh Graham, I don't know, I know it's not all your fault, but then again what the fucking hell. You screwed your sister and if you had not done that then he would not be here now and all this would not have happened, would it? So in that sense I blame you, but, oh I don't know." She shook in confusion and bewilderment bowing he head. Graham rubbed her shoulder and felt the hurt rise again in his heart. He did not know what to say; he did not want to run the risk of sounding pathetic by saying sorry all the time, but he was, so bloody sorry for it all.

She lifted her head and looked at his tearful eyes. She smiled slightly and then took a sip of her tea. She loved this man, she had married him, and he had shown her a great life. She did not want to lose that, but she was finding it hard to come to terms with what he had done what taboo he had committed drunk at the time or not.

"Gloria, I made a stupid mistake, alright it was a fucking big one, and I suppose a disgusting one. I was young, drunk and not in control, but for God's sake don't torture me with it. Please, don't use it as a stick to beat me to death with." He spoke gently at first but his voice began to rise at the end of the sentence.

"Graham, what am I suppose to do? I don't know, your sister?" She shook her head. Graham stared down at his wife. He was about to snap. He spoke to her in a raised voice firmly and determinedly but still in control.

"Alright for God's sake, I made a fuck up. Yes, I fucked my sodding sister once, under the influence of booze. Fuck, I didn't even know what I was doing; she had to tell me the next day. I fucking fell unconscious most of the time, I mean it was a mistake.

A mistake, Gloria It isn't as if I did it all the fucking time." He strolled round the settee and back again in a small but controlled rage. "Once, one stupid little mishap alright it is having fucking big consequences but Christ do you think I could have helped that? Do you think I'm enjoying all this? Christ, woman I love you, but I can't go on like this. It is too much hurt for me to take. If you can't forgive me then fine, but I will not have it rammed into my face all the fucking time. I need a friend right now, and you are, or were, the best one I ever had. This is tearing me apart and the worry if I still have you is worse. If you have come here to end it then do it, it will rip my insides out, but at least I will know, at least I will know where I stand. I'm sorry love, I'm, sorry. What else can I say?" He held out his arms and pleaded with her.

She had never seen him in such an outburst before and it shocked her She came over to him. He stood rigid to the spot looking through tear-filled eyes at her. She took his hand and held it tightly. Sam had come over knowing something was wrong. He sat and looked up at them both curiously; he always found human behaviour a little strange. Gloria tried to speak but had to swallow first. Tears rolled down her cheeks and she spoke in a cry of hurt and anguishto him shaking and her face full of hurt.

"Graham, I don't want to lose you, I love you, I always will. I'm sorry, I'm sorry for being so selfish. Please forgive me."

They burst into uncontrollable tears, holding each other long and hard. It was a good stress release for them both. Holding tightly, Graham ran his hands over her body and they pulled away and kissed hard on the lips. She felt so good and he could taste her salty tears as they ran down to their mouths while they kissed. He didn't mind and nothing would have parted them at that moment.

When they calmed down, they sat on the settee. They still held onto each other, as if their lives depended on it. They stayed on the settee for at least an hour just holding each other and being close. They felt the warmth returning to them and both welcomed it. If that had been lost then there would have been no hope for the relationship. It had been such a burden to them and it was a stressful time. But if they did not have each other then it would have been impossible and they both knew it. Sam wandered into the kitchen for a drink. He knew he would not be going out for a walk yet. It was nice to have Gloria back. He liked her, lying down in his favourite spot in the kitchen, just off to the side, where he could watch the back door, but also, he could see into the main room. He liked to keep an eye on things this way, keeping the family safe and free from harm. There had been a lot of upset lately, he didn't fully understand what was wrong but he would always be there and always be ready for them when he needed them. Resting his head on his paws, he lay on the floor looking into the room at the settee where Graham and Gloria were still sat, holding each other. He sensed the norm returning, but he still knew something was very wrong, something to do with that intruder he had attacked. He promised himself if he ever caught sight or smell of him again he would not get away. Next time he would get him and make him pay for the upset he had caused. His eyes closed and he was still and quiet for now, not sleeping but resting; his mind was alert.

It was good to have company again, Graham thought. He could tell she was not her old self but he knew it would take time. At least they had crossed the biggest barrier he thought, and at least they now knew they would stay together. Graham suggested a night out at a restaurant but Gloria declined and they ended up having an early night. They had told each other everything there was to tell. She told him about the kids, the holiday and how they would not be coming home until this freak was caught. Graham decided to tell her everything and hold nothing back. He had expected her to hit the roof and take the next plane out of the country, but like she said, he couldn't hurt the kids anymore and they were under surveillance so they should be fairly safe. When night fell and they went to bed, Graham noticed she left her knickers on. She had never done this before, except when it was the time of the month to hold her pad in place. He knew it was not that time. It was a sign she did not want to have sex.

He could understand this and said nothing. He gave her a little peck on the cheek and told her he loved her. She returned it and this made him feel a lot better He slept well that night, and cuddled up to his wife like they used to.

 The night was cold and sharp, the police surveillance team felt it, and made a comment about Gloria as both sat in the car passing the time describing what they would like to do to her if she was theirs to have. They were on all night and every now and then one of them had to get out of the car and patrol round the back, but not get too close to the house as the dog always sensed them and started to bark. But they did it night after night, day after day. Graham was never out of their sight; there was always someone watching him. They were getting nowhere and it was not good. They knew they should have had the man by now. All the forensic evidence told them it was the same man, the man they knew, the man they had a description of and they knew his background. But they did not know where this man was. His picture had been in the papers and on the police notice board. They had done a house to house with his photograph, but they had drawn a blank. Every policeman in the area knew what he looked like but nothing had been accomplished. Even an appeal on the local news produced nothing. With time going by, it was now becoming old news and the papers moved on to new stories.

But for the police it was a long battle, following up leads, meeting informants, checking out possible sightings. But it was, up to now, to no avail. And at the helm of all this was Peter. He was becoming more and more frustrated with the lack of progress of the case. He knew he was lucky to be working on it at all, with the personal involvement he had with Graham and Gloria.

His boss was not happy with it but he had persevered and had got to keep the case. But he knew if he did not come up with something soon he would be replaced and someone else would have a go at it. It was never a good or pleasant thing for a detective to be taken off a case and it was hard to live down. He had taken the piss out of many a colleague who had been in the same position of having their work passed on to others. It was embarrassing, to say the least. It might not bother many, but it would bother him and he was not going to let it happen. It had never happened before and that was not going to change. No way was he having his work passed on to someone else to work with, and possibly get results he most desperately wanted. But with this new threat he had to work fast and he knew it. All his experience was coming into play; his gut feelings and the tried and tested ways of police work. He had done them all; all his informants had been contacted and instructed, all his avenues were becoming exhausted, and he was to.

The next morning Gloria had got up first and made some breakfast. She had put on a good spread considering Graham did not have much shopping in, but he was more than pleased when he walked down to a cooked breakfast for a change.

She ate with him and they sat opposite each other at the kitchen table. After their meal they had coffee. Gloria smiled and laughed at a thought she remembered then shared it.

"Do you remember that bloody breakfast you cooked when we were first married and you burnt the sausages, broke the eggs and cremated the bacon? God that was a breakfast to end all that was."

They both laughed as they remembered. Graham laughed out loudest, rolling his head back, and saying as he did:

"Tell you what I found funnier was, when you insisted on having the least burnt sausage, because that was the one that rolled off the plate when I put it on. It fell on the floor and rolled under the cooker. I dusted it off and put it back on the plate." He laughed again and she joined in on the joke. It felt good for them to remember.

They washed up, and then rang the kids, and Gloria's mother mid morning. Graham even forgot all the worry and fear he had. He had his wife back and it meant more to him than anything else in the world. It was not long before Peter was knocking on the door. They only knew he was there because of Sam telling them. They were in the back garden, weeding and getting it straight, Gloria had let it go somewhat and she wanted it to be put right get it back to its former glory and brilliance.

Graham was doing as he was told. He knew nothing about gardening, but enjoyed helping his wife. She loved it and it showed in her enthusiasm and dedication to detail. If it was going to be done, then it was going to be done right.

Graham went and let Peter in. They came through to the back where Gloria was. She looked up and came over to join them. She was wearing torn jeans and an old jumper.

These were her dirty gardening clothes, the ones she always wore.

"Hello, Peter," she said, unemotionally, as she came up to them.

"Gloria," he nodded and then looked at Graham as if to say, 'do I go on?'

"It's alright, I have told Gloria everything," Graham reassured him.

"Right, ok, the heart is of a Labrador dog. We have intercepted another package. It was part of the same dog, a brain, with a note that said, 'give this to your policemen friends. They will need it because their brains are shit if they have not even got close to me yet.' He stopped, and looked confused. He pulled a small notebook from his pocket and read from it silently for a moment then out loud again. 'I'm still watching you and when I get chance I will come and say hello daddy. In fact you are so weak I am ashamed to call you daddy. The game will hot up now, enough playing around; your time is coming, your time is coming.' He put the book away. He was irritated and mad.

"We are working with the post office. Each package has been posted at different places, nearby but not the same place each time. He is obviously in disguise so we do not know what he looks like. We have a lot of CCTV footage to search; we are checking derelict buildings and houses, and we are going over rented accommodation again with the estate agents and landlords. We will get him; it is just taking some time." He did not sound convincing, and Gloria did not like it. She sighed and said, annoyed:

"How long have you all been saying that Peter, he is nearby and you all have no idea where he, is have you?" She looked at him sternly and confrontationally. He didn't need this and was in no mood for it.

"We are trying our best Gloria. We're not just sitting down doing nothing. There is a bloody huge operation going on round you at the moment. Do you realise how much man power and time it takes to organise something like this? Believe me, love, you are well protected." He was sharp and his voice had a tone of annoyance.

"Maybe, but you are still no closer to catching him, are you? It is going to be a stroke of luck, or a mistake on his part isn't it?"

"Possibly, that or some hard working copper doing his job right."

Peter defended forcefully

"Now come on, lets' not fall out, united we stand, divided we fall, let's not forget that."

Graham insisted and tried to lighten them both up a little. He could sense what was coming and he didn't like it.

"Yeah and let's not forget there is a fucking lunatic out there who wants you dead, and the only thing between him and you are us. Anyway, I have just come over to let you know, here this is the rest of your mail." He brought out some envelopes from his inside jacket pocket and handed them to Graham.

"Cheers mate, and let's not fall out over this." Graham looked at them both in turn. They were looking at each other with more than a hint of contempt.

"Right, I have to go, I'll be in touch. I'll see myself out." He left and it was silent until the front door slammed shut. Gloria shook her head and looked a little confused at Graham.

"What was all that about love?" he asked her

"They have nothing Graham, nothing to go on; he is making them look stupid."

"I'm sure they are trying their best, love."

"Well, it's not good enough; they must be doing something wrong. I'm not happy with the way it is being run. I know he is your friend Graham but I'm not happy with the way he is handling this at all."

Graham shrugged his shoulders at her.

"What else can we do?" he asked

"Well, I think it is up to us to catch the fucking freak, the police way just does not work. It is over a month now and they are no nearer catching him now than they were then. No, I think some drastic action is needed. I'm sick and tired of hanging around waiting to see if they get lucky. They should have him behind bars by now, what is needed is to flush him out, make him make a mistake. We have to get him before he harms anyone else. At least keep the fucker occupied and his mind off what he is planning on doing. Christ, we can't just sit round and watch him kidnap another poor girl, or a little boy. He is cutting up a dog and sending it through the post for God's sake, and he tortured and killed your sister up in Keighley. Fuck knows what else he is willing to do. He has to be stopped now; we can't just wait round like this. It is bloody stupid. What if he just goes away and leaves? What if he does not get in touch for another year? I'm sick of their set patterns and explanations, and psychological breakdowns of this sort of person. What if he does not fit any of their bloody textbook cases? No love, I'm going to do something with their help or not." She was angry and walked past a dumbfounded husband. He watched her march into the house; he had to admire her courage, and thinking about it there and then, she was right.

He had been that worried about his marriage that he had not given the police operation much thought, but now he did. He could see her point. He followed her into the house and walked upstairs. She was in the shower, so he went to the bedroom to change. It looked like the gardening was over for today, more important matters were on his wife's mind, and he knew when she set her mind to something it would be done. He also knew it was not a game. It was dangerous and possibly the wrong action to take, but like she said, something had to be done. What if he kidnapped someone else's child? They would have to go through what they did when Lisa was taken and no doubt the family concerned would blame them for it all. He was going to get strong, get tough. He was not going to let this madman break him down anymore. The tables had to be turned and he found the strength to do it right here and now. He got changed into some more comfortable clothes and stood ready to go back down to the kitchen for a drink, when his wife came from the shower with a towel wrapped round her. Her hair was wet and she looked sexy and voluptuous in the towel. He could see she was naked under it and it excited him. He could smell her and he wanted her like never before. He smiled as she walked past him and to her wardrobe and said:

"What we need is some plan to get the fucker out in the open, or somewhere we know we can get him a certain time. Then the police can pounce on the little shit. What we need is bait, or something to bargain with. We have got to get some plan together."

She unwrapped the towel and started to dry her hair with it. Graham found this very stimulating; her firm, well-made body moved like poetry to him. As she rubbed her hair with the towel, her large, firm breasts swung with grace and he felt his manhood responding to it all. But, thinking she did not want, and was not ready for sex with him right now, he turned and went out of the room. In the old days they would be having sex right now; they would not be able to stop themselves. Slowly, he walked towards the stairs to give her the privacy he thought she wanted He stopped when she called his name and an excited shiver ran through his body. He turned and asked:

"Yeah, want anything babe?" He stood motionless and listened.

"Come here," she shouted from the room. Slowly, he walked back in and looked at her lying on the bed, naked, with one knee up and the other leg flat down on the bed. She propped herself up on her elbow and was looking at him with a little smile on her face.

He smiled back and his heart beat faster.

"Graham, why don't you go and get a shower? Freshen yourself up and then come here, and refresh me with the monster you have in them pants. I can see it wants to get out."

He felt so happy and relieved at that moment. She was like her old self and he went to the shower to have the fastest one in his life. He returned within five minutes, naked and wanting. He jumped through the air from the door and landed on top of her. She put her arms round him and they kissed hard and long. Passion was high; she felt so good to him again. They always had a good, if not terrific sex life, and it was back.

It was something he had worried about not ever getting again, but he had no worry now.

It was like their first time again; they could not keep their hands off each other; kissing; licking, and caressing their bodies She also had missed him and it showed. The sex they had that afternoon was some of the best they had ever had.

It was late when they finally went back down to the living room and Gloria rang her mother and the children. She told her all was getting back to normal and she and Graham were going to have some time together, but didn't mention time away. She had not forgotten the phone was being monitored. Her mother was pleased and the kids were pleased.

Graham talked to them and it did them all a world of good. There was no awkwardness, or blame; he was happy and it was as if a weight had been lifted from their shoulders. Something in the tone of his, and their mother's voice told the children it was getting back to normal. The experience would never leave them but it was being dealt with now, and they all could work on it together, as a family. Sebastian asked about Sam, and he missed him. He wanted to come home. He'd had enough of Spain, but it was decided for them to stay just for a short while longer. Gloria was taking no risks at all with her kids. She knew deep down they were going to enter a very dangerous situation and she did not want her children anywhere near it. She felt they were safer where they were; she wanted the family she loved so much back, and she was going to get it anyway she could. If it involved risking a lot, then she would do it. No more was she willing to be held prisoner, when she had done nothing wrong.

She was not the criminal here, but it was her who had to be watched every step; it was her who was being observed like some sort of animal in a cage, while the real man they wanted was walking round free doing anything he wanted. To her this was not right, and she was going to change it. Graham was on her side and found strength with having her back; they were a unit again together and going to sort out this whole mess.

They hugged after hanging up the phone. Holding each other, they gently swayed where they stood. She snuggled into his chest and felt the security she had always felt. They said nothing, and didn't have to. The love was there as was the power and will to go, and that was all they needed.

Graham was not happy about going back into the electrical shop, not after the episode with the computer screen He waited in the car for Gloria to go in and buy what they needed. He waited and watched life go by in the little street. He noticed a blue car pull up about fifty yards to his right. Inside were two men looking at him. They were the watchful eyes of the police. It was comforting in one way but becoming annoying in another. He and his wife had a plan; they were sick of waiting around, and decided to try something. He watched the people walking past; knowing one of them could be his son and he didn't know it. One of them could be the man they wanted. He wondered what he would do if he saw him, if he could recognise him. He thought about briefly, shook his head and forgot it. He looked into the shop and saw his wife paying for something at the counter. She came out wearing a skirt, which was slit at the side. She knew she was showing a nice piece of leg and strolled back to the car. A slight breeze blew and the front of her skirt flapped, exposing her shapely thigh. The two policemen were pleased and smiled as they took a good look. It was all part of the plan and she just hoped it would work.

She got back into the car holding her purse and a box about twelve inches square. It was in a plastic bag, and no one could see what it was.

"Always trying to sell you cover, for this and cover for that in that bloody shop. All bloody smiles and trying to look at your tits, frigging little perverts."

"Yeah, they do that to me as well when you try to take something back."

"What, they try and look at your tits?" she said, with a grin.

"Have you seen them two over there?" Graham nodded to the unmarked police car.

"Yeah, they took a good look at my legs, perverts." She didn't look over at them, but at Graham, who started up the car.

"Let's hope so." He drove the car away slowly and headed for the supermarket. They went in and bought some food. They were conscious they were being followed, but it was the police after all. They split up and Gloria wandered off to look at women's things. It was Graham who was followed and watched. Soon, they rejoined and paid then left the shop. Graham put the shopping in the back of the car and they headed home, followed as usual by the police car. When they got home, Graham locked the door behind them and put the shopping away. Gloria took what she had bought from the electrical shop into the front room.

When Graham returned from the kitchen, he could see she had got it set up. He saw that the small black plastic box was an answering machine.

"Are you ready then?" he nodded and sat down next to her on the settee. He swallowed and his tongue licked the corner of his mouth for a moment. It was a nervous reaction he had acquired.

"How do I do it?" he asked, as he leant towards the machine.

"Right, you ready?" she said, pressing the button.

"This is your father you little fuck; now listen and listen good. I'm not here anymore, I'm with Rumbold, the giant who likes to throw stones. You should know where that is, if not then tough shit. You're not telling me what to do anymore. If you want me then come and get me, it is no use staying round here anymore. I'm not here. So, if you have the guts to face your father, come and see me. I doubt if you will have the courage to face me so probably this will be the last time we get in touch. If you don't come I'm going away, far away. This is your last chance so you better make good use of it, because you have done a fucking shite job so far. If you think you're scaring us then you're wrong. You are an annoying little child who must be punished. Come and see if you can take your dad. I'm waiting; I'm alone, no police and no one else but you and me. See you there if you have the guts." He lifted his head and backed away from the machine. Gloria stopped pressing the button. She looked down and then pressed the button which said announcement record check. The little tape automatically started to rewind and then stopped suddenly.

She made sure the sound wheel on the side was turned up and then they listened to the message. They looked at the machine and then at each other when it stopped and set itself to receive calls.

"What do you think?" he said, looking her in the eye.

"I think we have to do it, have to coax him out "

"What if he does not call again? What if he just keeps sending things through the post? How do we know he will call?" Graham suggested

"He will, eventually. He won't be able to resist it. It has been a while now so I would say he will be phoning very soon; he will want to tell you what he will be doing and will try to scare you by the power of suggestion. He will want to tell you personally what he is doing. I would say we are going to have to go tonight.

"Ok let's do it" Graham said with a determined sigh

"I was right about seeing my dad in the supermarket on a Thursday night. He said he would lend us his car so that will be parked round the back. It's up to you to fill it while our little distraction goes on at the front to keep our perverted friends occupied."

"Right, tonight it is then, and let's hope this all works. I still think we should tell Peter, just in case"

"No way love I don't trust him anymore. I don't think he is up to the job, to be honest. He would stop us, you know he would, and once we were gone he would be powerless to stop it, so let's take the bull by the horns and get the fucking job done. Then, we can put all this behind us and we will be able to get back to our lives again." She reached out her hand and took his. He smiled at her and nodded. He was willing to give it a try; he would have done anything for her, and gone along with anything she said at that moment.

That night it was all to happen. If it failed then it could be the last thing he ever did, but both of them were now at the end of their tether. They had to do something, knowing they could not go on like this anymore.

It was becoming late afternoon and they were packing their bags. They took their essentials including their money and credit cards. Graham mentioned that they would be able to be traced through the cards as soon as they used them, but Gloria did not bother about it and said to hell with it, so he did the same. It should not take Peter long to figure out where they had gone anyway, and if it didn't then Gloria was right: he was incompetent.

They were packed and ready shortly afterwards. They had three holdall bags by the back door. They did not know how long they would be staying away which is why they made sure they had plenty of money. It was set, and they were almost there.

Sam was again confused by what was going on, but he just followed and did as he was told. He did not waste his time worrying about what humans did; he never could understand them anyway. After some tea, they washed up and made sure all the windows and doors were securely locked. They did this discreetly and without drawing attention to themselves from the watchful eyes outside. Then, they waited until darkness fell. This was to be their ally and hopefully, their cover to slip away. Gloria was sure her father would not let her down. He was against the idea but went along with it. She could always get her own way with him and she knew it. She always had from being a little girl. He could never say no to her, even when her mother did. She would come to him and he would melt. He was soft with Gloria and could not help himself; the car would be there for sure.

It was cramped in the police car. They did not have much to do, and the nights were becoming very boring. It was dark and they sat there. Both were tired and sick of the stakeout. Rob, the older one, knew it was his turn to patrol the back. It was a ball ache he said having to walk round the bloody back every half hour. Trev, his partner, at least had an hour before he had to get out of the car. He had brought a book with him tonight but knew Rob would not let him read it.

"Tell you what, he is never coming back here," Trev told his partner as he looked up at the house from the street.

"You know that, and I know that, but the great one back at the office knows better my friend. Never been out on the fucking street most of 'em, but they can tell you how it all works; how to do your job you have been doing for the last ten years. Makes me sick, all of 'em." He slumped down in his seat and rested his arms on the steering wheel.

"Tell you what though, she looked lovely today in that bloody skirt, don't ya think?" He smiled as he remembered the scene; his partner smiled also nodding his head at him in agreement and had a childish grin on his face.

"Yeah, she is one fine woman that, don't know what the hell she saw in him though would be better with a hard working police officer like me."

"He must have a big dick," Trev said, plainly.

"No, he has got a big bank account. Owns his own business, doesn't he?"

"I bet he has a constant hard on living with that woman."

"You never know, he might be bored by it now."

"Don't talk so bloody stupid. Whoever gets bored of a woman with a body like that is not a man, he is a fucking idiot." He raised his voice but quietened down on his last word.

"You have a sick little mind, and you a married man at that."

"Christ, my missus is slack where she should be firm and hard where she should be soft, a right mess. She has really let herself go just lately."

"Not enough sex that, I've told you that before. You're not doing your job, Trev."

"Not much chance, sat here every fucking night." He sighed as he looked down into the foot well not really focusing on anything.

"Well, if you ever want a hand with her let me know."

"No thanks. Anyway isn't it about time you checked the back?"

"Oh fucking hell!" He was about to get out of the car when he noticed the bedroom light go on. He looked up, as did his partner, who had leant forward.

Gloria was in the room and did not close the curtains. She started to undo her blouse. Both men sat up and smiled at each other.

"She has forgotten the fucking curtains Rob," Trev announced excitedly sitting up in his seat expectantly.

"Yeah, come on baby take it off." Both men were transfixed. She walked to the side and behind the curtain, but her silhouette could still be seen. She undid her skirt and it fell to the floor. She stepped out of it and proceeded to take off her knickers. The two lecherous men in the car knew they would see her as she walked past the window, and were silently praying she did not close the curtain.

While this peep show was going on at the front of the house, Graham was slowly and quietly leaving at the back door. He had the bags in his hands and went down the garden, noiselessly and unseen. He jumped over the fence, pushing the bags over before him. He saw Gloria's dad's car parked by the side of the pavement. He walked to it and went to the back and, as arranged in the supermarket that afternoon, the keys were in the exhaust pipe. He took them and opened the boot. He threw the bags in, closed it and locked it again. He went back, got Sam and brought him round. This was going to be difficult but he managed it by lifting the baffled dog over the fence and letting him jump down the short distance to the pavement. He jumped back over and then opened the back door for Sam to get into the car. Once again, he locked it up and went back inside. Out on the front, the two lustful police men were prying and willing Gloria to move to her left past the open curtain. But she put on a robe before she did. It disheartened them slightly but she walked past the window and out of the room. Then the bathroom light was switched on. They could see it from the side.

"Shit, fucking robe," Trev said, punching his fist into his palm of his hand.

"Yeah, but she has to come back yet my friend and then we will see, I hope. She will disrobe and we will have a lovely sight. She might even come out naked and go right past that window," Rob said.

"Pity you won't be here, isn't it?" Trev smiled at him.

"Bollocks to you as well I'm not going anywhere until she comes back, I tell you that no bloody way, not giving you all the fun."

"The boss will be mad if he finds out you didn't do your rounds."

"Well, he won't bloody know, will he?" Both looked at the window and waited, all night if necessary, Rob thought. He fancied Gloria, had done since the first time he saw her which wasn't strange most men did.

Gloria at this point was getting dressed on the landing. When she was ready, she went downstairs to the kitchen. She was dressed in a dark sweater and black jeans and followed her husband out into the garden. The door was locked and they slipped away down the garden and over the fence. Gloria drove and they pulled away in the opposite direction of the house. In minutes they were heading for the motorway to Keighley.

It was some time before the two in the police car got sick of waiting. They had sat there, eyes fixed on the window, each as excited as the other, but the excitement began to wear off and frustration took over, then boredom.

"She must have gone downstairs Trev," Rob said, disappointed.

"Yeah fucking hell." They shook their heads and sat back. They kept having a look up at the window. It was like a drug they had to keep coming back to and they could not help it But nothing else happened and both became annoyed.

Meanwhile, Gloria was driving to the motorway with Sam in the back and her husband by her side she drove carefully and they were quiet until Gloria asked.

"Did you put the light timer to come on and off?" remembering she had not done it

"Yeah, the one in the bedroom will go off about twelve and the one downstairs is fixed with a light sensor, so when it's dark it goes on, and when it's light it goes off, all clever stuff." Graham informed her.

"Good, wonder how long it will take for them to notice? Probably won't, the way they handle things," she said, shaking her head slightly.

"Wonder when he will ring?" He looked at her and she glanced across at him, giving him a reassuring smile before concentrating on the road ahead. It was not too busy and she stayed at about sixty miles an hour on the motorway most of the time.

"So where are we staying, exactly?" Gloria asked.

"It is a pub in a place called Goose eye. It's nice and they are dog lovers so Sam will be fine. They have some barns out at the back and have converted them into rooms. It's very quiet and out of the way. It's like your own little place."

"What like an apartment?"

"Well, almost. You will see it is cosy and there is tinker not too far away."

"Tinker? Like, taylor soldier, spy?"

"No, not quite, it is a wood. I used to play there all the time when I was a kid. It is very nice, there is a river running through it and the walk is very stimulating. Sam will love it. I used to take my dog down there when I was a kid."

"Lovely, so who is this Rumbold character?"

"It is a statue in the town centre, legend has it he was a giant who lived in Keighley tons of years ago, and got pissed off with his wife. So he used to throw bloody big rocks at her. Everyone in the town knows him and he is always getting painted on, and graffiti plastered all over him, the poor chap. It won't look out of place to have some writing on him."

"Sounds like a really nice person, throwing rocks at his missus."

"Just hope I can do it without getting caught."

"What are you going to write?"

"Keith Leigh, Tinker Bridge."

"Yeah that is like leave him a message there?"

"Yeah, just hope it will work, just hope he will come."

"Well, he has no choice has he? If he wants you he is going to have to come to you. It is no good staying down there if you're not there. The only way he can get in touch with you is to come here."

"Well, I just hope we are right, and we're not making a big mistake, that's all."

"We are right, I can feel it. The bastard is not getting away with anything else. We will keep the fucker occupied so he can't hurt anyone else."

"Well, we will see." He looked out of the window and across the field they were passing, lost for a moment in his thoughts.

"Don't you wonder what he looks like?" she asked, curiously.

"No, I just want him out of our lives forever." Graham said no more on the subject and Gloria asked no more about it.

The night traffic was light and soon they were heading out of the county. For Graham it was old ground, but Gloria had only been up a few times. She was never impressed with the place at the best of times, but she was with her husband and they had an important job to do, a job that could turn out fatal for them both. But they had to do something; to fight back in some way. Maybe, this was the wrong way, but at least they were doing something, and that held them together. It was better than just sat around doing nothing and waiting. That was the hardest part. At least this way they had something to focus on.

Graham had to put her right at a few junctions but they were soon pulling into Keighley. Graham saw so many things, but Gloria saw nothing but a building, a pub, and shops. To Graham, this pub had meaning; it was where he went for his mum when he was a child. His dad had worked on the building, restoring it. Graham had been so proud of his dad, up on the roof working away as he went past and waved up to him all those years ago. Lots of things had meaning to him these were the good ones and he blocked out the now bad ones.

Gloria looked over at him as they stopped at some traffic lights; she smiled to herself as he looked round like a kid lost in his own little world.

"You can take the man out of Yorkshire, but not Yorkshire out of the man, eh?" she said to him as they drove away from the lights.

"Yeah, a Yorkshire man's roots are strong. No matter where they go it is his roots that matter."

"If you say so darling if you say so." She agreed and smiled to herself knowing she had heard it all before many times.

"It's true, you Midlanders don't know who you are, you're not southern, you're not northern, you are in the middle, no real side, a bit of this and that."

"I believe you, honest I do," she said, shaking her head. She had never really understood his fascination with his hometown and his roots as he called them. It made her wonder why Yorkshire men ever left Yorkshire if what he said was right.

But this was neither the time nor the place to have this conversation about why he would want to leave the place they had come back to. They'd had some very bad experiences here and she did not want to dwell on them too much.

She drove up a steep hill and was heading back out of town, it seemed. Graham was giving her directions. He told her to take a little winding road. She did not like it very much; it was very tight and hard to manoeuvre the car round but she did it. She headed back down into a small valley where Graham pointed to a large pub. He seemed to know where he was going so she left it to him and just drove. Gloria waited in the car while Graham went to the large, wooden door. She had stopped in a car park, but it was just a yard in front of the old building. Most of it was in darkness and she could not make it all out. She noticed the fields to the right. It was an old place and probably looked beautiful in the daytime, but it had an eerie look about it in the dark. She shuddered and rubbed her hands together, and stretched out the best she could in the seat. Graham was in there some time but eventually came out. He pointed round to the side, so she pulled off slowly from her parked position. She went over cobbled stones and round the tight bend of the building into a courtyard at the back. A dim light was all that was there to illuminate the whole area. Totally inadequate, she said to herself. Along one side at the side of the pub was a stone wall. Graham was walking towards some white doors to his left. Another car was parked up and a light behind some closed curtains indicated there was life here after all. Gloria followed Graham who walked to the end door. She pulled up slowly and parked outside the door. She stopped the engine and looked around once again from inside the car. She was not too impressed with the place, but Graham seemed content. He let himself into the room and disappeared inside. Gloria let Sam out. He instantly sniffed a wall then urinated against it. He shook himself and stretched out long and dug his claws in the floor. He pulled back and started to explore this strange place.

Gloria got the bags out of the back and locked up the car securely. She shouted Sam and they went in through the white door, closing it behind them.

Inside it was very comfortable. Graham was stood by the bed. He looked out of the small window then at Gloria as she came in with the bags. She looked round; it was basic but very nice. She had to admit that the place was clean and warm, well looked after and everything you needed was here: a bed, a small kitchen, a microwave and gas cooker, a small television and two chairs. It was just right as a base to come back to after a day of exploring Yorkshire countryside. She nodded and showed her approval. Sam again was off sniffing everything he could; a lot of new smells to sort out and a place to explore.

Graham smiled and took her hand. He led her to a small, brown, wooden door and opened it. He pulled a light switch cord hanging from the ceiling, and on flickered a strip light. This was the shower, again well looked after, clean and tidy.

"What do you think?" he asked, apprehensively.

"It's alright yeah, not bad." She came back out and looked round the room once more, noticing from this angle the lovely wooden finish of the roof and beams running across it and down the side of the wall. It grew on her and she felt warm and safe. Graham sat on the bed, bouncing up and down.

"Good bed," he said, smiling. She said she would do some supper if they really wanted it.

"I know a chip shop that will be open if you fancy any. We do get a breakfast here as well."

"Oh, I'm not hungry, are you?"

"Not really, no." He seemed a bit disheartened and was wondering if he had done the right thing and chosen the right place. Gloria sat next to him. She put her arm round his shoulder and pulled him closer, dropping her head into his chest. He put his arm round her and squeezed softly.

"The place is lovely darling," she said, lovingly.

"Good, if you hadn't liked it I would have got somewhere else. It is used by ramblers and people wanting long walks over the moors and all that. They let you keep dogs as long as they're kept under control and do not mess in the rooms." He spoke as if in someone else's voice and was mocking the woman he had obviously just been talking to. She smiled and held him tighter.

"I bet it is used by lovers and cheaters alike as well."

"Yeah, well probably, but it is out of the way and they ask no questions, t is just right for what we wanted, I thought."

"Yeah, you're right." She looked at Sam walking round and lifted her head

"I think he wants some water, love, he is bound to be dehydrated you know."

Graham got off the bed and searched in one of the bags for a moment before pulling out Sam's bowl. He went to the sink next to the cooker and turned on the old fashioned metal tap; water gushed out at a force he hadn't expected. He filled the bowl and put it down for Sam, who gladly took a long drink. Gloria was laid out on the bed on her side looking at him. She had a schoolgirl innocence about her.

"We could go for a drink, if you fancy?" he asked.

She smiled and shook her head. He looked at her, still the most beautiful woman he had ever seen, and he considered himself to be the luckiest man alive to have her. He walked silently to the door and locked it. They were in for the night and didn't want to be disturbed. Sam soon settled down. He found his spot and laid on it.

He could see the door and the bed from where he was, which suited him and he felt alright about it. He had left his mark and scent outside and would go and check on that in the morning. He glanced over to the bed. He knew the signs; he knew there would be no more activity for him that night. He looked up as he heard a sound outside, but then put his head back down. This seemed like a nice place and he was with his two male companions so it was not too bad at all. He liked a change and sometimes liked to get away as well. Slowly, he fell into a thoughtful sleep and wondered what the next day would bring for him and what he would be able to find if he went looking and searching long enough.

When morning broke, the two police officers in the car were tired and ready for the relief shift to come on they had not seen Gloria go back into the bedroom and decided she must have slept downstairs with Graham. Nothing seemed out of the ordinary and they had not realised they had been looking after an empty house all night.

The day was breaking into another fine one. The weather forecasters had been right for a change and the good weather they had predicted had arrived and was staying; it was to everyone's delight. It was mid morning, while the second shift was on, that something dawned on them. The milkman had been and the milk was still on the step, but there were no signs of life. They had been doing this long enough now to know the routine, but this morning all had been too quiet and still. They gave it another hour, then one of the men decided to go and take a look. He walked up to the house and saw the curtains were still drawn. He went to the side and round the back. He expected the dog to bark like it usually did when they got too close, but nothing, just silence, unnatural silence. He did not like it, and walked briskly back to the car and called in to talk to Peter.

"Well sir, we have seen no movement at all, and I have been round the back and it is all quiet. The dog didn't even bark." He spoke into his car radio while his friend and colleague kept a look on the house for any movement.

"For fuck's sake, have you rung them?" Peter enquired.

"No sir, I was hoping you could do that, you being a friend and all that. If they are preoccupied like, you know …" He was a little apprehensive about it in case he was wrong and overreacting.

"For fuck's sake, I'll pissing ring, let me know when you want a shit and I will come over and wipe your arse for ya." The line went dead and he put the radio microphone back into its seat on the radio.

"Sarcastic bastard," he said, annoyed at the radio.

"Yeah, well, he is getting a lot of stick over this. It is costing too much and he is getting nowhere, is he?" his friend told him, not taking his eyes off the house.

"Don't give a shit, there is no need to take it out on us, fucking tosser." He folded his arms, sat back in the seat and looked over to the house and waited, hoping he was not wrong, and in for another telling off.

The household had two phone calls that morning. The first was from Peter, who, when he heard the message, hit the roof and stormed round. While he was on his way there was a second call; this person listened to the message and said nothing. They simply hung up and the line went dead once again.

Peter's car was screeching round the corner and he was not in a good mood. He had already phoned the two men who were on duty the night before and they were waiting for him at the station. Both had been woken up and were told to wait for him until he returned. Neither of them was looking forward to it. They spent the time they had getting their story right, for when they were asked why the two people they were supposed to be keeping under surveillance could just leave when they were there all night and saw nothing, it was not good and they knew it. Desperately, they were trying to think of something, anything.

Peter got out of the car, slammed the door shut and marched over to the house. The two policemen got out and went over with him. He stood at the door and hammered away at it with his fist. He knew they were not, but he hoped they were still there and had not gone yet. He pointed to the back, and said to the officer who had just come over from the car.

"Go round there and see if you can get a response." He did as he was told and moments later he could he heard knocking hard on the back door. All it did was to alert the neighbours to their windows and doors. Peter took a long, exaggerated sigh, and shook his head in disbelief.

"Where do you think they are, sir?" the second officer said, rather cautiously.

"Fuck knows, of all the stupid fucking things to do."

"We saw nothing this morning."

"No, it's the fucking night shift that have fucked up. Stay here and await further instructions." He went back to his car and was gone. The second officer came round when he heard the car leave and had a smirk on his face.

"A little pissed off, is he?"

"I'd say."

"Well serves him right, he should treat people right, deserves all he gets if you ask me. What are we to do now then?"

"He said wait here for further instructions." He shrugged his shoulders.

"Oh great." He put his hands in his pockets and stretched, then followed his friend back to the car. They got in, knowing they could be there for quite a while.

whilst driving back, Peter got a message on the radio. He picked it up quickly to answer.

"Yeah, what is it? Good news I hope."

"No sir, I don't think so; there was a second phone call after you left for the house. Nothing was said, they just listened and then hung up; it was a local phone box call. We got there too late, I'm afraid."

"Fantastic," he said, sarcastically. He threw down the receiver and shook his head. He could not believe what was happening. As if things were not bad enough. He drove fast, heading the way he had just come and back to where he knew the two night shift officers would be waiting for him. He could take out his anger and frustration on them and he was going to make sure they suffered for this one, as he knew he would from his boss.

He had also to think his way out of all this. He knew he was on the edge as it was, on borrowed time. He just needed that one break: that one little thing to turn it all around, that one mistake, that one sighting, that one bit of luck, that one anything. He was getting more and more annoyed as he drove. He thought about the mistakes he had made, the mistakes his team had made. This man was hiding in plain sight and should have been locked up long ago and he knew it, and he knew his superiors knew it. They were not happy and when they were not happy it made his life miserable and hard, and he did not like it, not one little bit. He hit the steering wheel with his fist as he thought about it all, cursing and gripping the leather-covered wheel. He was driving too fast, but not caring. He needed some luck but just did not know where to look for it.

At this time, the duck feeder was sat on a bench in the town centre. He did not know what to make of the message he had heard on the phone. He looked up as a car sped past at a ridiculous speed. He only got a glimpse of the driver, but he recognised it as Graham's policeman friend, a slight smile came across his face as he realised that he also must have listened to the message. He peered at the passers-by through his plain glass glasses. His wig was tight and his beard itchy, as he looked at people going by doing their own thing, getting on with their lives. He watched a small girl run from her mother to look in a window at some toy. He stared at her as her mother rushed up and told the child off for running away from her grip. She started to cry. He stood, turned away from them, and slowly walked down the street, deep in his own thoughts. He did not lift his head; he did not know what to do. He did not know if it was a trick, maybe it was a big con to try to get him out into the open. Slowly, he strolled around the town lost in his thoughts and oblivious to the rest of the street, as the people on it were to him, no one knowing what he had done and no one knowing what he was capable of. He stopped by a shop window and saw his own reflection in a mirror. He looked at the image looking back at him, slowly took off the glasses and stood there looking at himself for a while. A smile came across his face; it turned into a broad grin and then a laugh. Putting his glasses back on, he turned and walked away briskly, his head up high. He took deep breaths and headed through the main town centre. He was heading home, home to his little basement room. He had made his decision and was ready. He went on and was looking forward to the challenge, a smile was on his face and he began to get a bounce in his step. As he went on his way, he swung his arms and looked content with life. No one would suspect him and he knew he always won, so he had nothing to worry about. This was going to be fun, he thought, and he looked forward to it, to the new chapter in his little game After all, they had not caught him and he had been here all along, right under their noses., They were no closer to catching him now, than when he first started. He had loads to smile about now and was already thinking of new ideas, new ways to make his father pay. Yes, he thought, it was good that this had happened, something new, something to make him think and something for him to enjoy. Let all the policemen here look for him, he would no longer be here. He would be going home, to where it all started, very fitting really. Just right for the game to end, where it began he knew his way round there and he had a few ideas already, a few plans to put into operation. Yes, he could not wait now, he wanted to be there and get on with it. He broke into a run and felt so alive and good, so ready for the final chapter, for the final curtain, the final blow. His father was not going to know what had hit him.

He ran faster and faster, laughing as he did. He could not help himself; he was laughing uncontrollably, and running home. He had things to do and could not wait to get on with them. He had a place to go and could not wait to get going on his way. Breathing heavily, he had not run like this since he was a child. Moments later, he disappeared into his rented room and the door was slammed shut.

CHAPTER TEN

After a basic, yet full English breakfast, Graham and his wife went out with Sam for a walk in the woods, the same ones where he used to play when he was a child. He did not know why they called it Tinker; they always had. It was an idyllic spot, and in summer it was a popular spot for walkers. The river ran through the length of it and ended up going through the town centre and into the river Aire. It came from far up past Laycock, where he used to live, and up past the teapot dam, named because it was in the shape of a teapot.

Graham loved this place and had many memories. He held his wife's hand and they walked along the firm, but uneven ground. It seemed to anyone that they didn't have a care in the world. Sam ran off to investigate all the new smells and scents he was picking up with his sensitive nose, it was exciting and all new territory for him so he was happy. The track along the river was well worn and well used. With it being so early, there was no one about and it was peaceful and relaxing. Graham was in his element as he pointed out many childhood adventures along the way. There was the tree where he used to tie a rope and make a swing; the bouncing branch that hung from another. They used to play for hours on it as kids. It was also the best part of the river for fishing. There was the time they camped out and a goat ate the ropes to their tent; the time they were shot at by some young men with pellet guns; the walks he used to have, and times he played there.

They reached the small bridge across the river, only wide enough for one person at a time. It was old and looked different to him. As he remembered it, it was wooden and had seen better days, but this was the bridge where he was going to meet the man; the man who had brought so much pain and suffering to his life; the man who was his son.

They stopped on the bridge; stood side by side, looking up the river, the way they had come. Behind them was the dam, used to power the mill beyond it many years ago. A small waterfall was off to the left just before the dam where the river changed direction and headed off into town. Two old green iron gates stopped it and held the water at bay on the other side, creating the dam.

When Graham was a child he had been petrified of these gates. They were old and looked menacing, the water it held back was dark and stagnant. He had walked across its narrow top many times as a child, being careful of his footing as he did so. It had always scared him, even now thinking about it brought a shiver to his back. He had a fear of falling in to the dam and drowning. The water always looked impending and intimidating to him. He did not like it then and thinking about it, did not like it now. He put it at the back of his mind, took deep breaths of the crisp, fresh morning air and put his arm round his wife. She did the same and they felt good together just like before.

"I wish I had brought you here in happier times," he said, with a hint of sorrow in his voice and a sadness in his eyes.

"It is very nice." She nodded and looked up into the trees to her right.

"This is where I'm going to get the bastard to come, right here on this bridge."

"Do you think you will be able to leave the message alright? Without getting caught, I mean."

"Should do I will go tonight and write on the rear end of the old feller. People are always writing on him anyway."

"I'm coming when he arrives," she said, in an inflexible way.

"Do you think it's wise?" he said as diplomatically as possible because he didn't want her there.

"Yes, I'm going to wait up there in the trees." She pointed up a distance to a wooded area. "I will have Sam and as soon as you give a signal we have the bastard." She nodded in satisfaction at the idea

"What about the police?" he asked, unsurely.

"No, Peter in my book, is useless. We can do a better job than the police and I want this bastard. I want him to pay for what he has done to me and my family. How dare he fuck with my life." She sounded very vengeful and Graham had to look at her twice before she smiled and hugged him. He held her tightly and they enjoyed the moment.

Sam came along glancing up at them both. He was panting as he walked down to the side of the river and took a drink of water. The running water tasted good and refreshing. He laid down looking at Graham and Gloria stood holding each other on the bridge. He liked this place and wanted to stay a while. There were lots to explore and do here; it was fun exploring and he enjoyed himself hoping he could return, which he would but did not know it yet so was making the best of it right now.

Rolling over, he scratched his back on the grass as he moved from side to side with his legs up in the air. He had what looked like a grin on his face and his tongue was flopped out on one side of his mouth. He shook and sniffed the air, and then went to smell the grass, trees, and anything else he could find.

"Well, Sam is enjoying himself at least," Graham said.

"He is a good lad, old Sam; he loves it here, doesn't he?"

"He is the best, our best friend." Graham smiled. His wife looked up at him and deep into his eyes she smiled and melted him with her gaze for a moment.

"Are you my best friend?" she asked, quietly

"Yes, of course I am"

"And am I your best friend?"

"Yes, of course." He pulled her tight and held her securely.

"I do love you so much, you know," she said, softly and quietly.

"I love you more than anything."

"I have never met anyone like you, never loved anyone like you and always want you with me." She stared into his eyes.

"I will always want you too, and please don't ever leave me. It was the worst time of my life when you were away and I thought I had lost you."

"You will never lose me." She lifted her head and kissed him on the lips. He kissed her back and they held each other closely.

"So long as I have you then I have everything I could ever want." She smiled and buried her head into his chest. She felt closer to him now than she ever had. She wrapped her arms round him, closed her eyes and felt his body heat and the love they had for each other. Nothing or no one would ever break that; she had made up her mind about that. Whatever happened, she would always want to be with him, and she knew he felt the same they were inseparable.

Peter had finished with the two nightshift men, and it put him in a worse mood than he was before. He soon found out about Rumbold, he checked locally, then rang Keighley police station, who told him about the statue in Keighley town centre.

It was all he wanted to know, and he decided to go visit the place himself. He felt he had to get away anyway; it had all been bearing down on him lately and he wanted a way out, even for a day at least it would be something. He was even sure what he was going to do when he was up there, but he was soon on his way and at this point he did not much care.

Graham came back early the next morning. He had been out for about an hour, but had now returned safely. He locked up the car and went into his wife, locking the door behind him. Sam came for a pet and got one, his tail was still wagging as Graham took his coat off, and walked over to his waiting wife, who said:

"I was getting worried; you said it would only take about twenty minutes."

"Yeah, well, there were some bloody kids playing about, I mean at this time in a morning, they want a kick up the sodding arse most parents nowadays, letting their kids out roaming the streets at this God-forsaken hour. Anyway they pissed off and I had to dodge the bloody CCTV camera they have put up. None of all that in my day, anyway, I have done it, I've written it on the back so when you walk past it you can see it plainly."

"What have you written?" she asked, calmly.

"Keith Leigh, Tinker bridge noon, I'll be waiting."

"So all we do now is wait?"

"I will have to be there every day now, until he shows, if he shows."

"He will, I know he will he won't be able to resist it. Anyway, he has no choice"

"I bet Peter knows by now. The police watching the house must have known something was wrong, a long time ago. I bet he has called and heard the message. Christ, I bet he went mad with the poor fuckers waiting in the car. Bet they had a right blocking, them two." Graham said with a sigh.

"Good, serves them right. If they did what they were supposed to be doing, instead of watching a woman undress in her own bedroom, then they would not be in trouble right now, fucking perverts, call themselves police officers, they couldn't catch a fucking cold, "

The rest of the day was uneventful but full of tension and anticipation. They had their doubts and both had their misgivings, but stayed strong for each other.

Sam was taken for a walk and they had a quiet day. After a light evening meal in the pub they went back to their room, and watched a little TV, but nothing interested them and they had an early night. They held each other close, both thinking about the same thing but in different ways.

They had decided to go into town the next day to buy some food and rations. They wanted something else besides the pub food.

Gloria wanted to go to the house, Graham's old house, but he did not want to go back there, far too many bad memories. She insisted and he reluctantly gave in. This did not make him look forward to the next day at all, He stayed awake in bed thinking about it He did not want to go back into that house, but he knew he would have to, to keep his wife satisfied. In a way he could see why she wanted to visit the place but then again he couldn't.

She fell asleep in his arms and he stared up at the ceiling wondering how it would all end, wanting it to be over, wondering how going back to the house would affect him. Would he be able to do it? Why was Gloria so adamant about going? She had not really explained why she wanted to go. He still had the keys and now wished he hadn't. Deep down, he was always going to go back, that was why it had not been put up for sale yet. He just could not, but knew he would have to; no way could he ever live there again.

He did not think it would have been so soon that he re-entered the place, the dark haunted house with terrible memories. It would never be the same, never be a home again for him. He wanted to sell it, and would, but a strange fear, or clinging entity seemed to make him hold on to the place. Fond memories of a childhood, but a nightmare in the last few months, he shook his head and tried to make it disappear from his thoughts. The image of his sister started to pop back into his mind, something he would never get rid of or come to terms with. He didn't think anyone would be able to forget that sight; he didn't think anyone was capable of such atrocities, and to think he spawned the beast who did it, made him shake and a shiver ran down his back. He looked round the room, shadows had appeared and it took on a different guise in the night. He saw Sam sleeping on guard and smiled to himself. Instantly, it made him feel better. He had fears that lurked in the shadows and he knew he would always have nightmares. It would be something that would be with him until he died.

 He dismissed the counselling they'd had and thought he would do better handling the situation in his own way. He knew they were experts, experianced doing their job and trying to help, but he did not like it and ended the sessions before they were done. They said they would always be there, but he knew he would never contact them again. The more he thought about it the more he remembered the questions and the things they told him to do: write things down, empty your thoughts, will them away, put them at the back of your mind, it's not your fault, don't blame yourself, admit the situation. He'd had enough of them after the first few sessions, but he did it for his family, his wife and children. That was the only thing that mattered to him then, and now. He shook his head and leaned back into the pillow, then lifted his head. Too many things were running through his mind, too many thoughts, too many worries. He breathed out and took a deep breath back in letting the air out slowly. He watched his wife's head lift as his chest filled with air then settled her down again as he breathed out. He was so glad she had seemed to forgive him. He loved her and knew he could not live without her She looked so peaceful and tranquil in her sleep, and he wondered what she was dreaming about, if at all. Gently, he kissed her on her forehead, and looked at her, long and hard, knowing he was a very lucky man to have a woman like her by his side. It made him feel ten feet tall and able to do anything.

He closed his eyes and tried to fall asleep, but it was not easy. There was too much running around in his mind, too much keeping him alert. He did fall asleep, but it was not until the early hours of the morning when exhaustion forced itself on him and his body demanded it.

It was a drive he was not looking forward to. He pulled away with his wife next to him and the dog in the back seat. It was a short drive to his old house but he wanted it to take a very long time. In fact, it was only a matter of ten minutes.

The house loomed, Gloria was transfixed on it and said nothing. This was the place her little girl had been held all the time and where she could have been killed. It had been Graham's nightmare and now he was going to face it.

He felt a cold shiver run down his back, an icy streak of soft pain as he remembered the day he found his daughter there. Slowly, he pulled up and parked outside the house.

It was cold looking and had seemed to have a life of its own. He no longer saw it as a place he spent his childhood, but as a place of fear and death. His sister had been tortured in there and he did not want to go back in. He looked at his wife and asked in a plain, calm, yet powerful voice:

"Let's go, I don't want to go back in there." His face was pale and his eyes sad.

"Come on, you have to face your fears if you are to overcome them." She took his hand and gave a slight squeeze. She got out of the car; he looked toward her for a moment then followed, telling Sam to stay where he was. He locked the car and hesitantly strolled up to the large house, which seemed to get larger all the time. It was looming down on him like some sort of grey monster ready to pounce at any moment. He looked round and felt a little bit of fear run through his body, followed by a larger, stronger bolt of fear. He did not really know why he felt so bad about it, it was only an empty house, but it held a lot of terrible memories, which it would never let go of, and it was these with which he was fearful. They reached the front door. He put his hand in his pocket and pulled out a small, worn key. He put this into the Yale lock, pushing and turning at the same time. The door opened and a cold blast of air hit

278

them. It was damp and smelt of some sort of disinfectant. He had told the police to get the place cleared out after taking his sister away. It was empty now, and he owned it. What to do with it he did not know. Gloria walked in and Graham followed .She stood just inside the doorway, closed her eyes and lifted up her head.

"What is it?" he asked.

"You can tell horrible things have happened here, you can just tell." She walked into the main room. Graham followed and glanced up the stairs as he walked past. The room was empty and bare now it had been cleared out. Graham put his arm round his wife.

"Are they all coming back?" she asked him.

"What?"

"Memories, you must have a lot."

"Yeah, but not many I want to remember." She turned towards him. She saw the pain in his eyes; he did not want to be here. She gave him a gentle kiss on the lips and looked directly into his eyes.

"You must have some good ones?"

"Not many I can remember right now. Can we go?" He walked to the door to leave. Gloria came up to him and took his arm.

"Take me to where he held Lisa."

"Oh come on Gloria, what is this?" His protest was felt but met with equal determination to go on.

"I want to see Graham, show me!" Without saying a word, he walked up the stairs she followed and he took her into the small room He went in and straight away noticed the hole in the wall where Lisa had been chained .Gloria walked in and looked round the desolate, small room. She went to the window and looked out across the fields. She turned back and leant on the window sill. She shook her head in disbelief, and looked at Graham, who was looking right back at her.

"We were lucky, weren't we? To get her back." she said

"Yes, we were, very lucky. If you want to see the other room you will have to go yourself, I'm not going in there." She put her arms round him, holding him tightly. She hugged him and swayed a little from right to left.

"No, I don't want to go in there. Why don't you sell the place, then we never have to come back here again." She spoke without looking up at him, and he answered the same way, hugging her tightly.

"Yeah, I will. I don't know why I have not done it straight away. I will, I'll sell it."

She saw his eyes were full of sadness and the torture he had suffered in the last few months showed through them.

"Now I have seen, shall we go?" They walked out of the room and down the stairs again.

He took one last look round and a thought rushed through his mind. "I wonder if he was still here when I came for Lisa? I never searched the place. Maybe, if I had, he would be sent away by now."

"I doubt it. If he knew you were coming he would have legged it."

"Yeah, maybe." They left and closed the door, leaving the emptiness to linger on after they had gone.

The cold of the house swept through it like a spirit; a draught was coming from the back, a draught they had not noticed. It was sharper as you got to the kitchen. The window was not shut right and on closer inspection you could see why - it had been forced. Surprisingly, the glass was not broken but the window was. Someone had forced it, someone was in the house, someone was in the loft and had heard every word that they had said. The loft hatch opened and a pair of legs came down, hanging from the hole, they were lowered down and fell to the floor, banging on the bare floorboards. It was Peter. He had been waiting in the loft. He went to the front window and carefully looked out from the side He saw the car pulling away down the road. He went back down the stairs. He walked into the kitchen and looked at the window. He had noticed it earlier. He had not forced it but he had a good idea who had, and when he returned he wanted to be here to welcome him. It could be a long wait but that was why he had brought some food and water which was in the loft. He was working on a hunch, a saying that the criminal always returns to the scene of the crime. He knew that was rubbish but he still thought that his man would return here and he was hoping he would find him before he found Graham.

As they drove away, Graham seemed to have a heavy weight lifted from his shoulders. He was going to sell the house. He smiled at his wife, who smiled back. She looked at her watch and saw it was eleven thirty.

"We'd better get to the bridge love, its half past eleven." He headed off and it wasn't long before he was strolling along minding his own business by the bridge. Gloria was sat out of sight in some trees, holding Sam back. He was wondering what this game was all about. It was quiet and there was no one was about. Graham walked onto the bridge and looked at his watch. It was ten to twelve. He stood silently and looked at the water passing under him, wondering if he was doing the right thing. It was fifteen minutes later when his heart missed a beat by a figure walking towards him from a field. He could not make out who it was. It was a man. He licked his dry lips and swallowed. Could this be him? He began to breath faster. The man climbed over a fence and was coming down towards the bridge. Graham was convincing himself this was him; it had to be him.

The man reached the bridge and stopped. Graham saw it was a pensioner and gave a sigh of relief.

"Are you coming or going lad? I want to cross like," the man said, looking annoyed at Graham blocking his way.

"Sorry." Graham walked off the bridge and let the man pass. He went on his way and off down the side of the river.

Time passed slowly and it reached an hour later. Gloria was getting cramp and had to stand to stretch her legs. Sam was laid out, bored with this game. Graham decided that was enough for one day. He walked off the bridge and off up to the trees. He came to where Gloria was crouched, holding Sam still.

"I think that's enough for one day, he is not coming. We will come back tomorrow. I will go the opposite way and you give it ten minutes and meet me at the car, just in case he is watching me from somewhere." He headed off down the hill and it was fifteen minutes when they met up at the car. Gloria opened the back door and let Sam in, then got in herself. Graham was already in there waiting.

"Never mind, he will show, I'm sure of it," she said putting on her seat belt.

"We'll come back tomorrow." They drove away and decided to go for some lunch. It was a good, fine day, but the weatherman had said it was not going to last. Rain was forecast and was due that night.

"Where are we going for some food then, I'm starving?" Gloria asked, stretching her legs out to get the circulation going again.

"A little pub I know. It sells lovely food, well it used to. We can sit outside so Sam will be alright, it's not far and won't take long."

"Good, I'm bursting for a pee." She crossed her legs and had a twisted look on her face.

"You should have had one in the trees."

"I will not, you men might do that sort of thing but not us ladies, thank you very much. I will have comfort when I pee, I tell you."

"Whatever you say my love." He looked at her and felt all the love he had for her pumping through his body. She had always made him feel good and she always would.

He knew that. He just had to see her face and his life was brighter. He considered himself very lucky to have her and even more luckier to be able to hold on to her, especially after what had happened. He drove into the town and then through it, heading up a steep hill and off to the left. The pub was a popular place to those who knew it was there. It did not advertise, worked by word of mouth and did good business.

Graham slowly took the sharp bend and pulled up next to some wooden benches. With great urgency in her voice, Gloria asked: "Where is the ladies?" She had her legs crossed and her face began to screw up again in a painful twist

"Er, now let me see." Graham took his time on purpose.

"Sod it, I'll find 'em." She rushed from the car and went for the pub entrance.

"Straight through to the other side of the bar," Graham shouted after her She waved back and then was gone. He got out and locked the door, assuring Sam he would be back shortly. He walked towards the pub and remembered the time he first came here with his young friend and they had eyed up these two women all night, Eventually, they plucked up enough courage to speak to them but were told to get lost.

It made him smile at the thought of it; how stupid you were when you were young. He had lost touch with his friends from those days but now wished he hadn't. Looking up at the old style windows and thought the place had not changed much. Paint was peeling off the outside wall and the roof had repaired slate here and there. He looked back out across the car park and noticed Sam with his nose up against the window watching him. He pulled open the two stiff wooden doors and went into the warm, friendly place, it was just as he remembered it.

Their meal was nice and Sam got a long drink from a large clean ash tray filled with water, and some left over's from their plates They sat outside and were on their second drink; the table had been cleared and it was so peaceful and quiet. The pub was away from the mainstream and not near any main roads. Graham liked it here and Gloria had begun to. She gave him a crooked smile.

"What is that for?" he said, looking back.

"Free," she said, breaking into a wide smile.

"When all this is over I want to take you and the kids away somewhere, just us as a family, away from it all."

"I think they will be glad to get back here to tell you the truth. I will have to ring them today, by the way."

"Yeah and tomorrow, and the next day after that"

"You know that river by the bridge, Tinker?" she asked

"What about it?"

"Where does it go?"

"Oh bloody hell, all over the place. It goes down under the old mill and the other side of the dam, down into town, under the streets, opens up through a wide tunnel and then underground again. I think it ends up in the river Aire. We once went down it as kids in a little boat we made, but when it went into the tunnel we shit ourselves and gave up. Bloody big rats were in there and God knows what else." He shivered at the thought.

"Is the mill still working?" Gloria enquired interested all of a sudden.

"No, it was an old wool mill but it closed years ago. It's abandoned now. Why?"

"Oh just wondered, no particular reason."

"I'm surprised Peter has not caught up with us by now, even though we have turned off our phones."

"Probably does not know we're gone yet," she said, sarcastically.

"He has gone down in my estimation, I tell you, the whole bloody police force has for that matter." She took a drink from her glass and put it back down again.

"I'm sure they are doing their best, love."

"Well, it's not good enough., they caught the Yorkshire ripper faster than this" She looked at Sam and reached down to stroke him. He wagged his tail at the attention. She looked back at Graham who was finishing his drink and then asked, nodding at her empty glass:

"Do you want another one?"

"No, that's ok. I've had enough thanks, I'm full and refreshed." He put down the glass and took a deep breath, letting it out slowly. They stayed for only a few more minutes then left Darkness fell quickly that night as the clouds closed in and rain was ready to fall. Peter was uncomfortable and still cramped up in the loft of the house, but he did not mind. He was listening very hard and thought he could hear something. He glanced at his watch with his little penlight torch. It was nine fifty. He knew it would be dark outside and it was raining. He could hear it dancing on the tiles of the roof only feet above him.

People didn't seem to be as observant in the bad weather; they just wanted to get home and into the warmth. He listened again. There it was, the sound, more distinctive this time. It was the second time he had heard it. He froze and listened, straining his ears. He could hear his own heartbeat; it was that silent. His breathing was hard, but he tried to hold it in almost, he tried not to breath and not to make a sound. The rain was hitting the roof in a methodical tone and he found it hard to listen out above it. But suddenly, there it was a definite thud. Someone was in the house who he did not know. It was night time; it was cold and damp and he was tired and stiff. But he knew he could now only be feet away from the man he was hunting; the man that was ever increasingly hard to find; the lunatic he was after, who they were all after. Could this be his chance? He listened and held fast. He did not have a plan just yet, and did not want anything to go wrong this time. This could be his last chance, and it was dangerous, and critical it was done right. The situation became menacing; he felt vulnerable but stayed in control. He leant back and got comfortable and thought about what to do, and how to handle the situation he was now in. He started to breathe easily again, thinking of the best way to handle his dilemma and when to make his move, he was not suppose t be here

288

and needed this to be done correctly so no one could say he over stepped and broke the law in the execution of his duty, no, this had to be done with no doubt and no mistake.

The next day it was raining. Sam and Gloria were waiting in the trees yet again. Graham was on the bridge, his coat totally inadequate for the weather. A summer jacket and shorts was not the ideal dress for this weather at all and he had not brought any weatherproof clothing. The rain was steady and becoming harder; his face was wet and his feet cold. He stood on the bridge with his hands deep in his pockets, trying to get some circulation back into his toes, and warmth back into his body. The water was like a torrent below him as the river swelled with the weather. It was twelve thirty, and he was ready for giving up. He looked round and what he saw made him shiver with fright.

Looking straight at him from only about a hundred yards away was a young man wearing glasses and a beard. He stood by a large oak tree, looking down at him. Graham had not noticed him there before so had no idea how long he had been watching. Slowly, the young man looked around as if to check the area. He was cautious but made a move to come out from by the tree, so Graham could get a good look at him. Deliberately, he walked down towards the bridge. Graham stared and could not move. He began to shake. He no longer noticed the cold or the rain anymore and he began to breathe faster. An empty feeling came in his stomach. The man was close now and he was staring at Graham with intense eyes almost demonic. He walked to the bridge and stopped.

Nothing was said for a moment and the only noise came from the pounding of the rain hitting the river and the wooden bridge. Graham sniffed up and asked:

"Who are you?" He waited for an answer.

The man took another careful look around the area, reassuring himself there was no one about He pulled at his beard, and it came off, dropping to the muddy ground. He took off the glasses, smiled and said in a northern accent Graham had heard before so many times on the phone, and hoped he would never hear again.

"I'm your son, daddy."

"You're an evil bastard." His tone was offensive and angry.

"Like son, like father." He put his hand in his pocket and pulled out something. Graham could not see what it was at first but when he held it up Graham saw that it was a small pair of knickers

"I took them from a little girl in the play area. These are her piss-stained knickers. Would you like to smell them? She pissed herself when I took her and told her what I was going to do to her. I told her, if this was a trap, she would die."

"Christ, you are sick." Graham shook his head in disbelief.

"When you have nothing to lose, you can't help but win daddy. I will always be around, even if they get me. They will do all their tests, all the questions and I'll get diminished responsibility. I'm mad, insane. They will put me away in a hospital, a mental hospital, not prison. I could be out again in years to come, if I'm a good boy and answer all the questions right. No daddy, you will never be free of me I'm afraid. I will always be part of your miserable life, just as a son should be."

"You are never going to be a part of my life you sick little fuck." Graham spat out

"Now don't start calling me names, you know you are really stupid. Do you know that, really, really stupid? I'm ashamed to call you dad sometimes. Did you think I would come here with nothing to bargain with. I have a little bitch, here are her knickers." He held them up, then moved them to his face and smiled as he sniffed them. "If the police or anyone comes near me she will die. I have put her away so if I do not return within the hour she will be dead, and I will never tell where she is. All this is down to you, so daddy we're back where we started from don't ya think?" He smiled broadly.

"Why did you kill your mother?" Graham asked with pain in his voice and words.

"Why did you fuck her? She was your sister, you dirty bastard. She deserved to die, locking me away in that home, you not wanting

even to see me, you having nothing to do with me, your own son."
He shouted at him and sounded quite mad, which made Graham
flinch back in a defensive mode.

"Why?" he asked again, coldly.

"Because I could, because it was there, because I felt like it, I
fucked her as well you know, not very good was she? I wish I had
fucked my sister Lisa now, maybe next time. How is she anyway? I
still owe her for what she did to me the little slut, tart, bitch, whore,
fucking bitch." His voice became unstable and he began to shake as
he spoke. His eyes narrowed and he frowned and his voice raised
and calmed in the same sentence.

The rain came down harder and Graham did not know what to do.
He didn't even have a plan. He was going to restrain him and call
the police, but standing here now in front of him, he could not. His
legs were becoming jelly and he knew he was talking to an unstable
madman, a dangerous mental disturbed human being.

"So what are you going to do now son?" he said, while trying to
think of a course of action to take and get out of this horrible,
terrifying situation.

"Don't know daddy, the question is why you have brought me
here? There seems to be no one here, your family are in Spain, your
policeman friend is down in the next county,
so it's just you and me is it?" His voice was calm again.

292

"Just you and, yeah?" Graham took a step back.

"Going somewhere daddy? Thought you wanted to meet me? Well, I'm here. You said some very nasty things on the answering machine, I have not forgiven you for that you know. I tell ya, you are going to suffer in ways you never imagined possible, you fuck. I have seen things done to people in the homes and hospitals. You would be very surprised what the insane mind can think up, no remorse you see, no conscience, no give a shit."

He stepped closer to Graham who at this stage was frightened. He knew he was in trouble and wanted to get away, any way that he could. The young man stood in front of him had the devil in his eyes. He was insane and Graham was in grave danger. He knew now he would be no match for him, even if he hit him hard. The mind of the maniac would still go on and not feel the pain, still keep coming and do whatever he wanted. They were as strong as they wanted to be and this one in front of him now was determined to kill him.

He looked into his dead eyes. They were uncompromising, unforgiving and totally disturbed, psychotic, and staring at him. It petrified him and he froze with dread and apprehension. .This nightmare was real and there was no waking up. There was nothing he could do panic was about to grip him with a pincer grip.

Without warning, a voice bellowed down from a nearby field at them through a police loud hailer.

"Do not move, you are surrounded, this is the police."

Graham saw it was Peter. He had never felt so pleased to see someone in his life. Several policemen were coming down the field towards them. Graham looked at the man in front of him; there was no real reaction at all from him. All he did was hold up the knickers and smile, an evil smile.

"Peter stop! He is holding a small girl somewhere. If you come any closer he will leave her to die. Stop!," Reluctantly, Graham held up his hands in a stop gesture at the onrushing police and Peter, but they did not stop.

Graham felt an excruciating pain in his stomach and dropped to his knees. He had been punched there and it hurt him badly. He put up his hand up to stop any more blows. The duck feeder took hold of his hand and held it up. With the other hand he put his fist round one of Graham's fingers and with a sadistic laugh, he snapped it to the side, breaking it and causing Graham to scream out in pain. Before he could do anything else, he saw the dog, the same one that had attacked him in the house, the same one that had chased him over the wall by the fields. Now, it was coming for him again. He saw the police coming in closer. He gave a swift kick to Graham's head, which sent it reeling back.

Bloodstained and throbbing, he thought his brains were going to burst out of his skull.

"See ya later daddy. The girl is dead because of you. I will send you her in the post." He

laughed and ran off over the bridge. Sam was gaining fast and was not going to lose him this time. Graham pulled himself up and gave chase. No way was he going to have a girl's death on his hands. The pain was pounding in his head and finger. He cried out and as he ran the adrenalin pumped. Sam overtook him and was growling at the anticipation of getting his prey. Gloria stood and went towards Peter.

"What about the girl?" She screamed at him.

"I have her, she is safe, he left her in his mother's house," he told her as they met in the field and then all gave chase.

On reaching the dam gate, the duck feeder climbed up and over it. Sam was stuck. He stood at the bottom unable to get over. He barked fearlessly, but it was no good. Graham climbed the gate. He walked carefully across it, the same one that had scared him so much as a child. Sam went across the opposite side of the dam and ran parallel along it.

The madman did the same on the other side. There was about fifteen feet of water between them but Sam could not get to him for a wall. But he could see his man and followed parallel on the opposite side.

Graham was running fast and in great pain. The duck feeder had a loud, lunatic laugh. He was heading for the old abandoned mill. The ground was muddy and they slipped but didn't fall. Although it was difficult to run too fast, Graham was catching up quickly. Whatever his demented son was, he was not a fast runner. Graham did not know what he would do when he caught him but all he had on his mind right now was catching him up.

When he reached the old rundown mill, he ran through the wooden doors, disappearing inside. Graham was out of breath but kept going. He was almost there. Sam barked from the opposite side of the dam, frustrated and angry at not being able to cross the water. Peter and the police were giving chase, and Gloria was bringing up the rear.

On entering the mill, Graham was hit once again by surprise. As he ran in, the door was shut and a wooden beam was fixed into the ground and wedged against the Woodstock of the door securing it shut. Only a small hole in the bottom, where the weather and whatever else had worn it away over the years, showed any light through, the gound had been eroded away and there was gap. Graham stood and faced his heavy breathing son, who, with a demented laugh, lurched forward at him.

Graham dodged away and rolled on the floor. He turned and kicked out catching his son on the side of the leg. He fell on the wooden floor which creaked and splintered under the force of his weight. The place was old and not very safe. The river was rushing by under their feet as the rain made it more powerful than normal and the dust and dirt was being disturbed and pushed up into the air. Graham scrambled forward and kicked out again.

He caught his man in the ribs and sent him rolling back once again. He could hear Sam barking wildly from across the water and he could hear Peter shouting him. But right now, he was thinking of all the pain and torment that this man had caused him and his family. Fighting through his pain, he straightened up and came forward a third time, but it was not third time lucky for him. He was not prepared for the quickness of his son, who stood up like a bolt of lightning. His eyes were red with hate and he growled like some sort of wild animal. Screaming out and grabbing Graham's neck with both hands, he pushed back taking Graham by surprise and he fell back on the floor. The wood almost gave way under the crash of the combined weight of them both. Fighting a losing battle, Graham tried to get the man off him but could not. He was too strong, his finger was causing him excruciating pain, and tears appeared in his eyes.

Peter ran to the door and tried to force his way in but the door held solid with the beam of wood wedged behind it. He pushed and kicked at it, the other two officers joined in but it was no good it held solid. Graham was losing and he knew it. He was fighting just to breathe now, as the hands closed and gripped his windpipe tightly.

Gloria struggled to get across the dam gate; it was hazardous and dangerous but she was determined to do it and help her husband. Putting more power into his grip, the duck feeder could feel the strength draining from his father and he knew he had him. Sadistically, he said in his ear:

"The girl is going to suffer, I'm going to rape her and kill her, and do the same to all your family. Do you hear me? All of them everyone, very slowly, very painfully, I still have a key to your house, I took it from your slag of a daughter, and there is nothing you can do.

Time to die daddy, time to die." He laughed, but stopped suddenly. He looked up and a shiver went down his back. His grip loosened, which was good news for Graham, who managed to get a bit of much-needed air in his screaming lungs.

Scrambling under the rotten door was a soaking wet Labrador dog. It was Sam. He had swum the dam and got under the door. No one else could get in here but he had. He wasted no time. He ran and timed his jump perfectly. He hit his target smack on sending him spinning back. Graham was not sure what was happening; he was

298

only just conscious. He rolled over gasping for breath and coughed up his guts.

Sam had his man, and tore into his flesh. He held nothing back. His bite ripped at the man, who was fighting back by kicking and hitting, but Sam was tough and could take it. Blood was running down the man's arm and he tried to get away, but was painfully bitten again in the upper leg causing him to fall hard on the wooden floor. A piece of wood dropped down into the river below as he fell. The old floor was giving way under the strain, but Sam held nothing back. He knew this man was evil, knew he had caused pain and upset to his family. He wanted to kill him. He did not know why he was evil, he just knew, his instinct told him.

Tearing a lump of flesh from the man's leg with his powerful jaws, he shook his head and dropped blood-soaked flesh on the floor. Blood was pouring from the dog's mouth, but, again and again, he went in biting and tearing. He got hit and kicked but didn't give up his quest. He had lost this man before and was not going to lose him again. His sharp teeth embedded into soft flesh, and his powerful jaws ripped and tore at it. The noise of him growling and snarling was frightening he was fast and ferocious.

The duck feeder was screaming out in a demented roar. He kicked out and punched and made Sam yelp in pain, but it did not stop him from sinking its teeth into his flesh once again. Sam lurched and got him round the throat. He struck the dog in a frenzy of punches but it did him no good. He stood up and the dog went with him, hanging on determined not to let go. They crashed to the floor which finally gave way. The old rotten wood could no longer take the strain. It made a snapping sound and splintered. As his body fell through the hole that appeared he desperately grabbed out and with inhuman strength managed to hold on to the side with one hand. Sam let go and jumped free. He only just managed to get free and away from the hole. The water was gushing past and the drop looked dangerous. The rotten wood splashed down into the river and was instantly washed away, smashing into large rocks protruding from the side and bottom as it was swept away downstream He was holding on with one hand and could not hold on much longer. The gashes and bite marks over his body were painful and he was losing blood fast. Swinging precariously above the rushing river below, he looked down then up again. His eyes were wild and bloodshot; his breath was uneven and he was snarling like a wounded animal.

A panting Sam was exhausted and in pain. He walked to the top of the hole, looked down and saw his man bleeding and holding on for his life. Feeling the energy draining from him, the duck feeder looked up into the eyes of the growling dog staring down at him. "I should have killed you the first fucking time," he said at the animal. He slipped and his grip gave way slightly. He saw the red blood dripping down into the rushing water. He was getting weaker all the time, but could hear Peter shouting and hammering on the door. He could hear Gloria screaming out and saw Graham's face appear over the hole.

Carefully holding on to the edge, he too, was gasping for breath. He looked right into the eyes of his son. Sam growled and crouched down ready to finish the job.

"You will never hurt my family again. Where is the girl?" Graham croaked out of a sore throat and neck. The pain was intense and throbbed hard in his throat.

"She will die. Help me up and I will tell you, daddy." He began to cough up blood and could not hold on anymore. He looked up right into the eyes of his father and gave a loud and sickening laugh as he fell silently into the rushing water below. It seemed to embrace him. Sam barked at him as he rolled over in the river and hit the rocks with a sickening thud. His body went limp and he was carried off in the torrent of water. Graham watched him go with painful, sad eyes. He could not stay there and he rolled back onto the floor holding his neck. It was hurting and he found it hard to breath. His head hurt and his finger was tremendously painful his heart was beating hard against his rib cage.

Sam licked at his paw and then came up to Graham. Sitting next to him, he lowered his head and sniffed at him. He wagged his tail at Graham's whisper of "Good boy!" Sam was the old family dog once more. They looked up as the door finally gave way under the force of Peter and the other two men. Peter ran in and told the other two to search the place. He came up to Graham and looked down the hole.

"Where is the little fuck?" he asked, loudly.

"Down there," Graham croaked, and then pointed down the hole "We have the girl. He left her in your old house, and I have her safe.

Graham was so relieved. He had to cry because the emotion was too much for him. Gloria came dashing in and frantically looked round. She saw her husband on the floor.

She rushed over, sat next to him and put her arms round him. She too was crying. They held each other tightly and did not want to let go. Sam licked his sore paws and back leg. He had taken a beating and could feel it more now he had calmed down.

The two police officers came back from looking round. They saw Peter carefully peering over the hole into the raging river below. He could see nothing but knew a search would have to be made all the way down the river until the body was found.

"Well, I think we can say it is over Graham. It was a stupid bloody thing to do, but it is over now. He will not survive that. We will pick up the body in a day or two down river. Now, it's time to start rebuilding your life."

Gloria kissed her husband and he felt the pain in his body even more. He could not move without hurting. He swallowed but it was also painful. He nodded to Peter and tried to stand, helped by his wife, Slowly, they moved from the place and headed back to the door, which was swinging on its broken hinges. The rain was coming in and wetting the dry wood inside. Peter took another look down the hole. He saw the water rushing past in an unstoppable thunder of noise and power, dark and unforgiving, dangerous and full of peril. He saw nothing of the body that had fallen into it. He turned to one of the policemen with him and asked:

"What do you think?" He looked down the hole.

"Dead, smashed up, sir."

"Yeah, I hope so." They all walked to the door and a limping Sam went with them. They made their way back out into the rain and down along the dam. One of the officers volunteered to lift and carry Sam over the dam gate, something Sam did not mind. He was too tired to complain anyway. They made their way back up the hill, Gloria helping Graham who was finding it hard, his throat hurt and he was gasping a little for breath. It

did not take long to reach the road where the police cars, Peter's car, and the police patrol car had been parked. Peter took Graham,

Gloria and Sam, who got in the back and laid down for a much needed and well deserved rest. Gloria got in by his side, stroking his head as she sat with him. Graham was in the front. They watched as Peter finished talking to the other two policemen and joined them. The car was warm and welcoming from the weather. The other two policemen went in the patrol car and were soon gone. Peter turned to Graham and asked:

"Nearest hospital?"

"Airedale, I'll show you," he croaked out, pointing straight ahead. Peter started up the car and pulled away. He drove his friend to the hospital and got Gloria checked over while they were there. He knew that there was now all the paper work to do and a massive search for the body. It was a mammoth task and he was not looking forward to it. The paperwork never was his favourite time or part of the job.

Every action had to be explained and written down, every detail evaluated, from start to finish. Was the right procedure adhered to? It was a right pain in the arse.It had all come out good in the end, but it could so easily have gone wrong. He still thought it was a stupid and dangerous thing for them to do. He did not go on at them right now; he felt the time was not right. He would have his say, he was sure of that, but he saved it. It was over. It was not the best of his cases and not one he wanted to repeat, but he would have to, at least on paper, for his report and to his boss. The rain did not ease up all day, and Graham stayed in hospital overnight. Gloria stayed with him for as long as she could, then went back with Sam to the pub,. She finished up there the next day paying the bill and collecting their things and then went to collect her husband. Thankfully, it was all over, and they could now get on with their lives. She drove into the hospital car park a much happier woman than she was the day before. She walked into the hospital to see her husband, the man she loved and would never leave again. They had statements to make and submit, interviews to give. The children to bring back and get some normality back in their life. Graham was feeling much better but still his neck and throat was very sore they were happy to find out no permanent damage was done. They both wanted to get away from this place and back home and Gloria made sure they did.

CHAPTER ELEVEN

Gloria had to help him; he could not do it by himself. The banner was too long. 'Happy nineteenth birthday' it said. It was for Lisa. She had done them so proud by going to university and doing so well. After pressing the drawing pin into the wall with his thumb, Graham got off the ladder and looked at the banner. He gave a nod of acceptance and Gloria came over to him.

They looked round the room and were satisfied it was right, not too childish, but just right for a nineteenth birthday party. She wanted to share it with her family and had grown so close to them all. She had become a fine, young, mature woman.

"What time is the train, did you say? I should have gone and got her," Graham asked

"You have about an hour. Stop worrying, I won't let you be late."

"No, I know love. I will pick her up from the station and bring her straight here. Where is Sebastian?" He looked round and saw Sam lying on the floor.

"I don't know. He said he might be a little late. I think he will make it in time, you know what he is like when he gets round to his friend's house, internet mad. I'm glad we stopped him going on it here, dirty little sod."

"Yeah, but he had fun." They smiled and she hugged him tightly. He responded similarly and they stood there in a clinch for a short while saying nothing, just enjoying each other's touch each other's presence and each other's warmth.

"I love you so much Graham, even after all we have been through. I'm so glad we stuck it out and got our lives right again"

"We said we would not talk about that part of our life again."

"I know, but I still have the dreams, bad dreams. His body was never found, was it? I'm still having the nightmares." She shook her head at the thought as if to shake them away out of her mind.

"He is gone, dead. It has been three years and nothing. The river is treacherous; the rats would have got him. There is only a certain part of the river they can get to anyway. I told you it goes under the town and all over the place. There are hundreds of places where his body could have gone. No, my sweet, we will never hear from him again." He squeezed her tightly and she smiled up at him, kissing him slightly but lovingly on the lips.

"Shall we have a quick one while we are waiting?" she said, pushing her breasts into his chest and provocatively licking her lips at him. The phone rang at that precise moment and stopped the proceedings.

"That will be Sebastian wanting a lift I bet," Graham said. He went to the phone, picked it up and put it to his ear, but it went dead as he did. He put it back down again.

"What is it?" Gloria asked

"They hung up." He shrugged his shoulders then the phone rang again. He picked it up straight away and listened.

"Dad its Sebastian." The voice was strange and made Graham frown in confusion. Gloria came up to him and asked with a worried tone:

"What is it?"

"You alright son?" Graham said into the phone.

"Dad, I'm sorry" The phone went dead and what Graham heard next sent a cold chill through his veins. It was a northern voice, one he had heard before, one he thought he would never hear again. He recognised it instantly, the same cold northern tone.

"Hello daddy, it is your number one son. I'm back. I have him and now the game starts again. I will be in touch."

The phone was quiet and Graham dropped to the floor in a state of shock. Gloria picked up the receiver and listened. She put it back when she heard nothing. Scared, she looked at Graham. He was shaking and she knelt down, worried and concerned

"Darling what is it? What's wrong?" she asked, frantically.

"He, he..." trying to speak Graham felt his mouth go dry. Gloria picked up the phone and pressed for the caller's number, but it had been withheld. She turned back to her distraught husband. She was beginning to panic and get nervous.

"What is it, Graham? Tell me!" she shouted at him. He turned with terror in his eyes and she knew, without any words being said. She knew.

"Oh no, not Lisa, no, not my baby," she screamed, uncontrollably shaking, not wanting it to be true she fell to the floor and sat down in tears.

"He has got Sebastian," was all Graham said. She looked at him and screamed out again, and again. She was uncontrollable; it was the nightmare she always had; it was here; it was true. Her life again was ripped open, the horror of it all was back and this time it was to be worse.

"Gloria, Gloria," Graham shouted and held her as she woke in a panic .She was sweating and shouting.

"Sebastian! Sebastian!" she shouted out as she awoken

"Baby, you're dreaming again." Her husband's voice calmed her as she realised she was in her own bed. It was dark and she was next to the man she loved. She sat up taking deep breaths and calming herself, letting her eyes adjust to the darkness. She made out Graham was next to her. He leant over and switched on the bedside light. The room filled with soft lighting and she gave a sigh of relief. She had been dreaming. She smiled at him and he asked her in a low voice:

"Are you ok?" His face was friendly and she lay back. "Sorry," she said and rolled her head to the side and looked at him.

"That's ok babe, are you alright?"

"Yes, it was just so real."

"You're safe." He lay next to her and put his arm round her. She snuggled up to him and listened to his calming voice.

"Don't panic, we have Lisa home tomorrow from university for her birthday party. We will have a great day and a great time. Nothing or no one will ever hurt you again, my darling. I promise."

"Thank you, I do love you, I love you all." She closed her eyes, and was calm and Tranquil again, Graham switched off the light and they lay together quietly. He closed his eyes, and tried to drift off to sleep, when suddenly the phone rang ...

The end....

Printed in Great Britain
by Amazon

26785160R00179